WORLD WHISPERER

RACHEL DEVENISH FORD

SMALL SEED PRESS

First published in 2016

Copyright © 2016 Rachel Devenish Ford

Small Seed Press LLC

racheldevenishford.com

PROLOGUE

The woman held her breath as she approached the high walls of the village. The walls shimmered with heat. She walked toward them slowly with the great desert at her back, two of her three young children stumbling along behind her. She carried the sleeping nearly-five-year-old on her shoulders, the weight lodging a painful kink in her neck that pinched and trailed down her spine under the merciless sun. The woman's name was Amani. In one hand, she held a bow, and her back was bent under the weight of a large satchel she wore slung over one shoulder, all their possessions. When she reached the wall, she found that it was taller than her and made of thick stone. She placed her free hand on the wall and flinched as she felt the demon magic seething within it. Her shoulders slumped, and she pulled her hand back from the wall. Beside her, her six-year-old boy whimpered, and at the sound, her eyes flitted to him

1

and his sister, seven years old now, though when they had started their journey, she was still six, and he was five.

The two of them stood leaning on each other, dusty tear tracks showing on the girl's cheeks, which were much hollower than a child's cheeks should be. All three of Amani's children were so thin, no matter how much of her own food Amani put into their wooden bowls at mealtime. A slender, white-barked tree stood nearby. Amani knew the little ones couldn't walk much longer.

"Here, sit in the shade. Isika, you sit there," she pointed to a spot that seemed clean and soft. "There's room for Ben too. That's it."

Amani carefully lifted the sleeping toddler from her shoulders, laying the tiny girl in a hollow between two roots of the tree and unwrapping her long headscarf to cover the little one.

"Wait here a moment," she told the two older children. "Mama is going to take a little look at this wall. Have some water. Drink carefully and share!" she said, then smiled at them. "Play the water game." In the water game, the sister and brother took turns having sips of water, the tiniest they could manage, passing the water skin back and forth between them. It used up time and kept them from gulping water, which could be dangerous in the scorching desert that had been their home for many months.

Isika's eyes lit up at the mention of a game. She was the older and braver of the two. The woman stroked her daughter's hair and touched her cheek gently, and tapped the boy on his chin softly with her knuckle, before straightening and turning, her eyes on the wall.

The walls that surrounded the village made her sick to her stomach. The city they had fled, many months ago, had also been surrounded by walls. Amani had hoped to find a new home, free of poison, but it didn't seem possible here.

She approached the high barrier again, one hand on her belly, which went before her like the prow of a ship. The baby moved heavily within her, and she flinched as an elbow or foot knocked her ribs. She knew it wouldn't be much longer until the baby demanded to come into the world, and she felt the familiar tendrils of panic reaching along her spine and flickering into her mind.

She walked along the length of the wall, ignoring her fear and exhaustion, looking for any sign of a breach. She only wanted to see within—she didn't want to be seen before she was ready to show herself. She walked a long way, searching, and it was after her children were out of sight that she found it: a large crack in the wall, just enough of an opening to gaze through. She put her eye to the wall, registering a market square with stalls of food and goods.

She gasped, drawing back, one hand on her heart and the other on her belly. After a moment, she laughed at herself. It was silly to be afraid of any person. She heard the words of her deceased mother in her head, chiding her for being scared. But these weren't the people she was looking for.

For seven months, Amani had been searching for her mother's people, the place where Amani had been born. This wasn't it, even at first glance, Amani knew it because the people she saw through the wall had pale white skin. Amani stared at her own hands on the wall, as dark against the sandstone as black tree branches against the dawn. She lifted a hand to her face and looked again through the crack in the wall. The people were the palest Amani had ever seen. Of course she had seen white people in the walled city, but one or two maybe, and at a distance. Never so many at one time. Her courage faltered. She wondered if the people of this village had ever seen a woman with black skin.

There were about a dozen men, women, and children, in the market square before her. The women wore heavy, long dresses that covered their bodies from wrist to neck, neck to ankle in dark, dull material. They had long, straight hair that didn't look real to Amani. She wondered whether they were wearing wigs, to have hair in such strange colors, hanging limp, like a cloth on a clothesline. She reached a hand to her own head, where her short, tightly curled hair was slowly growing out after she had shaved her head to make it easier for the journey.

Amani stared at her hands again, seeing the way her wrists jutted from her thin arms. Her hands looked impossibly large. They had been walking for so many months with little more to eat than the occasional rabbits she could kill with her bow. The baby shifted in her belly. She sighed, and the sigh came from the deepest part of her. This was the end of wandering. She couldn't go farther, she had no more strength. She had run away from the walled city, desperate to protect her children, and here they were, at this village that reeked of demon magic.

It was this or death. She only hoped that they were merciful here, merciful to those who looked different, merciful to strangers. It didn't appear that they were kind, she thought, craning her neck to look at the broken glass stuck along the top of the wall. But she would have to use everything she had left within her to gain their trust.

"Help me, Mother," she whispered, feeling the familiar ache of loss. If only her mother was still here—she would know what to do.

THE REACTION of the villagers was even more intense than Amani had feared, though thankfully, they did not become violent. As Amani and her children walked through the main gate of the village, the littlest girl on Amani's hip and the older two holding hands tightly beside her, people stopped what they were doing and stared, terror plain as daylight on their pale faces.

The village children wailed, and a few women picked up babies and ran headlong, in a panic. Amani thought wryly, that, seeing their reactions, she had been right to wonder whether the people of this village had ever seen black people before. She was almost certain they hadn't. She stood as straight as she could, her head high.

"Do you see how silly it is to be afraid, children?" she asked in a low voice. "You must never give in to fear."

"They look so strange, Mother," her daughter replied in a whisper.

"Don't fear what is different, my love," Amani said. "This is another game. A chance to learn." She cast her eyes around for someone who might be brave enough to offer a cool drink and answers to Amani's questions. She spotted a tomato seller at a stall nearby, who was standing her ground, though her face was pale and set. She had hair of a color that Amani had never seen before; bright orange, pulled behind her, curling in tendrils like the creepers of bean plants. Amani walked toward the stall, and though the woman took a step back, she didn't flee.

"Greetings," Amani said. The woman nodded swiftly, tears standing in her blue eyes. "Don't worry," Amani said. She couldn't help herself. "I'm only a person as well. Not a demon or a ghost." The woman lifted her head and dashed at her cheeks with the backs of her hands. She gave a short bark of laughter, not meeting Amani's eyes.

"I should be ashamed of myself. Please, mother, sit. You look as though you've traveled far." The woman fetched four cups of water from a bucket behind her while Amani sat. For once, Amani didn't make her children play the water game. She watched in silence as they gulped. Now that she was seated, weariness crashed into her with such force that there was every chance she would not be able to find them the shelter they needed.

Summoning her strength, Amani asked her question. "Who is in charge of this village?"

"The priest," the woman said, her eyebrows shooting up. She glanced away and used her chin to point somewhere in the distance behind Amani. "But you won't have to search for him, because here he is, coming to us."

Amani looked. In the distance, a building rose from the earth—a strange red cube—and from it strode an old man. He wore deep black robes that contrasted heavily with his pale white skin and even paler hair. Amani felt stirrings of understanding within her, and she bowed her head, taking a long, deep breath to ready herself for this last effort to save her children.

PART I

CHAPTER 1

S*EVEN YEARS LATER*

Isika looked nothing like her father. It was an awareness that had always hummed underneath the regular work and sleep of her daily life, something the neighbors watched and gossiped about, something she brooded about during the evening offering, peeking from beneath her eyelids as she bowed her head. Isika's skin was dark, like the large sooty garden moths. Her father had long, papery limbs, pale as the moon. Lately, her father's face had a gray tint that alarmed Isika. He was sick, possibly dying. That day, the day everything changed, fourteen-year-old Isika was already familiar with fighting off fear.

The morning started out like every other morning in the Worker village. When dawn came, she woke, put on her outer dress, and rolled her sleeping mat to store it in the corner of the room. She left the house on soft feet to begin the day's work. Her seven-year-old sister, Ibba, had finally settled into sleep after a restless night that involved a lot of murmuring and thrashing about, until Isika had been tempted to tie her sister's legs together. The house was quiet. Outside, the sky was pink, the light barely bright enough to outline the walls, but already Isika's youngest brother, Kital, was out playing. He threw a ball for a street dog, hurling it again and again with his thin arms. He grinned every time the mangy dog brought it to him.

"You know you're not supposed to play with them," Isika told her little brother, her voice stern, and he turned. For a moment, his eyes were wide with guilt. Then he grinned at her, his dimples appearing and disappearing in his small face. He knew Isika wouldn't stop him or tell on him, so again, he threw the ball as far as his short arms could manage, and laughed as the dog ran for it. Street dogs were like rats to the Worker people, but Kital had always loved them. If he could get away with it, Kital fed them tiny bits of fat from his meat when he thought no one was watching, and Isika didn't have the will to keep him from doing as he wished.

Kital was only four years old, and he was the boy of her heart. Their mother had died soon after he was born, and Isika had raised Kital from the time he couldn't even pick his head up off her shoulder. She knew every part of him, from his high, round forehead to his tiny square brown toes.

She touched him briefly on the head, something Workers were only allowed to do to a younger person, and walked across the yard to reach the tall iron gate. Their family wall was broken, which was how the dogs got in, but keeping the gate closed was one of the strictest rules of the Workers. It was how they kept the sacred boundaries, how peace remained in the village. Each family had its own island with honored borders that other Workers did not violate. It was wrong to tread on another person's home ground.

As soon as Isika left the walls of her family's ground, a familiar weight settled on her. She looked down the long road that swept from the temple and the priest's grounds toward the village square, out to the harbor beyond the village. Walls of different shapes, heights, and thickness lined the road, separating each family's ground from the ground beside it. Every family wore the responsibility for its own walls, but no family had lifted a finger to build them.

The walls were gifts from the goddesses, breathed straight from the four deities, without help from the people of the village. Isika had seen it happen; waking in the morning, you might find a foot added to a neighbor's wall that hadn't been there the night before. The walls were a blessing, and Isika assumed that their wall remained broken because of her father's sickness. The goddesses were visiting some kind of anger on her family.

Many eyes turned toward her as she walked. Even though she was as familiar as the sun to the people on her street, they always stared at her, one of the four black-skinned villagers, before giving the traditional nod and looking away politely, eyes on the dust at their feet. Isika nodded back, looking down as well. Holding eye contact was impolite, a violation almost as bad as walking on another person's ground, something Isika's father had spent years trying to get through Isika's head.

When she was younger, and her mother was still alive, eyes had fascinated Isika. Her mother's eyes were black as the night sky, and they shone like mirrors in moonlight or sunlight. Isika's eyes were dark brown, and her father's eyes were light grey—startling, with black rims around the irises. Some people in the Worker village had eyes that were blue, or even a mix of green and blue. Isika longed to stare at all the different colors, to study the rays that seemed to sit in some people's eyes, blooming like flowers. But if her father caught her looking too long, he put his hand on her head, resting it there or pushing her, to let Isika know she was trespassing on the person's soul. Whenever she looked away from a person's eyes to the dusty ground and her own bare feet, she felt a sense of loss. Isika didn't know why the rules came so hard to her. She knew she hadn't always lived here. Maybe something from before made her different.

Seven years ago, Isika's mother had walked out of the desert and into the Worker village with her children. Isika's new father, the priest of the village, had taken the family in and married her mother. There was still a lot of talk about why, exactly, he had done it. Isika flinched away from the gossip, murmurings of strange magic that her mother had cast over Nirloth.

They had wandered in the desert for months before finding the Worker village. Before the desert, they had been in another place, but though Isika tried, she couldn't remember it well. She could picture eyes and faces, blurs of color. It troubled her because she knew she should remember. She had been old enough—she was six years old when they left that place. She remembered high walls, much higher than the walls in the Worker village. She remembered her mother singing, or sometimes crying. She remembered being alone and afraid, and that was all she knew before her memories of coming to the desert and playing with wandering herds of goats. After the desert, they reached the Worker village, and it had been their home ever since.

Isika stumbled on a stone in the road, her mind still busy with trying to remember their past. Sometimes trying to remember consumed her. Benayeem, her brother, didn't like to talk about it at all. Just a year younger than Isika, he should also be able to recall it, but he shook his head when she prodded him.

"Mother didn't want us to talk about it, Isika, you know that," he would say.

She only wanted to know if he remembered anything at all, but Ben refused to say. Her younger brother was the most frustrating person, more frustrating than either of the other two. At one time, there had been five siblings, but Isika shrugged the tight, sad thoughts of her sister, Aria, away, as she always did when she remembered her. She thought of Ibba, instead, born shortly after they had reached the village, and Kital, the son born to her mother and her new father, the priest. Thinking about Aria couldn't bring her back.

Isika reached the edge of the woods and walked between the trees slowly and carefully, watching for snakes. She began to gather the dead sticks that lay on the ground, keeping her eyes open for larger sticks that would burn longer. Many people in the village bought wood, but Isika's father wanted their family to gather first and buy wood only if they couldn't find any. It was *the way*, he said, an old Worker tradition; his answer for most hard things in their lives. Isika's limbs were sluggish, exhaustion trickling through her body. She had only sipped a little tea before she came. The Workers ate only one meal—the day's food—at midday; it was the way. She felt the slow, hungry, feeling of the morning overcoming her even as she tried to hurry. She blinked and rubbed at her eyes, bending to pick up a stick that was wider than the others.

"Ah!" she said under her breath, happy to find such a large one. Just then, she heard a sharp crack as someone stepped on dead wood behind her.

"Give it to me, Loshy," a voice said. Isika sighed and hesitated. The voice went on. "Actually, give me all of it."

"No," Isika said, straightening and staring into the eyes of a tall, wide-shouldered boy. His name was Jak. She knew him from her time in the village school, and from seeing him strut around the village, knocking baskets out of the hands of younger boys, or throwing stones at street dogs. Isika knew he was from a pig-raising family and that they should have more than enough money to buy their own wood. She saw again that his eyes were a dark blue, deep-set in his face, caught in an expression halfway between cruel and excited. She kept staring until he looked away.

"Get your eyes off my soul, Loshy," he said, his voice fierce as he looked down at her basket of sticks.

"My name isn't Loshy, and where were you this morning, Jak? Dead asleep from overeating? You should get out here earlier and find your own wood. You know you can't take wood from a temple daughter."

He spat at the ground then, and a tiny drop caught in the wind and flew up to Isika's cheek. She took a step back, finally looking away from his face, wiping at her cheek with the sleeve of her dress.

"You're no temple daughter, what a joke," he said, his eyes bulging as he kept them trained on Isika's shoulder. "And your father is dying— his well-deserved punishment for bringing foreigners into the temple."

Isika felt as though he had slapped her. A bird cried out, and the sound echoed around the quiet forest. The losh trees were bare at this time of year, tall, with long black limbs and hardwood that was perfect for burning. "Loshy," they had called Isika in school because her skin was the darkest out of all her siblings, nearly as black as her mother's. She looked at her hands now as she clutched the old basket, and remembered her mother's hands holding hers before she died, her mother, wasted away, commanding her with feverish eyes to take care of her brothers and sisters.

The terrible fear she felt now at the possibility of her father dying was even greater than the daily dread she felt at him continuing to live and breathe and be disappointed in Isika and her siblings. He had taken them in and cared for them, and even though his care was hard to perceive sometimes, without him, Isika knew the village would not keep them. With her mother dead, Isika didn't know where they

17

would go. She knew that her stepmother, Jerutha, could not change the minds of the Workers. Jerutha would try, because she was brave and kind. She had moved into the house of a priest and four black children, a house of mourning and bad luck. She had moved in even after one daughter had been given over, and the mother had died of grief. She had married the priest out of pity for the children, and she would stand up for them out of love, but there was only one of her and too many villagers. Many of them had no mercy in their hearts. Isika's father couldn't die.

"You know nothing about it," she said, but she was shaking, and she could hear the fear in her individual voice.

Jak smiled, his eyes narrowing. "Oh, really?" he said. "Is there another plan? One we haven't heard yet? I haven't heard bells yet, but maybe they'll ring soon."

Isika moved before she thought, her hands itching to knock the smile off his face, but she stopped in time, tightening her hands on her basket to keep them still. She gulped large breaths and tried to calm down. It was as though he had found her greatest, most secret fear, and prodded with something sharp. Terror washed over her like cold water. Her worst fear was not the possibility of being alone at the mercy of people who had never trusted them. Her worst fear was the bells. But no! She shook her head against it. The goddesses had never forced any family to give over more than one child, and this was the truth she clung to, even when sharp dreams of boats woke her in the night.

"One child has always been enough," she said.

Jak smiled wider, leaning against one of the stark trees of

the forest. His feet were bare, like Isika's. His family might have enough money for wood, but not for shoes, and that made Isika and Jak more alike than different. But he was glad to see her panic, and she told herself there was nothing similar between them.

"Your 'father' is a priest, and he is dying," Jak said. "Do you think he'll keep foreigners safe rather than appease the goddesses? He has no priest trained up to follow him—if he dies, the Workers are left without the offerings. He knows his duty."

Worse, Isika thought. Her father was afraid of dying. She could smell his fear in the nighttime when he got up and paced, and her own terror grew until it was as large as her chest and leaked out through her eyes, making damp spots on the pillow beneath her head.

Jak laughed. Isika remembered that he had been especially cruel to Benayeem, who had learned to fight for his life in the village school after they came out of the desert. Jak reached out and pulled the basket from her shaking hands. He emptied every stick but one into his own basket.

"I'll be waiting for the bells," he said. And he was gone, stomping away through the forest. Isika could hear him long after she couldn't see him anymore. She began to gather wood again, taking deep breaths to calm herself and drive back her anger. The sun was barely up and already it was hot on her head, so she put her headscarf on, tucking it under her heavy hair. After another half hour, she felt she had enough. Her stepmother had slipped a few coins into her dress pocket the night before—"In case you can't gather it all," she had said, and Isika decided to buy the rest of the day's wood. Her father would never know. He wasn't the same as he had been in the past, when he oversaw absolutely everything. Since he had become sick, he rarely checked the wood to see if it was forest wood or the shorter, neater logs the woodmen sold in the market.

Isika put her basket on her shoulder and left the forest to walk on the road. The dust swirled around her feet, and the sun pounded on her head, its rays glistening on the dangerous broken glass that adorned the walls on either side of the road. The houses behind the walls seemed heavy and quiet, as though no one was in them, but Isika knew people lived behind the closed doors. She watched the wall glass sparkle in the sun until she reached the market square. She wandered through the market and bought tomatoes from Faiza, the kind woman with the bright red hair who always pressed her hand gently as she passed Isika her change. The tomato seller had been friendly with Isika's mother.

Then Isika bought goat milk from the man with the long nose who had repaired the temple roof two months ago. His twins were sleeping under a tent behind him while his wife sat spinning goat wool. She looked at Isika briefly, nodded, and looked away.

"May your eyes be guarded," the man said in the traditional greeting. He passed her the goat milk in a leather bag.

"And your speech kept safe," Isika replied, taking the bag and handing him a few coins.

She wandered around the market as long as she could, purchasing a bag of wheat to pound and a small packet of meat for the day's meal. She would help Jerutha harvest greens from the garden plants that still struggled along in the season of hot sun.

At home, she let herself in through the gate and brought the wood to the kitchen. Jerutha was standing over the sink, washing dishes. She leaned over to lift more plates from the pile on the bench beside her and sighed. Her belly was round, and Isika knew her back hurt her. Her time was growing near. Together, she and Isika had been preparing the birth space, a small room on their grounds, the custom for Worker women when they gave birth.

Isika laid the sticks beside Jerutha on the floor and bent over to make the cooking fire in the grate. They would begin cooking the day's meal soon. But Jerutha turned to Isika as she pulled the larger sticks from the basket.

"Your father wants to see you," she said. "I'll ask Ben to make the fire."

"Benayeem? Make a fire?" Isika said, her voice incredulous.

"You know he can do it," Jerutha said, her voice reproachful, but she was smiling.

"When have you ever seen him make a fire?"

"He has his temple work. It keeps him busy there."

Isika looked at her stepmother with raised eyebrows. Jerutha smiled at her. "Go to your father."

Then Isika realized what she was saying, and her stomach clenched with dread.

"Why does he want to see me?"

"He didn't say." Jerutha's voice was light, but Isika saw the frown on her face. She mulled over the different reasons that her father could want to speak to her first thing in the morning, and none of them were good. Scolding... a work assignment? She shrugged off the idea that came next. An announcement. It couldn't be. She stood and shook herself, standing as tall as she could before walking to her father.

CHAPTER 2

*H*er father's sleeping room smelled like sickness. Jerutha helped him up to bathe often, and Isika changed the sheets under him daily, but the odor persisted, and Isika hated being in the room more every day. The light hurt her father's eyes, so the curtains were pulled tight over the windows, and Isika could barely see him as she walked in. As her eyes adjusted, she saw him sitting up on his mat, his legs crossed and tucked under him, his eyes closed. She recognized his praying posture, so she waited for him to acknowledge her.

Finally, he looked up.

"Isika. Did you get the wood?" he asked. His eyes were shadows in his face. She couldn't see into them at all.

"Yes, Father," she said. She found that her hands were shaking, and she grabbed the right one with the left to make them still.

"I called you in here..." he paused and coughed, "because today I want you to make the offering at the temple."

"Why? That's Ben's job," Isika said before she thought, then flinched, knowing her father would be angry. He didn't move toward her, though, only looked at her. She couldn't see his expression.

"Go now. Don't come back until the noon meal." He bowed his head and returned to his prayers.

Isika felt frustration burning through her. Her life was a series of commands without explanation, rules without the ability to understand. She was always confused and struggling with the way Workers did things, and why. Why was their house tired, old, and sad? Why did her father refuse things that helped with the work, like buying wood? Why did they wear dark colors, and why weren't they allowed to bring flowers into the house or climb trees? The answers she got, when she got answers, were unsatisfying. She ached from wanting to speak, to say all the words that were silently building up inside her, but she knew by now that speaking would mean a burning cheek and a bruise the next day.

"Yes, Father," she said. She bent her head and turned to go.

HER FEET DRAGGED in the dust as she walked to the temple. Isika had never liked doing temple work. Benayeem didn't like it either, but he didn't have a choice— Nirloth, their father, had decided that Ben would be the one to become the village priest when he died. Isika doubted that the villagers would ever allow a foreigner to become their priest, but still Benayeem did the temple duties, day after day. It seemed to Isika's eyes that her brother accepted everything that happened with silence. He never spoke out, the way she did. She couldn't tell what he truly thought about anything. It was almost as though he could button himself up inside his skin, shrink into himself so that nothing of his true character was visible. Isika sometimes thought that she would love him more if she actually knew who he was. They were very different. Isika lived with more risk, unable to hold back her thoughts unless she clamped down on herself hard. As a result, it wasn't strange for Isika to be in bed with a cold cloth over her face after her father struck her.

The temple of the four goddesses was the one bright point in the Worker landscape. Their village and the surrounding plains were flat and dry, with scrubby bushes, the Losh forests, and a few Yuci trees that didn't add much color, with their gray, washed-out trunks and dull leaves. And Workers didn't like to use too many colors because it was said that the goddesses were jealous of bright things. Their temple, in contrast, was dazzling, painted red with gold accents on all its square corners, a large red cube that rose suddenly out of the brown dust. Isika went in quickly and felt the darkness envelop her as she left the burning sunshine. The air was old with incense, and cool, despite the small sacred fire that was always kept burning. The stones were smooth beneath her feet. She walked toward the terrifying statues and picked up the bells, ringing them to wake the four goddesses. She began to light the cubes of incense, chanting the words for the morning offering as she did so.

Power, fate, independence, wealth, four sisters, four realms, I bow to you.

I bow to you, power, for you hold everything in sway.

I bow to you, fate, for you have written the end.

I bow to you, independence, for you hold up our heads.

I bow to you, wealth, for you feed the bellies of men.

She said the words quickly, and as she chanted, she frowned, the familiar anger rising in her.

Isika's mother had died during the famine of the deaf ears, three years after they arrived in the village. There had been a drought for three long years, with no rain falling on the earth to beat back the terrible dust or allow the crops to grow. By the third year, the Workers were starving, and they offered more children over during that time than they had sent out in a hundred years. The boat makers frantically hammered together the tiny boats that the villagers used to send their children out to the sea where they died in the waves as an offering for the goddesses. Despite the children they received that year, the goddesses hadn't heard the Workers. They turned deaf ears. Many more children starved.

The goddesses even turned their backs when Nirloth decided that Isika's younger sister Aria needed to be given over. Aria was nearly eight years old, far too old to be sent out, but Ibba, three years old and the right age for the sacrifice, was their father's favorite, and he refused to give her over. They sent Aria out in the little boat. Isika could see her face to this day, quiet, asleep after the offering tea that sent the children to sleep, mercifully, so they didn't have to be awake for the moment they were pushed out on the sea to die at the goddesses' hands. Isika still remembered the dread in her stomach, the prickling all along her arms and legs that meant something was terribly, horribly wrong. Paralyzing fear had surged over her, and though she wanted to change something, anything, she was helpless. She had no power or ability to change the world or even Nirloth's mind.

Isika's mother, Amani, went into labor that very night and baby Kital was born. Amani lived for only two more weeks. She died of grief, Isika knew. Losing Aria —and the wrongness of her death—took their mother from them. Even all her other children, even her new baby, weren't enough to make up for her sorrow, to keep her with them. Isika hadn't been able to do anything about that either.

She chanted the words again, thinking of her mother in bed in those last days, how small she had become, shrunken and frail as she refused to eat. She gave Kital, the little brown baby she had just birthed, to ten-year-old Isika, and then she gave up her life and floated away.

Kital became Isika's truest love, even as he wore the life straight out of her. Isika remembered the wild predictions of the villagers before Kital's birth. Kital was the son of Nirloth and Amani, and no one in the village had ever seen the offspring of a black person and a white person. The egg seller had gone far enough to suggest that he would be striped, like a cat. But Kital came out a lovely, soft brown, and then Isika stopped going to school, staying home to watch the baby. She looked on with pride as his scrawny little body became a decently meaty body—not fat, never fat—as the famine lessened, too late to save Aria or her mother.

Isika walked with Benayeem and baby Kital over the endless brown fields of Worker land, trying to tire her horrible grief right out of her body. When Kital got older, he toddled around in the trees and went with Isika to gather sticks in the morning. He made everything better, though it had seemed like things would never be okay again. Isika hadn't known how she could ever survive the loss of her mother, who had been the sun in the morning. She made everything bright, even on the dullest day when nothing else penetrated the thick haze of the sky. Amani had helped Isika to understand the people of the Worker village and why they looked at the little family with suspicion.

"They are afraid of what they don't understand," she told Isika. "And they don't understand what they have not experienced, because they haven't ever tried. I know it is hard, but you need to learn from the way it makes you feel. Learn to live without fear."

Isika told Kital the same thing, later. "Mama's mother always told her this, when she was a little girl: *Fear is the thing that grips the heart and ties the limbs. Live without it, and you can truly love.*"

She finished the chanting in the temple, the words still echoing in the smoky, incense-scented air. *Power, fate, independence, wealth.* The four goddesses they were taught to fear. No one questioned them and their cruel demands. Before Aria was sent out, Amani had been mostly happy in the Worker village. She had her small kitchen garden, she coaxed flowers from the earth where no flowers had grown before, though she never was allowed to gather them and bring them into the house. But Amani quailed before the goddesses. She didn't like to go to the temple; one of the few things she and Isika's father argued about before Aria and the sending. She remained at the doorstep to the temple, her head bowed.

"These are not the beliefs of my people," she told Nirloth, pleading with him when he insisted she come in.

"You can't even tell me who your people are," he replied. "You don't know where you came from. And you're here now! The people notice you and wonder who this priest has taken for his wife, that she refuses to enter the temple."

He had been right about that. Isika placed the bell back into its alcove and pulled the broom from the space behind the altar, sweeping the ashes into a neat pile, then slowly cleaning the interior of the temple where the feet of so many people trod each week, looking for reasons for their failures and pain. *More, more,* the goddesses cried, *more worship, more sacrifice.* Isika felt their hunger in the stones under her feet. The blame for the Workers' pain fell squarely on themselves. Isika shuddered and left the temple with relief. She started across the field that led to the house, and just as she did so, the wailing began.

CHAPTER 3

"*B*enayeem!" Jerutha called from the door to the house. Ben heard her from behind the back wall, where he sat looking out over the fields. He was putting off his ordinary job of doing the temple work, which he hated with a loathing deeper than anything, except, perhaps, the memories of the walled city, memories he tried to keep shut away. Day after day, though, he was stuck doing something he hated. It was that or suffer consequences from his father.

Benayeem shrank from conflict or physical pain, so he went to the temple like a good son, though his heart wasn't in the motions his hands made or the words he mumbled. He could barely make his hands move to build up the sacred fire. Ben knew his father felt scorn for him as he watched the slow way Ben lit the incense and cleaned the idols with the soft cloth—that was the worst, he hated touching the statues—but his father didn't know about the ringing that seared his ears and brain while his feet were touching the temple floor. *Wrong... wrong,* he heard, the words taking shape as soon as he reached the threshold.

Ben's secret was that he heard music that wasn't there; ringing bells, gongs, discordant screeching, and notes that grated across his mind while he did his work in the temple. The goddesses stared down at him with baleful eyes full of malice. They weren't fooled by his blind obedience to his father. They knew he hated them. He learned to be invisible, and he had taken to hiding when he knew it was time for temple duties. But Jerutha's voice was too loud to ignore, and he sighed as he went to face his stepmother.

The discordant music was something he had heard all his life. It pressed on him at all times, making his life miserable. He heard it when he saw someone in the market give someone else the wrong change, he heard it when his father hit his sister. He didn't know how to stop the way he sensed people, the knowledge of their hearts, or the way his skin burned or the sick feeling in his stomach when he perceived wrong being done. So he tried to disappear into himself. He withdrew farther and farther away from the world, not taking notice when bad things happened, turning away and closing his eyes. He went to the market only when he needed to. His life became a circle between the temple, the school, and his home, and in this way, he dulled the voices and the sounds and kept them quiet enough that they didn't deafen him.

Jerutha stood in the entryway with her hand on her belly. Her eyes brightened as she spotted him, and she smiled.

"There you are, Ben."

He nodded, looking at the side of her face to avoid her eyes. She looked away as well but reached one hand out to touch his shoulder gently.

"Your father wants you to build the kitchen fire today."

Ben straightened, surprised. "What about the temple?"

"He sent Isika to work in the temple," Jerutha replied. She grinned. "You're free for today."

Ben felt relief soaking into him. He followed Jerutha into the kitchen and bent before the fire. He loved being in here, partly because when he was around his stepmother, the pressure on his mind lessened. His sense of her was calm and sweet, and she rarely did anything that brought the gongs booming into his head. Unlike his father.

"Isika wasn't sure you would be able to light the fire," Jerutha said. She stood beside the washing bucket that sat on the large stone slab she used to prepare food, washing the mugs from the morning's tea.

Ben snorted, pulling the logs out of Isika's gathering basket. "I'm sure she wasn't. Isika's only a year older, but she thinks she's the only one who can do anything." *Wrong, wrong,* chimed the voice in his mind, this time like tiny, piercing bells. Ben winced.

"Besides," he said. "I take care of the temple fire every day."

"True," Jerutha said, drying the mugs with a faded cloth, "but that fire is already lit."

Ben pulled bits of a stick apart to make kindling, shaping a little nest and placing the larger sticks over the top, like a tent, the way his mother had shown him all those years ago in the desert. Ben still made fires the way she did. He felt a familiar stab of pain at the thought of his mother and shrugged the ache away. He adjusted a few logs, wishing this was his regular job. Ben loved making things, doing things with his hands, but when he turned thirteen on his last birthday, his father had determined that he would be a priest, and now Ben faced a lifetime of prayers to goddesses he hated.

He had just coaxed the spark into the kindling and was sitting back to admire the crackling of the fire when his father entered the room. Ben looked up, shocked. He couldn't remember the last time his father had been out of bed.

"Nirloth!" Jerutha exclaimed, rushing to hold her husband's arm. He was shaking, and his skin was gray, but he looked as stern as ever. Ben shifted to make room as they walked past him. Jerutha helped Nirloth into a chair.

"Where is Kital?" Nirloth asked.

"He's playing in the yard with Ibba," Jerutha said.

"That boy plays too much, he should work more," Ben's father said. "But never mind now, just bring them both here, please."

Jerutha left at once to find the children, and Ben was alone with his father. He closed the door of the stove and sat back with his hands on his knees, not looking toward where his father sat, just a few feet away. With the music droning in sickening loops, Benayeem sensed his father clearly. Everything in Ben screamed with dread. He felt like he would throw up.

"This will be for the best, son," Ben's father said. "You will see."

Ben's eyes flew up to his father's face, and he had his mouth open to ask *what* would be for the best when Jerutha came back into the room with the little ones. They were giggling together, but they stopped when they saw their father sitting at the table.

"Father!" Ibba cried out. "You're better!" She ran to him and hugged him around the waist. Nirloth smiled, but pulled her arms off of him.

"Not better, dear one. I have something to tell you." He turned to look at Kital and gestured for him to come closer. Kital was the only child who was actually Nirloth's son. His skin was a little lighter than Ben's or Ibba's, but for all that, he didn't resemble his father or even seem to feel much of a connection to him. Kital's bubbly four-year-old energy was too joyful to be comfortable around his stern father.

"Kital," Nirloth began, but then he needed to pause and take a breath, and Ben's stomach began to squeeze into a ball. Ben slowly stood. Nirloth went on as Kital looked up at him. "You are blessed, son, and you live in service of the goddesses, as do all the Workers. Your service is changing, growing, as of today."

Ben glanced at Jerutha and saw her standing, bent over, gripping the back of the chair opposite Nirloth's, her knuckles white. He couldn't see her face because her head was bowed, and her hair fell around her like a curtain. Ben was paralyzed. He thought that if he could keep his father from speaking, he might be able to stop this from happening. He understood, suddenly, why his father had sent Isika to the temple today.

He forced his mouth open. "Father," he said, but it was a

whisper, and one glance from his father had him as silent as the heavy stone table his father now thumped with a fist.

"Silence! Benayeem, if I want you to speak I will command you to speak. Kital, you will enter the service of the goddesses tomorrow. You will be sent out, as appeasement, for the health of the priest and thus the health of all the Workers."

Kital blinked up at Nirloth, his eyes large. He didn't seem to understand. He turned to look at Ibba. She retreated from their father and stared at him with a shocked face. She knew. The blood left Ben's face, and the pressure on his whole being was like a huge gong ringing. He heard screeching, discordant music. *Wrong, wrong, wrong, WRONG,* it shouted. Kital looked at Benayeem, and when he saw the look on his brother's face, he understood that something very bad was happening, and he began to cry. Ibba started crying as well, and the two of them ran to Jerutha, clinging to her skirts.

"What are you saying, husband?" Jerutha asked Nirloth, her voice a rasp, her face paler than usual. She put one hand on her belly and sat down abruptly.

"You heard my words," Ben's father said. "I am giving Kital over. I am the priest of this village, and if I die, the whole village will die. Benayeem is not cut out to be a priest; there is no one I can pass my duties along to. If I had known, when I took Amani in, that her children wouldn't even find it in them to give the goddesses proper respect," he spat the words in Ben's direction, and then Ben truly wanted to disappear, "maybe I would have reconsidered and sent her away."

Ibba and Kital kept crying, and the pressure on Ben

continued. He knew it would continue as long as he was in the house with this great horror. So he left. He walked through the kitchen and out the door, ignoring his father's shouts. "Even now?" he yelled. "Even now, you run away? Get out of my sight, boy! And don't come back until I am asleep, or you'll be sorry!"

Ben didn't look back at the house. He focused on moving his arms and legs under the pressure that had now built so much it threatened to flatten him. Ugly, horrible music made the ground swim before him. *Wrong, wrong, wrong.*

What do you want from me? He called out in his head. *What am I supposed to do? Of course it's wrong, but nothing can be done!* There was no answer.

As he ran across the yard and said the sacred words to leave the walls of their ground, he spotted Isika coming back from the temple, and he ran even faster. He knew what was going to happen, almost as if it was written out in front of him. He couldn't be there for what would happen next. Isika never tried to disappear. Isika dove straight into whatever trouble she found, no matter how afraid she was, and she suffered for it. He kicked at a rock on the path and kept running.

CHAPTER 4

The crying went on and on as Isika ran toward the house. Benayeem burst out of the front door and ran to the gate, fumbling with the latch until he finally got it open. He flung the gate wide and ran out into the street without closing it behind him.

"Ben!" Isika called, and he paused to look at her with wild, red eyes, then kept running.

Truly alarmed, Isika walked to the house, her stomach rolling and tossing with fear. Her body went cold when she saw Jerutha sitting in the kitchen garden, rocking back and forth. The walk to the door seemed very, very long. Had Nirloth died?

In the clean, swept earth before the door, Ibba and Kital sat with their arms around each other. Ibba was crying. Kital's eyes were wet, wide, and shocked, the color of morning tea in his light brown face, shaped just like their mother's.

"What happened?" Isika cried, falling to her knees to put her arms around the two of them. "Is it Father? Is he... did he...?"

But whatever had happened, he hadn't died, because there he was at the door, looking down at her, standing for the first time in weeks, though he held tightly onto his cane. His white hair stood up from his head, and steely gray eyes flashed from his set face. A deep dread filled her as she stood to face him.

"What is happening?" she asked, remembering to aim her eyes away at the last moment. It was unspeakably rude to ask a question while looking into someone's eyes, it was the most invasive thing you could do toward a person's soul.

"I feel strong," he said, almost to himself. He lifted his head. "The strength I feel confirms my decision," he said, and she couldn't help it—her eyes flew up toward his. He was looking off into the distance, toward the temple. "I will give Kital over at dawn, the day after tomorrow."

The world blinked red.

"No," Isika said, and her voice seemed to come from somewhere old and dead. Ibba began to wail again. "No," Isika said one more time, her voice increasing in volume on the word until she was screaming and screaming and screaming. Her father withdrew into the shadow of the dark house, and she followed him.

"You can't!" she shrieked. "You can't!"

"It's done," he said. "I announced my intention while you were away. Great downfall will descend on the whole village if I turn back now."

He had sent her to the temple so he could announce this evil without her there to stop him. The blood left Isika's face, and her legs shook as though she would faint. She sat on a nearby chair with a thud. She watched, unbelieving, as he limped to the house altar and picked up the small brass horn. When she saw his intention, she leapt up to stop him, but she was too slow, and he sounded the blast. The horn rang out, signaling to the village that a child from this house would be given over. Isika listened to the shrill sound in stunned silence. When it ended, Nirloth put the horn back in its place on the altar and leaned heavily on his cane.

"We gave Aria over," she said, pleading now, tears running down her face. "No family is expected to give more than one child over."

"Except in times of extremity."

"Extremity? Your illness? An old man dying is not extremity! You'll give his life for yours?"

Isika flew at him to grasp his sleeve and beg for her brother's life, but he lifted his cane and struck her on the side of her head. A blast of pain echoed in her ears, and she fell to the floor, holding her hands over her head, trying to block the cane that came down on her, again and again. And still, she wailed and shouted. "He's not yours to give over! He's mine!" Until the cane struck her above the ear, and all was black.

WHEN ISIKA OPENED HER EYES, Jerutha was bending over her, weeping as she wiped her face with a cold cloth. Isika winced as the water stung the many cuts where the cane had dug into her skin. In the past, her father had slapped her or used his fists on her, many times over, but he had never done this. She didn't know what was happening to him. He had always been serious and hard, but never cruel.

Kital's life for his. Tears came to her eyes again, then spilled over, burning the scrapes on her face.

"Hush," Jerutha said. "You must not fight this, Isika. It is the way."

"The way?" Isika's voice was rough from screaming. She sounded broken.

"Hush, hush."

"Where is Kital?"

"Sleeping beside Ibba," Jerutha said. "They're worn out." She put a hand over her full belly, her face falling, her kind blue eyes filling with tears. She stroked Isika's face. "I'm so sorry, my love."

"It must not happen," Isika said, clenching her fists, wincing with the pain of moving her mouth. She wondered whether she would be disfigured. She lifted her hand to her face and lightly touched it.

"You will heal fine," Jerutha said, taking Isika's hand and moving it away. "The scrapes are shallow. Oh, Isika, little sister. How could you rush toward him? You know better."

"It must not happen," Isika repeated, but she felt a deep sense of panic. It was happening again. She had been too small to stop Aria being sent over, too young to prevent her mother's death. Deep shame washed over her, the familiar sense of not deserving to live because she hadn't been able to save their lives.

"There is nothing for it," Jerutha said. "We must accept this."

Through the door, which was still open, Isika saw the last rays of the sun touch the kitchen garden. Her mother had made flowers grow where flowers had never grown. People had whispered that she was a sorceress, to make colors come from the dull earth, but she shook her head and laughed. "Treat the earth well," she told Isika, "and it will respond to your hand. This is the true way." But when Isika pressed her for more, she had shaken her head and pinched her lips, looking distressed as she glanced at Nirloth, who sat in the shadow of the porch.

In the afternoon light, Isika saw the bean vines glowing, soft and golden, the curling tendrils of green grasping at one another, holding onto each another in their urge to grow tall and reach for the light.

"This must not be," she repeated.

Jerutha sighed and shook her head. She washed the cloth out in a bowl of water and dabbed at Isika's neck.

"We have work to do," she said.

There was preparation to be done for the sending. Jerutha and Isika needed to make the sleeping tea, and fold the cloths they would put in the boat—red for penance, white for purity, green for the envy of the goddesses, envy that prompted the Workers to assuage them by giving their children over. Isika thought she might vomit.

"Jerutha," she said, reaching out to touch her stepmother's

hand. Her voice was choked and low, and the room swam in front of her. If she wasn't careful, she was going to pass out again. She realized that she was half lying on Jerutha's crossed legs. Isika's stepmother stroked her forehead gently with her free hand. Jerutha had always been so kind to the children, ever since she came to them when she was barely more than a child herself.

"Jerutha, Kital is my baby. I can't give my baby over. This will be your child one day, Jerutha! Everyone gives one child, that is the way. It is not the way to give over so many. He won't stop! What if he wants to send your baby out, once it is the ripened age?"

The Workers didn't give their children over before the age of two. The goddesses cruelly insisted on the bonding between mother and child before snatching the children from their parents.

Jerutha's face paled, and she gripped her belly with one hand. She carefully lifted Isika's shoulders off of her lap, shifting so she could heave herself to her feet. Her belly stood out against her thin body like a melon. Jerutha was only ten years older than Isika, but she had lived a lot in a short time. Her mother was one of those who couldn't accept the life of a Worker, destined to feed the goddesses with time and sweat and children until death. Jerutha's mother had been altered, even broken, when her oldest daughter was given over many years before Jerutha was born. Her mother had later given birth to Jerutha and two other children, but she hadn't been right in her mind. Finally, she had wandered out into the wilderness, never to return. Jerutha had taken care of her younger siblings for much of her life. She and Isika were alike in many ways.

Jerutha paced, gathering the things they needed for the sending preparation: herbs for the sending tea, colored cloths. She opened drawers, searching for items they hadn't used in four years; she pulled bundles of herbs out of dusty baskets.

In between, she paced. She walked from one window to the other, gazing out at the garden, her hands spread over her belly as though she could guard it against the world.

She looked up at Isika, who hadn't moved from where she sat.

"Rest, daughter," she said. Her voice was very quiet. "I'll finish here."

ISIKA STOOD and limped toward the main sleeping room. In his sleep, Benayeem had rolled himself into a corner. Ibba and Kital were asleep, piled like puppies on the center mat. No, Isika realized as she drew near, Kital's eyes were open. He turned toward Isika, and she hurried to curl up beside him.

He caught her hand as tears came to her eyes again.

"Don't cry, Isika," he said. "I am not afraid."

She looked at his small, beloved face. His tea-colored eyes and perfect little nose, the small gap between his teeth, his long eyelashes. She thought of all the nights she had held him as a baby, while those eyelashes drifted shut ever so slowly and then opened wide again as he jerked back to wakefulness. She remembered her exhaustion, singing him endless lullabies, rocking him back and forth and trying not to nod off to sleep before he did.

As though he knew what she was thinking, he began to sing one of those lullabies, his voice soft and sweet. It was the song their mother had sung to her, the first thing she could remember beside the calm of her mother's face.

"Water flowing between earth and sky
Bright day, old night, gentle and wise
Birds on the wing, fire in the stars
Oh, high one, earth is in your hands
Oh, true one, we are in your hands."

The words had always been mysterious to Isika, and now she felt a spark of longing—frustration at her lack of understanding. The song had come down to her from her mother's mother, and perhaps it came from farther back than that, but Isika knew nothing of her grandmothers, and she was adrift in a time when the words made no sense.

They must both have fallen asleep because the next thing Isika knew was Jerutha gently shaking her awake. Kital was curled in a ball against her stomach.

"Wake up, Isika," Jerutha said, her voice urgent. "We don't have much time."

It was still dark, but Isika followed Jerutha. She groaned softly as she stood, the memory of her father's decision slamming into her as she felt the bruises on her shoulders and legs, the cuts on her face. Her heart burned with pain. Jerutha led her into the garden, and they huddled between the bean plants.

"You must," Jerutha whispered, "come to me if I ever send word that I need you. You must help me if I ask for you." Her eyes burned into Isika's, and startled, Isika looked away.

"What?" she asked. "I don't understand—"

"Hush. Wait and listen. The gates to the village will be closed tomorrow. There's no way out on a sending day. But you know my brother has many boats. I have tied one of the oldest boats to the dock that lies twenty steps beyond the last fishing house, out of sight, behind the tallest rocks. It is very near the sending ground. You will wait only until the sending boat has been untied and pushed off, and then you will run. Get the boat, follow him. Get him back. But you can't return. And I—" she sobbed and covered her face with her hand. "I don't know what your father will do as punishment, so all of you need to go. You can't come back, Isika, do you understand?"

Isika nodded rapidly, her heart hammering, her mind sluggishly trying to understand what her stepmother was saying.

"Take Benayeem and Ibba," Jerutha continued. "You will need Benayeem, he is strong and smart. And Ibba needs to go with you. But I don't know what you children will do after you get Kital out of the boat. I don't know where you will go." She stared at Isika, her face stricken and pale. "You'll have to figure that part out," she whispered.

Isika stared at her stepmother in shock. Jerutha was telling them to leave the village and never return. Jerutha's face twisted, and tears spilled out of her eyes, which were already red from crying. Isika drew close and wrapped her arms around her young stepmother. Jerutha was beautiful. She had always been beautiful in Isika's eyes, ever since she had intervened when the village kids were keeping Isika away from the water pump, back when Isika was twelve and Jerutha was not yet her stepmother. Isika remembered her then, the older girl's face flushed with anger as she sent the children running and held out her hand for Isika's pail, filling it herself and helping her to carry it back to their gate. It was the moment that Nirloth had first taken notice of Jerutha.

"I can't leave you," Isika said.

"You must."

Isika shook her head. Then, suddenly, she understood. She knew why Jerutha wanted her to promise she would come and help. One day Jerutha's own child would be given over, and she wanted a way out. She wanted Isika to help her leave, on a bleak day when her own child was sending age. The weight of the dreaded brass horn hung over all of them.

"What is out there?" Isika breathed, her eyes wide. What did Jerutha expect her to find?

"I don't know," Jerutha answered. "I don't know what is beyond our village. But I know you, sweet Isika. I know you will find a way to do this thing."

To live alone in the wild? To build a new life with only children to help each other? Isika weighed it against letting Kital die in the waves. She thought of the grief and helplessness she had felt at Aria's sending. It was not a hard choice, no matter how unknown the future would be.

"I will come back to you," she said. "I will fly to you when you need help."

"I know you will," Jerutha said. "And I know something good will come of this, of you, Isika. There is something special in you, something pure and strong. Now quickly, you must tell Benayeem and Ibba and we will prepare for the sending. We must gather food and hide it from Nirloth. And, little sister, you need to act as though nothing has changed. Don't let him know that you have any hope at all."

CHAPTER 5

*I*sika woke Benayeem and whispered the plan to him in the garden, just as Jerutha had done for her. When she finished, he straightened and looked at her.

In some ways, Benayeem and Isika were the closest of their siblings, because they remembered their mother and the desert, but in some ways, they were as distant as two stars, because they were so different. He was quiet and tall, self-contained, and often withdrawn, while Isika was impetuous and reactive, quick to blame or cry, ready to make up right away. Ben had taken this terrible news of Kital's sending, and he had run. Isika had stayed and blown up at her father and received the penalty. Now she saw Ben trying to make sense of what she was saying.

"Just... leave?" he whispered.

"How can we let them take one of us again?" Isika said. She used what she knew would shake him. "Our mother's last baby?"

Deeply protective of their mother, Ben had been devastated by her death. He nodded, staring at his hands, long and deep brown, wrapped around his thin legs.

"We'll need my bow," he said. Every year the men of the village hunted when the deer came through in the hot season, heading north. Benayeem had gone out with them for the past two years. Last year he had taken his first deer. "And some rope."

He looked at her then, and she saw sorrow and guilt in his eyes as they skittered over the cuts on her face. He reached out to touch her hand, careful of the cuts on her knuckles, then he stood and went quietly toward the small shed behind the house. Isika saw him drawing himself together, moving into the practicalities of what they would need to pack. She smiled. Her face hurt as her smile pulled at the deeper cuts, but she knew that she had him beside her, and though Benayeem was quiet, with him, she felt they might have a fighting chance of surviving.

She told Ibba only that she needed to obey when Isika told her to run. Seven-year-old Ibba was tiny next to Isika and Ben, who were both tall for their age, and long-limbed. Ibba was petite and wiry, full of energy, her eyes huge in her small face. She had skin as smooth as silk, deep brown like the earth in the freshly plowed fields during the planting season. Isika whispered the words to her little sister as she braided her hair to prepare for the sending ceremony.

She smoothed oil through four large sections of Ibba's tightly curled hair, rubbing the oil into her scalp and smoothing the strands, then winding sections into long twists that fell to Ibba's shoulder blades. Isika had done the same with her own hair earlier, pulling it apart to get rid of the tangles, the way her mother had always done for her. Now she had to do it for herself.

"It'll be okay," she said to her small sister, lying through her teeth, because how could she be sure of anything, shaking with love and fear and energy to run? She was barely sure of her own name, and the ground under her feet seemed shaky and strange. Were they *leaving*? "Tomorrow, you only need to listen and be absolutely silent. We're going to get Kital back. And you can't tell anyone what I'm telling you now."

Ibba's eyes flooded with tears, and as Isika finished with her hair, winding a cord around the finished twist, Ibba ran back to her sleeping mat and wrapped her arms around Kital, who was napping. The little boy murmured and cried out in his sleep, and Ibba squeezed him tighter.

The ceremony would happen at dawn the next day. The rules of the goddesses dictated that the great field gates must be shut and locked until noon on the day of a sending, keeping everyone inside the walled village. The villagers would push the boat off into the black, choppy sea, then walk back through the sea gates, leaving their beloved children to drift off into the ocean. If they stayed to watch, they risked the anger of the goddesses. Jerutha hoped these rules would save Isika and her siblings; the people compelled to move back into the village. Perhaps the three children would not be missed until later, when it would be too late to stop them.

Isika was terrified, but she looked at tiny Kital on his mat and felt the heat of strength and resolve flowing through her trembling arms and legs.

The day passed so slowly that Isika wanted to scream. She made the breakfast tea and gathered the wood as usual. This time, she met no one in the forest. She used a headscarf to hide her bruised and cut face. Full of nerves, she couldn't look at her father as she brought his tea to him in his sleeping room. She hoped he would attribute her silence to yesterday's beating.

They ate the day meal. Ben tromped around the yard, gathering various supplies. Jerutha pulled the clean sending cloths off the clothesline, and Isika helped her fold them. Kital and Ibba sat in the garden, their heads bent together as Kital drew pictures for Ibba on the ground with his finger. The house was oddly silent. No one dared speak, in case the hope in their hearts was audible in their voices. Isika's father stayed on his mat all day. He had tired himself the day before, stomping around and swinging his cane.

In the afternoon, Nirloth called to Isika. She and Jerutha were quietly setting aside part of the day meal for the children to take with them. Isika looked at her stepmother, her eyes wide with fear. Jerutha looked back at her with steady eyes, then bent her head and whispered.

"Go," she said. "You must."

The room smelled bad again, and Isika felt reluctant to walk in, but her father beckoned her to his side. Pain rushed through her as she limped to him. She kept her face blank.

"Daughter," he said, his face a shadow on his pillow. "You

must resign yourself to the way." There was no anger in his voice.

Isika was silent. She stood with her eyes on the floor as a proper Worker would, though every cell in her body screamed in protest. She would not resign herself any longer. Isika had lost a sister and a mother to the way. She was finished with resigning herself.

"I have decided to train you up as a priestess, Isika." Despite her resolve not to look at him, Isika's eyes flew to her father's face. He went on. "Benayeem is not the right choice, I know this now. He doesn't have the heart of a priest in him. He will be nothing more than a regular Worker."

This was her father at his most appeasing, his rough voice as soothing as he could make it. He told Isika this news as an apology. He had hit her, true, but see, he was training her to take his place. A single square of sunlight shone on the dirt floor. Many people in the village had slate in their houses now, but Isika's father insisted that the old ways of dirt and stone were enough for their family's ground.

"Do I have a choice?" she asked, hardly able to get the words out. She dared another look at her father, now that her eyes had adjusted to the dim light. He lay in his corner on the bed mat, his face grayer today. His hands lay listless by his sides, and he looked out through the small window, rather than at her. He frowned.

"Of course not. You are a Worker. None of us have choices. We do what we are destined to do. The goddess, Fate, rules over us in totality. The only satisfaction is through following carefully in her footsteps. You may have questions,

Isika," now he looked at her, "but you are full of spiritual power, and you will be a great priestess."

She flinched when his gray eyes met hers. His words confused her. Everything had changed in the night. Yesterday she may have welcomed his words because at least being a priestess would set her apart, keep her from needing to marry. She knew that otherwise, she would be at a disadvantage, looking for a husband to take her on the merit of her cooking ability or her willingness to work hard. She was one of the black outsiders who lived with the priest, and no one would happily choose a wife who may bring bad luck, someone with the shame of being different. But today, the world had shifted, and Isika was about to spit in the face of the goddess, Fate. She thought of Kital, and confusion fled. Isika was utterly sure that she would follow her baby brother and get him out of that boat, goddess, or no goddess. She nodded to show she had heard her father's words, and looked down at the square of sunshine on the floor, silent.

"You may go," her father said.

The evening passed, and Isika lay down on her sleeping mat early, Kital in her arms. She stared into the dark, knowing she needed to sleep for strength, but she was nearly crazy with the feelings that washed over her; fear, curiosity, dread. What if they couldn't row hard enough to reach him? What if they died in the wilderness, what if one boy with a bow wasn't enough to care for them? Life had been hard but predictable just two days ago when all Isika had to worry about was whether her father would check the firewood. She couldn't imagine how to approach a new life. Workers were raised for obedience. What would become of them? It didn't matter. They were leaving. They could not abandon Kital to the waves. Somehow, Isika drifted off, into the relief of sleep.

SHE SLEPT ONLY a few hours before Jerutha woke her. In the dark of the early morning, they gathered what they needed. They would not eat or drink tea before a sending. Isika shivered without relief. She hoped that people would assume that she feared for her brother, which was partially true. Isika went over the steps in her head. They needed to push him out in the boat, then make sure they trailed behind the other Workers as the people filed back through the sea gate. Isika and the others couldn't run until almost everyone was back inside, and hopefully, they wouldn't be spotted.

Yesterday Benayeem had taken the bundle of supplies to the small boat that was hidden among the rocks. He was skilled at getting into difficult places without being seen. Isika supposed it was from trying not to be noticed for his whole life. Now, she saw Ben emerge from the sleeping room and met his eyes briefly. This morning he was responsible for ringing the bell to announce that the sending was imminent. Isika watched as Ben picked up the heavy bell. He held her gaze for a moment before turning and sealing their fate with six rings of the symbolic instrument. The bell rang out over the flat, dusty earth, vibrating to the sea's edge, to the boats on the harbor, all the way to the richer houses that sat at the borders of the village, far away from the stench of the fishing boats.

Isika thought she could sense people preparing themselves for a sending—scurrying around, opening the gates in front of their houses. Nothing would ever be the same. She knew nothing of the future. She felt that they were standing on the edge of a cliff. Perhaps she was leading her brother and sister to their deaths. She shook herself and gave Kital his sending tea, singing their song to him until his eyelids were too heavy to stay open. They drifted shut, his beautiful eyelashes resting on his cheeks.

Nirloth came out of his room, stiff in his long black robe. He walked out of the house without looking at any of them, leaning heavily on his cane. Benayeem followed. In the courtyard, Ibba fetched the donkey. Isika passed Kital up to Ben after he mounted, taking care to tuck Kital's head against Ben's shoulder so it wouldn't bounce around on the rocky path to the shore. Nirloth opened the gate, muttering the sacred words as they passed through the wall. Isika looked back at the house as she passed through the gate, a final glance at the place where she had last seen her mother, and then she turned to follow the others.

THE WORKERS FILED to the harbor from every direction. Some were missing, Ben could tell, from his perspective on the donkey. Even the richest of the Workers were not very wealthy. Still, they could afford to pay the temple for the privilege of missing the sending. Ben had witnessed the payoff happening many times in the temple, when the warning music vibrated through him at the exchange of money. But most of the villagers were present. Since he had become the priest's apprentice, Ben had never missed a sending. He felt a sudden hope that this would be his last. It fizzled when he remembered that first, they needed to escape, a dangerous thing. The people drifted together to the sea gate. Ben's father spoke the sacred words over the gate, and the Workers filed through with bent heads, walking out to the harbor. Ben saw Faiza, the tomato seller, put a gentle hand on Isika's shoulder. His sister flinched, her wounds hurting her, and Ben winced in sympathy.

"May your eyes be guarded, Isika," the woman said.

"And your speech kept safe," Isika replied.

The woman said nothing more, but she walked by Isika's side as they made their way to the harbor. Ben remembered buying tomatoes from Faiza on days when Isika was too busy to go to the market. He remembered her smile, back when her baby was small, before he was given over during that horrible season when Faiza's family farm had a tomato blight. She didn't smile much anymore. As Ben watched, she bent her head and slipped back into the crowd of Workers.

He caught a glimpse of the harbor as the villagers walked down, only a murmur here and there breaking the silence. Ben kept his eyes away from the dark shape of his father at the head of the procession. He didn't want to think of his father too much, afraid that he would lose the nerve to break free at the last moment if he considered his father's heavy anger. Ben's heart was pounding until it seemed that it would rise into his throat. He looked down at the sleeping boy in his arms, and as he did, he heard a clear, lovely note. The burst of sound surprised him, and he looked around, but soon realized that it had come from within him. His arms tingled with it. A single, centering vibration through him. *Yes.* Gazing into his brother's sleeping face, he felt it rise inside him, filling him with sound. It wasn't the painful ring of discordant music or ominous drums. This was peace, like sleep and waking all at once.

This was his hope, in leaving, the reason he had agreed to run with Isika. Ben wanted peace. Maybe he would find it somewhere far from this village. He lifted his head, staring straight at his father at the front of the procession, and the peaceful feeling didn't fade.

The water of the harbor was dark and foreboding. Sending day after sending day, the Workers sent their children out into the gray, rough sea, watching until the boats disappeared around the rocks into the open waters.

This is not the true way, Ben's mother had whispered to him on Aria's sending day. *This is not the way of the True One. Remember it, Benayeem.* At the time, Ben was crying so hard that he couldn't see. He didn't need her words to tell him it wasn't right; the wrongness of it shook him like a leaf, drums that rolled and threatened to tear him apart from the inside. Not today. Today his eyes were dry and hard, his muscles tense. Ready.

The sending boat bobbed beside the pier, tied by a single fraying rope. Jerutha looked at Ben solemnly as he passed

Kital to her to dismount. When Ben was on the ground, he took his little brother in his arms again, carrying Kital to the small boat and laying him inside, on the largest cloth, the red one for sacrifice. Isika and Jerutha arranged the sending cloths over him, taking care to wrap him loosely, so he could move if he woke up. The crowd chanted the dirge-like, mournful songs, beginning with the song of the goddesses and moving to the songs of sending.

Isika and Jerutha stepped back as the songs finished. Three strong men approached. They waded into the water and pushed the boat out toward the sea with great strength so it could reach the spot, beyond the small harbor breakers, where it kept going and didn't come back. Boats had washed back in the past, but the small vessels were only for sending, never receiving. The children were sent again, and it was even more heartbreaking the second time.

Kital looked small and pale in the boat, his brown skin lacking its usual warmth. His eyes were closed. *We will come for you,* he told his small brother silently. *Hold on, little one, we're coming.*

The men gave one last push with all their might. The tiny boat rocked for a moment, then righted itself and went out in the current, drawn toward the opening in the rocks and the great sea beyond.

CHAPTER 6

*I*sika's arms and legs burned as she watched Kital's boat bob on the dark sea like a small toy. She met Benayeem's eyes. The next few minutes were crucial. They needed to turn their backs, as was the custom. They needed to lag at the end of the procession. They needed to keep Ibba beside them. And then, rather than filing back into the village, they needed to escape at the last moment, through Jerutha's brother's fishing hut, and race to the old boat hidden behind the rocks at the harbor's edge.

The crowd sang the last song, the song of loss, and Isika joined in, her heart beating a hard rhythm as the three of them filed slowly up to the sea gate with the crowd, walking back into the closed village. The sky was still dark. They needed it to cover them when they rowed into the sea. It was Benayeem's job to lock the sea gate, and the people were not allowed to look back at the harbor; this would save Ben and Isika. If the Workers didn't look back, they wouldn't see the children run. But the plan counted on the obedience of the Workers. Obedience had never been Isika's particular strength, so she didn't know if she could count on everyone else.

Her heart jumped as the fishing hut became visible. *Now!* She looked at Ibba and put her finger over her mouth. Ibba nodded, her eyes wide. She would listen. Isika caught Ben's eyes, and they ducked into the doorway of the fishing hut. It was small and bare, empty, with sleeping mats still piled on the floor. The open door to the harbor was at the far end of the room. Having a door like this was a privilege held only by the fishing families of the Workers. They had access to the harbor when no one else did, and normally others would never dare intrude on their family ground. Jerutha had said that she would keep her brother away by walking back to the village square with him, but as Isika ducked through the doorway into the room, she heard a weak voice call out to them.

"Children?" Isika turned. It wasn't Jerutha's brother, but her old grandmother. When Jerutha was young, and her mother had gone insane and wandered into the plains beyond the Worker village, Jerutha's grandmother had helped Jerutha raise the family. The old woman had always been good to Isika and the children. She was toothless and bent, but strong, kind in her strange way, bringing tea to their gate when someone was ill, pinching Kital's cheeks when he was small. Her eyes were shadowed in the dim light of the room as she lay on her mat beside the cooking fire.

Isika kept walking, but she put a hand on her heart as

they went to the door that faced the harbor, outside the walls of the village. The old grandmother silently watched them go. She didn't make a sound, didn't shout or raise the alarm. Isika remembered the old woman's strong hands, patting her shoulders or touching her face, and felt a wave of gratitude.

But they were almost at the boat, and they needed focus. Isika saw it just ahead, nearly invisible in the rushes—an old boat that the family didn't use anymore. The three of them ran to it, the stones of the harbor loud under their feet. Isika hesitated for one instant, looking at Ben and then Ibba.

"Ready?" she asked, and at their sharp nods, she waded into the water. Benayeem walked behind her. Isika lifted Ibba into the boat and climbed in after her, settling herself onto the simple wooden bench. The wet wood creaked with her weight. Benayeem gave one strong push, then leapt in, and they were floating on the water, their very first time in a boat. It was scary, the wood creaking and swaying underneath them. The little thing didn't feel as though it was solid enough to support them. Isika gulped air as she fought to calm herself.

Jerutha had given Isika and Ben a short lesson in the garden. "You'll need to pick up the paddles, one for each of you, and grip them like this." She demonstrated, holding her two fists on the broom she carried so that the backs of her hands were opposite one another. "Put one on one side of the boat and one on the other, and dip them in the water, pushing back against the water to pull yourself forward. It's not hard, but your arms will soon grow tired. Try to do it together, you will go faster. And you'll need speed if you're going to catch Kital's boat."

Isika picked up the unfamiliar paddle and held it firmly in two hands. She worked hard at home and in the forest, and she had since she was small. She was strong. Benayeem was strong, too, from building and digging.

"One, two, three," she whispered, and they dipped the oars together. Isika felt the push of the water against the paddle and tried to lean into it, to pull forward like Jerutha had said. She lifted her oar and circled it ahead, then dipped it again. She heard Ben do the same behind her. Ibba was silent, sitting on the seat next to Isika. The boat began to pick up speed.

Isika's stomach felt sick from all the energy and fear running through her body. She waited for a shout behind them, but none came, and they pulled the boat swiftly through the water, following the distant speck of Kital's sending boat as it disappeared around the rocks. Her arms burned, and sweat collected under her arms and on her back. The sky was growing lighter, soon the sun would rise, and they needed to be around the rocks and out of sight when the harbor flooded with sunlight. Isika was breathing heavily, and she could hear ragged breath from Ben.

"Where are we going?" Ibba asked. She sounded as though she was crying.

"To get our brother," Isika said, her voice strained as she gasped for air. The sky got lighter and lighter, and Isika could see the monstrous rocks that leaned over the opening to their harbor like sharp teeth on guard dogs, sheltering the village from the fierce sea beyond. Isika and Ben pulled and pulled until they were even with the rocks. Behind her, she heard the shout she had been waiting for. It didn't matter, they were... out.

They paddled around the rocks just as she heard the alarm bells ring. Would the Workers send the fishermen out after them? Isika didn't know. It would break the laws of sending: the seas were off-limits until the next dawn after a sending, but then the children had certainly broken laws themselves. She had no way of knowing whether the Workers would pursue them. She looked around wildly for Kital's boat and spotted it in the distance to the south. The sending boats traveled quickly, shaped like leaves to carry children who weighed almost nothing.

They paddled toward him a while longer, and when they didn't see anyone coming, they sat back to rest for a moment. Isika gasped, amazement building in her as she looked around the boat. She had never seen anything so beautiful. Out here, the sea wasn't gray; it was a deep, intense blue, and it swept into the distance, blurring at the horizon. Behind them and on both sides for some time were the rocks and cliffs that hid the village from the sea. Farther along, to their left, to the south, she could see the faint outlines of trees lining the shores.

"Again," Isika said to Benayeem, though they hadn't rested long. Without a word, he began to paddle. The sun was up now, lighting the water from their backs, showing sea depths Isika hadn't seen before. She felt fear and wonder, but she stayed focused. They needed to catch Kital's boat before it was swept away from them. The little vessel continued nodding along in a southwesterly direction, along the faint line of trees on the shore, slowly drifting farther out to sea.

Isika and Ben gained on Kital's boat as they paddled hard. Ibba asked a steady stream of questions, and Isika answered some, ignoring others. "Why are we going to get Kital?"

"Because we love him, and we're not going to let him go."

"Whose boat is this?"

"Uncle's."

"Will we see Jerutha again?"

At that question, Isika gritted her teeth and paddled harder. They were gaining, they were getting closer. She could see the grain of the wood in the small sending boat. She could see Kital's face in glimpses as the boat tossed in the water. They were going to reach him! It was working.

"Isika, let's rest," Benayeem said, his first words since entering the boat.

"Okay. But only for a moment," Isika said. She sat back. Blisters were rising on her hands. They burned as she dipped them into the sea, trying to ease the pain.

"What's that?" Ibba asked, and Isika looked up slowly, wearied by her little sister's questions. Then she jumped, leaning forward to see, rocking the boat so that water splashed over the sides.

"Benayeem!" she said.

Boats approached swiftly from the south; long, graceful boats with both ends curving upward. Two men sat in each boat. Isika couldn't make their faces out. There was a strange mist around the sea vessels. She gasped. Sea animals swam alongside these new boats, like fish, but larger, gray and smooth, leaping and diving. They were beautiful but terrifying. Isika didn't know what they were.

"Isika," Ben said, wonder in his voice. "What are those?"

"I don't know," she replied absently, trying to see the faces of the people in the boats, then in a flash, she realized what was happening. "No!" she shouted. She had seen their purpose. They were headed straight for Kital. "Paddle, Benayeem!" she cried, but it was too late. Isika and Ben strained with the muscles in their thin arms, but the other boats were fast and reached him first. Isika could see the people now, four of them in two boats. One, a woman, reached into the sending boat and pulled Kital out, tucking him against her. Isika saw with a shock that the people had black skin, like Isika and her siblings.

The boats turned to the south again and rowed away as quickly as they had come. They hadn't once looked at Isika and Ben, perhaps blinded by the rising sun behind them.

"No!" Isika cried again. And then she wailed and shouted and screamed, rowing against the small waves the boats had left behind, rowing and rowing but never getting closer to the people who had taken their brother away.

PART II

CHAPTER 7

They rowed all day, always south, in sight of the shore, so they could see if the strange boats had pulled up anywhere. Ben strained his eyes for any glimpse of them. Ibba slept, curled at his feet. Isika laid her scarf over Ibba's face to shelter her from the sun. They rowed. Occasionally, they rested and ate a little of the food Jerutha had packed for them. Benayeem felt that he was in a dream world, overwhelmed by loss and the newness of everything, their sudden homelessness. They were lost and adrift; a fourteen-year-old girl, a thirteen-year-old boy, and their little seven-year-old sister. What good were they against the world?

"Who were those people?" he asked his sister, but she had no answer for him. He had never seen people or boats like that before, and especially never animals like those gray shapes swimming in the water.

"Ben," Isika said, her voice low. "Are they going to feed him to those animals?"

A chill made Ben's arms prickle. He felt sick. He glanced down at Ibba, but she was still fast asleep, exhausted from crying.

"Let's not think about that," he said. "It's too horrible."

"Were they slave ships, then?"

The Workers told stories about boats rowed by people who stole children to be slaves. Many parents didn't allow their children to go to the harbor. Unknown people were rumored to paddle in from the sea and snatch up unwary children, taking them to large ships filled with stolen children. No children had been taken from the Worker village for many years. Ben's father said it was because the sea gate was doing its job. Still, the slave ships lived on in the children's nightmares.

"The boats in the stories have strange eyes painted on them," he told his sister. "Those boats didn't have paintings, did they?" He felt nauseous at the thought of his brother being taken as a slave. He set his face and rowed harder. And if they reached the boats that had taken their brother? What would they do then? It didn't matter. He rowed.

In the late afternoon, as the sea was turning to gold, they pulled to the shore. Ben shook with exhaustion. One look at his sister told him she had no strength left. He looked around. Ben had never seen anything like the place where they landed. The shore was covered with a soft layer of pale golden dirt, which, when he looked closer, wasn't dirt, but a collection of the tiniest of rocks. They ran through Ben's fingers as he dipped his hands into piles of them. Ibba sat and began playing with the dirt immediately, scooping handfuls and letting the soft substance flow through her fingers.

"Sand," Ben said. "It's called sand."

Isika looked at him. "How—?"

"From the desert, Isika. You remember."

She stared at him, then laughed. "I remember dirt, brother."

"There was sand, too. And there was sand in the walled city."

He met her eyes briefly, then looked away and tried to rub the soreness out of his arms. His back burned and his hands were torn up and covered with blisters, some of them bleeding. They were lost, they couldn't go back, and they didn't have Kital. He glared at his hands, wondering whether he could tear a piece of his shirt away to bind them in the morning. He supposed they would keep rowing and searching for their brother. With his fingertips, he pulled one of Jerutha's parcels out of his pocket and found three helpings of the daily meal, wrapped in a banana leaf. His stomach wanted to eat right through his ribcage and continue to eat everything in sight.

"Why don't you ever talk about those days?" Isika asked. Her voice was weary. She had asked him a thousand times. He didn't answer. He handed her one portion of food.

"Ibba, go wash your hands in the sea, then come back to eat," he said.

As the little girl ran to do as he said, he looked up at Isika. She was still gazing at him, a stubborn look on her face, and he felt his own face soften as he saw her cuts and bruises again. He was sore from rowing. She must be sore from both rowing and being beaten, yet she hadn't complained. Ben admired his sister's strength, but he couldn't talk about those times. He couldn't talk about *before*. If his mind even reached toward the past, his whole spirit flinched away, the drums chanting doom. He had learned to make a box of it in his mind, keep any thoughts of that time tightly sealed away. It was the only way he could have peace.

"I've never seen some of these trees before," he said.

Isika turned her head, following the direction of his eyes. There were three types of trees in their village—the losh trees they used for fuel; the yuci, a tall thin tree with curved leaves and pale bark that added no color to the landscape; and the banana trees, which offered the treasured fruit of their village. But these trees were different.

They had landed on a short, curved beach that bordered a jungle jumping with color. There were trees with wide leaves that were almost blue, and trees with thousands of tiny round leaves and long, broad branches. One tree was so tall that Ben had to tip his head back to see the top of it. It dwarfed the other trees, with branches that curved, snake-like, spilling from the tree's long limbs and circling up to climb again. Isika limped up the beach toward the tree. As she moved toward it, a large creature exploded from the leaves and leapt away, farther into the jungle. Ben didn't see what it looked like, he had only the impression of size and speed. Isika turned to Ben, her eyes wide.

"This place is alive," Ibba said beside him. Ben nodded. The animal had startled him, but he felt wonder, rather than fear. Ibba came closer to him and put her small hand in his. He winced as she brushed against his blisters, but he didn't move away. His younger sister looked up at him, questions in her eyes. Questions he couldn't even begin to answer. The voices inside him were silent, a welcome rest. He wondered what it meant, that they were so quiet, but he relaxed into it, accepting the respite.

"Okay, let's eat," Isika said, walking back toward them. "Then sleep. We'll have a big day tomorrow—we have to find Kital. But we should sleep down here, on the *sand*. That jungle is a little too alive."

The sun moved slowly toward the horizon. They were exhausted after rowing under the blazing sun all day. As they sat with their cold porridge, Isika and Ben barely able to use their hands, Ben thought of his father. His house was nearly empty now, only Jerutha and her unborn baby left. Ben knew that his father's chief worry tonight, even as his children were in the wilderness, was that he wouldn't be saved from his illness after this giant rebellion against the goddesses. And who would he send into the temple to work at the shrine? Pregnant women were forbidden.

Ben didn't know whether Nirloth would miss them. But then a memory came to him. It was from the terrible days after Ben's mother died. The old man had passed by Ben and paused to let one hand rest on his shoulder. Ben had flinched, expecting a rebuke, but Nirloth had simply squeezed Ben's shoulder with a gentle hand, then kept walking.

Yes, Ben thought. He would miss them. In his heart, Ben

felt something like satisfaction. Perhaps his father would finally see the value in what he had lost.

"Let's go to sleep," Isika said. "Tomorrow, we'll keep looking."

Benayeem looked at her. The setting sun glowed on her face. A rush of things came to his mind, things he wanted to say, a thousand reasons this plan wouldn't work. They had already failed. But she looked both tired and very brave, so he lay down and arranged his cloak around him. Within moments, he was asleep.

ISIKA SLEPT A DEEP, dreamless sleep. When she opened her eyes, the sun was rising, and the last stars were disappearing. She was warm. She was too warm, actually. She pulled her cloak off and sat up. The air was wonderful on her face. Isika remembered that they hadn't found Kital, which gave her a momentary flash of fear. But despite the memory of the day before, there was a feeling in her heart that slowly grew. She almost couldn't name it. She sat and smiled for several moments before she realized that she felt... happy. They were outside, under a blue sky. The trees of the jungle shook lightly in a morning breeze.

She stood and stretched, looking around her. Ben sat at the shoreline, near the water. She walked to him and sat down. They looked out across the sea, so blue, as clear as the well water at home. Just beyond the breakers, which were about as tall as Isika's knees, fish darted in and out of plants that grew underwater, waving as the little waves shook them back and forth.

"Where are we?" she asked, her voice full of the awe she felt.

"I don't know," Ben replied, and she sat up straighter and looked at him.

Normally, he spoke quietly, and Isika often had to strain to hear or ask him to repeat himself. This morning was different. His voice rang out in the morning air, and Ibba stirred in her sleep.

"It's beautiful," he said, and she recognized the expression on his face because it was the same way she felt. It was peace. Isika felt the need to get going and find Kital, she knew they had to discuss the best way to do that, but for the moment, she felt peace.

Ben reached out and took one of her hands, turning it over, so the palm was up. She looked at him, then at her hand, and it took her a minute, but when she saw what he was showing her, she gasped and brought her hands closer to her face. Her hands were smooth and free from wounds—the deep, weeping blisters of the night before were gone, as though they had never been there. She didn't have an ache in her back or neck either, and as Ben lifted a hand to her face, she realized that the cuts and bruises her father had left on her body and cheek were gone.

"What *is* this place?" she breathed, and Benayeem shook his head at her, smiling.

"I hoped you would know."

"You hoped I would know? Do you think I've been

exploring magic landscapes while you've been sleeping? This is amazing, Ben, what is happening?" He shrugged, his eyes wide.

"It's like I want to worry about Kital, but I can't find the fear," he said. "I feel sure that we'll find him, but I don't know why."

Isika nodded. She felt the same way. She looked at the water. It was so clear she wanted to touch it. She got up and walked the short distance, splashing her hand around in the shallows. As she did, a strange feeling of joy bloomed inside her.

"Let's get into the water..." she said. "We need to bathe to keep from smelling enough to bring the villagers right to us."

Ben nodded. Just then, Ibba stood up, rubbing her eyes and walking toward them. "Bathe, where?" she asked.

"In there," Ben said, pointing at the calm, endless sea, and Ibba's eyes widened as her smile overtook half her face.

They stripped to their underclothes, and Isika felt like a tiny girl without her heavy dress, her arms and legs poking out of her sleeveless shirt and shorts. She looked at her long, skinny brown legs and Ben's long, skinny brown arms, and she laughed. Ibba danced on the sand beside her. They ran straight into the sea.

The water was warm, and it felt like the sweetest birdsong on the days when Isika could pretend that her mother was still alive. It was like the embrace of her mother. It brought tears to her eyes, so she blinked them away and moved her arms and legs. She dunked her face into the water. She surfaced, took a deep breath, then pushed herself straight down until she was eye to eye with the fish at the bottom. She swam. Ben and Ibba swam as well. They circled each other in the water, slapping at the surface, splashing. Ben was smiling so wide that Isika could see every one of his teeth, and Ibba tried to imitate the swimming of the fish-like animals they had seen the day before. All at once, submerged in water, Isika knew that the people who had taken Kital had never fed children to those animals. The gray fish couldn't live in this sea and eat small children. The whole sea was alive with joy, the water perfect; warm and yet refreshing. Tiny drops of water shot straight into the sky from the tops of the waves and caught the light, shining for a moment like stars.

Isika, Ben, and Ibba climbed out after a long while, lying in the sun to dry. Isika felt the sun's warmth on her face, and for the first time in her life, it felt friendly.

She was just thinking they needed to get back in their boat and continue the search when there was a sudden whirring. A breeze lifted fallen leaves from the sand. Something large flew over Isika, and she sat up, her heart pounding.

CHAPTER 8

Three enormous birds landed on the beach, not far from where Isika sat. Beside her, Benayeem slowly sat up. Isika could see the tension in his rigid shoulders. The birds were black, and their blackness was woven with lights like the jewels in the temple walls. They shone with blues and greens and a deep, deep red. When they turned and hopped around the children, they glowed with different colors as the sun moved over their bodies. They were larger than the eagles that circled the fishing nets at dusk when the fishermen discarded the bad catch onto the beach. But their beaks were straight, not curved sharply, like eagles' beaks. The large eyes of the birds focused directly on Isika and her siblings.

A shiver of fear or anticipation passed through her.

"Where do you come from, young ones?" one bird asked, and Isika leapt to her feet, astonished.

Benayeem stood beside her, and Ibba came and slipped her hand into Isika's, hiding her face behind Isika's back. The birds were so large they reached above Isika's waist. How had the bird spoken? Its beak hadn't moved, but Isika knew with certainty which bird had spoken, just as she knew instinctively that it was the leader of the three.

"We are Workers," she said. "We come from a village to the south."

The birds exclaimed among themselves, clicking and chirping, and Isika stepped closer to Benayeem. Was she dreaming? She must be. It explained their healed hands, the lack of pain in her back and face. She smiled, glad to have found such a simple explanation. Beside her, Ben shifted from foot to foot. The sounds the birds were making to one another sounded like speech, though Isika couldn't understand their meaning.

The leader spoke again, and Isika knew with sudden clarity, as his words reached out around them in the air and in her mind, that she was very much awake. This was no dream.

"You don't look like Workers," he said.

His speech was something that conveyed instant understanding, that showed her the intent behind his words as well as the words themselves, and as she listened to him, it was almost as though she could hear his day, his morning of flying over the sparkling sea, the fruit he had eaten, as though she could hear his kind thoughts toward the three of them.

It wasn't so much speech as a kind of closeness, a way of

being absolutely together. She gasped, from its warmth and its rudeness. In her village, to intrude on someone's thoughts, the way this bird was doing was worse than looking into someone's soul through their eyes. It was as though he was in her soul already and knew that she needed to be reassured. *Shield your eyes*, she heard her father's voice say.

"It's true," Ben said. "We don't. Our mother came from far away, but we have lived in the Worker village for many years." There was a bright exclamation from the birds again as they spoke to one another. Though Isika couldn't understand what they said, she could sense their surprise and curiosity.

"Why are you so sad?" the bird asked.

Though Isika felt less sad than she should in this beautiful place, his question brought their loss flooding back to her. She felt a stab of pain and fear for her brother.

"We tried to rescue our brother from the sea," she said, "in that boat." She pointed to their boat, which looked rather ragged and old in the bright morning light. "But people came and took him, and now we don't know where he is. We are desperate to find him."

A second bird answered her, and Isika somehow knew she was female.

"Was he outcast?" she asked, and behind her words, Isika heard deep anger, though it didn't seem directed toward Isika and her brother and sister.

"Outcast?"

"You would say 'given over,' perhaps."

"Yes, he was."

The birds clicked and rustled. "Then they have carried him to the place where the Maweel always take the outcasts. It is very far away, across the land. You cannot take a boat there."

Isika felt her stomach plummet. "How can we find him? Where have they taken him?" There was more rustling from the birds, their feathers gleaming in the sunshine. Isika rubbed her eyes. She was talking to birds, far away from her village, about people who had taken Kital far away. She knew she wasn't dreaming, but it seemed like a dream. She glanced at Ben. He was standing quietly, a strange look on his face.

"You will need a guide," the first bird said. "And I sensed your need before I reached you. So I have sent for a guide to lead you." He flapped his wings and hopped onto the branch of a tree to look into the jungle.

Faintly, Isika heard the whistling of a human. Someone approached through the trees. She looked around quickly for her clothes and pulled them from the sand, wrapping her dress around her a moment before the rustling reached the edge of the thick jungle. She took a breath. What was happening to her in this new place? Swimming in underclothes, talking to birds? She squared her shoulders and stuck her chin out, waiting for whatever would come through the trees.

Two boys, a little older than Isika and Ben, stepped onto the sand. Ben drew in a breath and took a step back. One of the strangers had very dark skin, nearly black, like a losh tree, like Ben and his siblings. Isika and Ibba stared at the boy with wide eyes, and Ben thought his own eyes might pop out of his head. It was the first time in seven years he had seen a dark-skinned person who wasn't a member of his family. The boy was extremely tall, with black, tightly curled hair cropped close to his head. He wore dark blue pants and a loose sleeve-less shirt. Thin bronze bands encircled his upper arms. There were patterns embroidered on the collar and front of his shirt. He wore tall boots on his feet, and he looked every bit as shocked as Ben felt. The boy with him was pale-skinned. He looked just like the people of Ben's village, but tanned from the sun, like a fisherman or a farmer. His hair was so blond it seemed to be white, and it didn't lay down, but pointed in every direction, mostly up, like a tangle of grass. The two boys looked at each other, and the blond one said something Ben couldn't hear.

The largest of the strange black birds spoke.

"These lost children need your guidance, Jabari, Gavi," he said.

From the first moment the birds had arrived, Ben had been riveted by their effect on him. Their words sang inside of him, and he could sense their deep meaning and the joy at their core. It was as though Ben was an instrument that rang with their joy. He found that he needed to hold himself very still, or he might do something crazy, like cry, or run, or jump in place. When the bird spoke now, the music inside Ben flared up again, and he held his elbows tightly against his ribcage, holding himself together. Ben didn't know what was happening to him.

"Who are you?" Isika demanded. She shifted her weight and put a hand on Ibba's shoulder. She looked as though she was ready to run or attack. Ben tensed, prepared to join her if she needed him.

The tall boy gestured at the bird. "Nirral just told you. I am Jabari."

Nirral. At the name, Ben sensed the large bird's spirit, taller than the highest tree on the beach. He shivered. The boy named Jabari seemed calm and unafraid. A small tendril of sound within Ben separated from the rest and chimed one quiet, simple note. He could sense the spirit of this boy, as well. Ben didn't sense danger. Could he trust his instinct?

"No," Isika said. "I meant, *who* are you? What are you doing here?"

"I should be asking you that," Jabari answered, his voice mild, a smile on his face. He stood straight and tall but still managed to seem utterly relaxed. "This is our land. We are seeking, which is our work. We don't normally find groups of children wandering around, do we, Gavi?"

"I don't think we've ever found a group of children wandering around," the blond boy said.

He looked vaguely familiar. Ben closed his eyes. It was all too much, as he began to sense vague shapes behind each person on the beach, words behind their words. He tried to calm the voices and sounds inside him. If Ben wasn't going to go insane, he needed to find a way through the ocean of music that was growing in him. He patted it down, the way he would calm Kital if the younger boy was frightened, and Ben's mind cleared. He opened his eyes.

The birds made clicking sounds, almost like a purr or a growl, and Jabari glanced at them.

"You're right," he said. "Sorry." He looked at the three of them. "Are you hungry? We were just sitting down to eat when we got Nirral's message."

Ben wondered what to answer, and how Nirral had sent a message, but he didn't get time to think because Ibba responded first.

"Yes!" she exclaimed, stepping toward the boys on the edge of the jungle, an eager look on her face. She was in her underclothes, just a sleeveless shirt and shorts, but since she was a small child, it didn't matter.

Ben glanced at Isika, who was still holding her dress to herself, her eyes flashing daggers at her little sister. Ibba's skinny brown legs had knobby knees. The hair that had escaped her long twist caught the light like a halo. Her eyes glowed as she looked at the boys and the bag of food they pulled from a pack at their feet. A wonderful smell filled the air, and Ben's stomach woke up. Isika was still frowning, but she joined Ibba and walked toward them. Perhaps her hunger wouldn't let her refuse. She disappeared into the trees for a moment, and when she came back, she was clothed.

The boy named Jabari spread a sheet on the sand under the large tree, and the one called Gavi set the food out. There was a stack of small fresh-baked loaves of bread that gave off the good smell that had enticed them, a tall metal jar with a lid, a bunch of bananas, and a wrapped package that Gavi opened, revealing soft white cheese.

After Gavi divided the food, Jabari handed each of them a loaf spread with cheese, and a banana. He opened the tall container and poured a golden, steaming drink into a single cup.

"What is it?" Ibba asked.

"It's a kind of tea," he said. "We drink it for strength." He passed the cup around the small circle. It was quiet as they ate. The bread was so soft and delicious; it nearly fell apart in their mouths, and the tea was hot and sweetened perfectly. The cheese was smooth and salty. It was the best food Ben had ever tasted.

"So," Jabari said, smiling over at the birds, who stood watching, flapping their giant wings occasionally. He looked back at Ben and the others, "Tell us your names."

Immediately, Ibba spoke. "I'm Ibba," she said. "And this is Benayeem and Isika." She pointed at each of them as she said their names.

"They are Poison-landers," said the female bird.

Jabari looked at the bird, frowning, his face thoughtful. Gavi looked up from spreading more cheese on his bread, his eyebrows raised.

"You don't look like Poison-landers," he said.

Isika shifted to sit with her legs tucked under her. "I don't know what you mean by Poison-landers," she said.

"You call them Workers," Jabari said. "You look so different from the others we've met."

"So we've heard," she replied, her voice sharp. Ben knew how she felt. It was more of the same. The refrain they had heard all the years they had lived in the village, *Black children, you don't belong*, except this time it was coming from this wandering boy who had dark skin as well. Someone who had happened to cross their path with a giant sack of food and was now sitting back and watching them, waiting, it seemed, for Isika to say more. But there was nothing more to say. They didn't look like Workers.

"What is this?" Ben asked, gesturing at the crumbs of the food left on the sheet. "How is it that you can eat in the morning?"

"Why not in the morning?" Jabari asked, frowning.

"Workers only eat once a day," Ibba announced, and Ben felt anger at the sudden pity that crossed the faces of the boys.

"Let's not talk about Worker traditions," Isika said, interrupting. "Let's get to the point."

"There's a point?" Gavi asked, surprise in his voice.

"Where is our brother?" Ben asked.

Jabari and Gavi exchanged looks.

"I'm afraid that you're going to have to fill us in. Who is your brother, and why would I know where he is?" Jabari asked.

"He was sent out," Ben said, "and we followed him in our boat, to get him back, but people came in their own boats and took him. They rowed away quickly, and we couldn't catch them. They didn't see us, and we shouted, but they didn't hear us. We don't know who they were or where they went, but we want our brother back."

There was silence for a moment. The boys looked astonished. Gavi's mouth hung open, and Jabari's brown eyes were wide.

"You followed the outcast?" Jabari asked, his voice almost a whisper. He leaned forward, his hands on his knees. Ben felt frustration welling up in him again. Kital was getting farther and farther away while they explained every single thing to the strangers, who kept using words that Ben didn't understand.

"I don't know about outcasts," Ben said, "or what you mean by that. Kital was given over, and we had a plan to get him back and then... well, I don't know what we were going to do. We couldn't go back to the village, we knew that. But then the people in boats took him. Can you help us? Because if not, we need to keep going. We need to find him."

"I've never heard of anyone following an outcast before," Jabari said.

"No," Gavi agreed, nodding and looking up at the branches overhead. "That's because no one has ever done it."

"How would you know?" Isika demanded. "Are you all-seeing?"

Ben privately agreed with the other boy, he didn't think anyone had ever tried to rescue someone who had been given over. No Worker wanted the wrath of the goddesses on him.

"No," Jabari replied. "We are not all-seeing. We are the Maweel. We rescue the outcasts and bring them to our land. Every one. That is why Gavi knows that no Worker has ever tried to rescue one. We would know if someone had, just as we are now finding out that you have attempted to retrieve your brother."

"What are you saying?" Isika asked. Her face was shocked. "Are you telling us you take every one of them out of the water like we saw yesterday?"

"Yes."

"Then, the goddesses don't get any of the offerings?" Ben asked.

Jabari's face changed so swiftly that Ben sat back, afraid of the anger he saw there.

"The goddesses," Jabari spit. There was a clatter and growl from the birds again. They flapped their large wings, stirring the leaves on the trees. Jabari stopped talking and watched the largest bird. His face became sad.

"The young ones know only what they have been taught," the female bird said. She turned and lifted her wings, and the light shone on the bluest part of them, then suddenly glowed brightly as she flapped them again. "All things will be made right," she said. Her voice was deep, and tendrils of wild song crept through Ben's tentative lid on the jungle of music. "The crooked will be made straight, the soiled will be bathed in light." Her voice changed back to normal. "Be patient, Jabari."

Jabari picked up a clod of hard sand and squeezed it. The sand ran from his palm to the ground. "I am sorry, Efir," he said.

Gavi looked up. "I was an outcast," he said.

All at once, Ben knew why he looked familiar. He looked just like a boy from school. The butcher's son. Ben stared at him. It was impossible.

"Then..." Isika said, then stopped.

"Yes," Jabari said. "They're all with us. They are Maweel now too, not Poison-landers anymore."

Ben lost control of the jungle completely then. Images, songs, shadows of past things flashed through his mind until he couldn't see. A name flitted through his head, a note of the saddest music. *Aria.* His sister's name. He stood shakily and gripped the tree branch. Everyone looked at him, but as he touched the tree, his head cleared, and the voices calmed. He took deep breaths, sure that he was going insane. Too many hours under yesterday's sun had burned the little sanity left after years of the bells of doom. He sat down.

Isika's spine was tall and straight. She stuck her chin out. "Take us to him," she said, and it was not a request.

Gavi and Jabari looked at each other. Jabari shook his head.

"It has never been done," he said. "We couldn't bring poison-landers to Azariyah, our royal city, or even deeper into Maween."

Gavi nodded, his brow creased. Ben took a deep breath, ready to argue. But Nirral gave a long, deep cry, and Jabari sighed and dropped his head into his hands.

"Come into the trees, and we will speak, Jabari," the bird said.

Jabari looked at Ben and Isika. "We go to talk with the

Othra," he said. "And we will come back when we have made a decision."

They turned and walked into the jungle, and with a breath, the birds lifted above the trees and flew a few feet above the jungle canopy, until they were out of sight.

CHAPTER 9

While they waited for Jabari and Gavi's decision, Isika helped Ibba back into her clothes. She was seething inside as she arranged the long skirt and shirt on her sister. Jabari and Gavi were taking forever to talk with the birds, and Isika buzzed with impatience.

She walked back to the large tree on the jungle line and tilted her head back to look at the branches above her head. The sun filtered down through the leaves of the strange, snake-like tree, casting patterns of shadow on the ground and on her arms and hands. It would be an excellent tree to climb, she thought.

She hadn't climbed a tree since she was very small, when they had first come out of the desert to the Worker village. She hadn't known then that it was forbidden to climb trees. She clambered into the tempting yuci tree with gray bark and wide branches near the kitchen garden. Her new father, Nirloth, punished her for it, but Isika's mother intervened quickly; he hadn't hit Isika more than twice. Everything had been easier when her mother was alive. Isika hadn't climbed a tree since.

She sat and waited, watching Ibba, who sat close to the water, patting piles of sand and smoothing them to form large round domes. Isika thought of what Jabari had told them.

All the children who had been sent out were alive. It was too incredible to believe. Isika had assumed the sent ones to be dead for so long, she found she couldn't believe him. It couldn't be true. She absentmindedly drew in the sand, thinking hard about all of it. She blinked and looked at what she had drawn. One word: *Aria*. It was the name of the lost sister who had been given over, breaking Isika's mother's heart. Could Aria be alive?

Isika blinked sudden tears out of her eyes. There was no use thinking about it. She knew from experience that hoping for things made disappointment more devastating. Aria was dead. With her own eyes, Isika had seen the boat tossed into the dangerous ocean.

Benayeem was sitting a few feet away, dreaming, it seemed, staring out at the sea, quiet as usual. Isika wished he was more talkative. She needed to talk this over with someone, and Ben was better than no one. She shifted and sighed.

"We'll go anyway," she said loudly, filled with sudden conviction. She felt brave. She stretched her hands out in front of her to look at them, then turned them over to look at her tingling palms. "Even if they won't take us," she continued. "We'll go after him anyway."

Ben turned his head and met her eyes. He looked impossibly thin and tall, sitting there on the beach. She wondered briefly if she looked that way from a distance. He nodded, slowly, and she knew he would come with her if they had to go alone.

She was pacing the length of the curved beach when she heard the long cry of the female bird and turned to see Jabari and Gavi stepping out of the jungle, the Othra swirling around them. She ran back to the boys and waited breathlessly. Jabari frowned, but Gavi was smiling.

"I don't know what the elders will think of this," Jabari said, sighing. "But the Othra have convinced us, and it seems that I am destined to push at the edges of what is allowed." He grinned, his face transformed. "We'll take you to Azariyah, our royal city, to look for your brother."

"WE START THIS AFTERNOON," Jabari said after Isika and Ibba had finished exclaiming over his words. He stood with one hand holding onto a branch that swung from the big tree. "For now, you should get some rest. You three look exhausted. It will be a long journey. The rescuers are ahead of us, and they'll travel quickly, with only one poison-lander to guide. We won't be able to catch them before they get to the city."

He reached up to the tree limb above his head and caught it with both hands, pulling his chin over the large branch four or five times before dropping lightly to the ground and walking away.

Isika frowned. He was showing off, and he had said that they looked tired, when Isika had more energy than she ever remembered having. And then she thought of something that nearly made her fall over.

"Ben," she gasped. "Their eyes! They haven't been shielding their eyes."

Ben looked surprised, then laughed at her. "Have you only just realized that? They've been meeting our eyes all day."

She had missed it. Why had she missed it? Was it because she had always strained against the rules? Or because she was sick with worry for Kital? But it was amazing, uncomfortable, breathtaking. A place where she could look into the eyes of anyone she chose. It was as unbelievable as the idea that all the sent ones were alive. After a moment, though, her excitement fizzled, and she looked at her feet. She missed Kital, and there would be a long journey before she could hold him again.

Isika tried to prepare, but there was almost nothing to do. She helped Ibba roll her clothing into a pack to carry. She pulled the boat farther onto the shore, wishing she could return it to Jerutha's brother, or simply thank him.

Her mind was disturbed, though, and she couldn't concentrate. She kept feeling a tugging on her mind like she was forgetting something. She had felt something similar before, faintly, in the losh forest near their home. Here, it was stronger. The feeling grew, pulling on the edges of her consciousness like something she should know or should be doing. She looked around, frustrated and puzzled.

Gavi was fishing, throwing a net into the sea, waiting until he caught something, then pulling the shiny fish out of the water and dropping it into a basket at his feet. Jabari was packing a bag and seemed to be arguing with the birds. Benayeem sat on the shore and stared out at the sea again. Every so often, he turned and drew something in the sand with his finger. Ibba sat beside Ben, singing. The feeling of pulling grew stronger and stronger.

Isika closed her eyes and tried to push it out of her mind, but as soon as her sight was gone, the feeling was even more potent. A clear direction and shape came to her. It was the tree. The tree was calling to her. The tree was calling to her! It was the one with long snake-like branches, the one that had seemed like a good climbing tree.

She opened her eyes and walked toward it. The pulling eased as she went, and the closer she got, the more she felt that going to the tree was the right thing to do. She put a hand on one of its branches and drew a sharp breath. The tree was *buzzing*. It hummed under her hand. She pulled her hand away but put it back when she realized it was almost painful to lose contact with it. The pulling came from its heights. Isika needed to climb into the upper branches. She picked up one foot and tried to put it on a limb, but her long, heavy skirt wouldn't allow her to stretch her leg very far. She paused.

It is not our way, she heard in her head, but then the humming of the tree brought tears to her eyes, and she grew angry with the voice in her head. She pulled her heavy over-dress off until she wore only the shorts and light shirt that were her underclothes. Ignoring everyone else, paying attention only to the call of the tree, she climbed onto the first branch. She felt a burst of joy like light flowing through her body. The light inside grew brighter as she climbed, and her limbs grew stronger as she went higher. She climbed until she reached the branch that sparkled in the edges of her vision, and she heaved herself onto it. She closed her eyes and tried to quiet her racing heart.

The humming of the tree filled Isika until she couldn't tell where she started and it stopped. It was more than the brilliant, joyful light behind her eyes, it was sound and motion inside her. Pictures began to flash through her mind, and she allowed them to draw her along a path of memory.

Her father beating her for not gathering enough wood in the morning.

Her father berating her for lack of reverence in the temple. Her mother's face as she lay on her bed, wasting away from grief. Isika's tears as she cared for Kital, the nights and mornings of walking with him. She saw herself exhausted and grieving, small and bent. She saw herself in the garden, her face wet with tears. She saw herself making the food. She saw herself as an old woman, though she was only a child. Jerutha coming, the tentative steps toward love for her stepmother, the way she might feel toward an older sister.

Her father beating her when she screamed against his decision to give Kital over.

The three of them running toward the boat, Benayeem and Ibba shadows behind her. Now she saw the birds flying overhead and spotting them, calling to Jabari. And the colors behind her eyes became wilder and wilder until she saw things that made no sense to her: A dark-skinned girl on a city street, a wall being torn down, a woman wailing, an old man with dark skin and a gentle face, a woman with a crown.

Isika gasped and opened her eyes. Though she would have sworn she had been flying, she was still in the tree. She picked up one hand and stared at it. All her life, she had been so, so tired. She was used to dragging herself out of bed in the morning, shuffling along, hunched over. The sun usually seemed to beat her into the ground. In her heart, the weariness went even deeper.

But now, as Isika opened and closed her hand... she felt great strength. She thought she could run to the city. She clambered down the tree and hopped up and down on her toes, reaching her hands over her head and trying to pull her chin over a branch, the way Jabari had done. Oof. Maybe not that strong.

She looked up to see the birds watching her, clicking at each other in that way they had when they were talking only amongst themselves. The smallest of the three cocked her head to one side, and it seemed for a moment that she was looking straight through Isika. Isika shook her head to clear it. Things had become so strange.

"Isika! Do you want to start the fire?" Gavi called.

She nodded, thankful there was some easy thing she could do; something familiar. When she walked away from the tree, she noticed that the feeling of being tugged had gone away completely, but the new strength didn't go anywhere. She straightened her shoulders and pulled her head up tall.

She scooped a small pit into the sand next to Gavi, heaping the wood into a little pile the way she always did. Building a cooking fire was no different from what she would be doing at home. What *was* different was the sea whispering gently along the shore, sparkling with thousands of tiny flecks of sunlight.

When she struck the flint, the fire bent obediently and flared up quickly, more quickly than she had ever been able to coax fire along. She sat back on her heels and looked at the little blaze, perplexed. She had just built a roaring fire in only a moment. That wasn't the usual way. What *was* this place?

Gavi roasted the fish along with potatoes he buried in the coals. Ben and Ibba and Isika ate most of the food. Isika could sense that Jabari and Gavi were holding back. She narrowed her eyes at them.

"You should eat," she said. "Don't let us eat everything."

"Don't worry about us," Gavi said. "You look like you haven't had a good meal in a while, and Jabari and I eat like kings. Plus, he," and he held his palm out toward Nirral, "would take me into the jungle for another talking-to if we didn't feed you well." The huge bird spread his wings just once, and they flashed green in the afternoon sun.

"TIME TO GO!" Jabari announced, sauntering over to them as Isika put out the fire, and Gavi and Ben washed their hands in the sea. Ibba was washing her face, dipping her hands in the crystalline water, cupping it to splash over her. She was wet from forehead to knees.

"Ready," Isika said, standing. Jabari held something out toward her, and as he stood looking at her, she felt her face getting hot. She was still wearing her underclothes after climbing the tree.

"Here's something easier for you to wear while we're traveling," he said. "Sorry that I only have boy clothes." He smiled at her, and she saw he had a dimple in one cheek. His hair was tight and curly, cut close to his head. When he turned, she spotted a scar on his back, peeking just over his shirt, near the base of his neck. Isika was bursting with questions for him, but she took the clothes without a word and went into the shelter of the jungle to change. Getting in wasn't as easy as Jabari and Gavi had made it look. As she tripped over a vine, she heard him call out.

"We'll walk along this way and wait for you in the first clearing," he said. "Ibba, go with your sister. I don't have anything small enough for you, but you can wear the little shorts and undershirt you have."

Inside the curtain of leaves under the tree she had climbed, Isika looked at what he had given her, Ibba drawing close like a curious little tree squirrel. There was a pair of grey pants. Isika put them on and found that they were wide-legged and made of a very soft, light material. She drew the strings tight, tying the pants on. Next, she wriggled into the short-sleeved tunic. It was light brown, with intricate designs along the edges, and far too big for her—she could have fit Ibba into the shirt with her. Largeness aside, both things were far easier to wear than the heavy skirt and tunic she had been wearing. The clothes were so light and airy that she felt as though she wasn't wearing anything. She walked back and forth, testing them out, and the cloth flapped pleasantly against her skin.

"You look nice," Ibba pronounced, jumping around like a puppy, arms and legs bare. She seemed completely happy and not disturbed about the changes that were happening to them. They grinned at each other for a minute. Isika quickly redid Ibba's braids, twisting and smoothing the stray hairs back in, and fixed her own hair, smoothing her coarse, tight curls, braiding them neatly.

She rolled their old clothes up and left them in a bundle at the bottom of the tree. Just before they turned to follow the others, she put a hand on the tree trunk. She felt the humming strength running up and down its branches.

"Thank you," she whispered, and they turned to follow the others deeper into the jungle.

CHAPTER 10

They walked all day. Ben and his sisters must have looked funny, stumbling along with their mouths open. Ben saw the comical look on Isika and Ibba's faces, and he felt the same expression lighting up his own. But he couldn't help himself; the jungle was amazing. Ben had never seen such a beautiful place. Ibba's feet hardly touched the ground as she danced and skipped along the path.

They walked along a road, little more than a path, with red, packed dirt beneath their feet. Trees leaned over them on each side, nearly touching, so that sometimes Jabari had to wait and hold back branches to let the others pass. The three birds flew overhead, stopping to wait in trees, singing as they swooped from branch to branch. Ben's heart rang in response to their singing.

There were so many trees. Some of them were tall, with white trunks and dark green leaves as big as people. Some trees had dark blue leaves, small and round, the trunks a deep red. There were trees with brilliant purple flowers and trees with white blossoms that gave off a fragrance that trailed after the travelers or beckoned to them around corners.

There were fruit trees, and at one point, Gavi stopped under a tree and picked five small red fruits. He handed one to each of them. The fruit was round, with tight skin and a pit in the center, tart and sweet on the tongue. It felt like drinking a long drink of water, or like swimming. Ben stood a little straighter. They all did.

Ben walked with Isika while Ibba ran ahead, pointing at things and running back to them. She was like a young goat. Ben felt the same way inside. He envied her freedom. Benayeem was nearly a man at thirteen years, and he was too old to run and jump and skip. But he walked with long swinging strides. He felt different, not slipping from shadow to shadow, trying to hide. His bow swung on his back, the satchel Jabari had given him to carry hung at his side, and he looked up, instead of at the ground.

The sky overhead was a deep, brilliant blue, with flocks of green, chattering birds streaming through the jungle from time to time.

"It's beautiful," Isika said, and sighed. "I wish there were better words to describe what it is. It's so much more than beautiful." Ben knew what she meant. The surroundings reached deep inside, somehow, like the bird's speech.

"How are you?" she asked.

He looked at her then, walking beside him, and he saw that she carried herself differently. Her strength seemed less like anger and more like grace. She held her head up.

"I feel more awake than I have in a long time," he answered her. "As though I've been half asleep, and I'm only now waking up." Ben frowned. There was so much more than that, but he had never told her about the torment of oppressive dread he'd endured in the village, so he didn't know if he could tell her about the way he was sensing things now. It felt like a jungle of music inside him, the world in duplicate, as though he could close his eyes and still see the heart of everything.

"I know what you mean," Isika said. She sounded surprised. She looked at him. "You don't normally answer when I ask questions like that," she said.

It was true. For a long time, speaking had seemed as though it was too dangerous, and Ben often chose not to talk through the voices in his head. No wonder she was surprised. She went on.

"I feel stronger, taller, happier, younger, and older at once," she said.

"You look different," he said. Isika's eyes were clear and dark, more alive. Her whole face was more relaxed and less pinched. The fierce look she always wore had receded, smoothing her forehead, she looked like someone you could approach easily.

"So do you," she said. They smiled at each other.

BEN'S SMILE was so unfamiliar that Isika realized that her brother almost never smiled. She felt a sudden flash of grief that made her gasp: sorrow for the small children they had been. They would never get a second chance at being little. And they had lost their sister.

"Ben?" Isika whispered. "Do you think they have Aria?"

He frowned and looked at the dirt. "It seems like too much to hope. I can't quite believe that they found everyone."

Isika agreed. She had thought of her little sister as dead for so long it seemed unbearable to hope that she was alive. They would have to wait and see. Because she was thinking of Aria, the familiar grief washed over her.

Sadness felt more real in this land, the same way pleasure and joy seemed to be stronger. Isika thought she would crumple under the sadness of loss, but the bird Jabari had called Efir passed overhead, coming so close that her wing brushed Isika's shoulder. Peace wrapped around Isika, entwined with the bird's song. Even after the bird flew away, Isika heard the intriguing song in her head. She decided to ask about the giant birds that Jabari called the Othra. She would find out who and what they were.

Around the time the sun was getting ready to set, Jabari held a hand up and stopped walking. Isika and Ben stuttered to a stop behind him, and Isika stared at Jabari's shoulders, square and tense. Her clothes were sticking to her. The day was still hot, and she was ready for a little evening coolness. She looked back at the path, at Gavi standing next to Ibba. He was tense as well, and he seemed to be listening to something. Jabari started forward again, and the others followed, whispering along the path until a house became visible in a little clearing on the right side. There was a short wall around it, half the size of a wall in Isika's village. The house could easily be seen behind it. To Isika's eyes, the half wall made the house look unprotected, almost naked.

"Wait here," Jabari said. "Gavi and I have work to do."

"Can we help?" Isika asked.

"You won't be able to help with this," he said.

The two boys walked ahead until they were beside the house, then put their hands on the wall. Isika took a breath. Touching another person's wall was forbidden. But then she felt a shock that vibrated from her eyes to her toes, as the two older boys began to pull at the wall. They grasped big chunks of stone, gripping it in their hands. It came away as though it was made of garden dirt. Isika was frozen, horrified. Both Gavi and Jabari broke huge sections of it away until it was open to the ground. She screamed. Beside her, Ibba was crying.

Jabari looked back at them, a puzzled frown on his face. Isika ran to him. "You cannot!" she cried, breathless. "It's sacred!"

His face moved into the same angry, hard look he had worn when they spoke of the sending.

"It is not sacred here," he said.

He and Gavi continued breaking large pieces of the wall, walking around the house, tearing every part away. The others watched in silence. All at once, Isika felt stunned and chilled. Too many things had happened in a short time, and she sank to the ground, where she sat, exhausted. All around the house, there was a great cloud of dust from the broken pieces of wall. The birds had flown off somewhere, so Isika couldn't even ask them to explain what was happening. Ben stood beside her, watching, his face set and quiet. Ibba still cried, though now she sounded like she was crying because she was too tired to stop. Isika reached out to squeeze her hand, and Ibba collapsed onto her. Isika adjusted so that Ibba's head was on her lap. She stroked her sister's hair absently, waiting for the wrath of the goddesses to fall on them, looking toward the sky to see if it would come from the open blue. Maybe it would erupt from the ground beneath them. She was momentarily distracted by the color of the sky. She had never seen such a deep blue before. It was so blue it seemed there must be another name for it.

"Isika!" Ben said suddenly.

She looked. The dust around the house was clearing. She could see that instead of rubble, there was nothing. The wall had completely disappeared.

"Where did it go?" Ibba asked, awe in her voice.

"I don't know," Isika said, shaking her head. Honestly, there were far too many things in the world that she hadn't known about, and it made her angry, but she didn't know who to be angry *with*.

Jabari dusted his hands off near the front entrance of the house, and Gavi paused at the doorway to touch the upper mantle with his thumb, before entering.

"He's intruding on their ground," Isika said dully. She stood and walked to where the wall had been, looking at its absence with a sick feeling in her stomach. She had been taught that the walls were sacred since before she could remember differently. Ever since they had come out of the desert to stay with the Workers, they had honored and said the sacred words over the walls every single day. The whole world felt like it had turned on its side, as though soon they would fall straight out into the brilliant, blue nothingness of the sky.

Jabari approached, and as he did, Ben and Ibba moved closer to Isika, Ibba slipping her hand into Isika's and leaning on her leg, so that the three of them were a unit, facing the strangeness of what the boys had done.

Gavi came out a few moments later, ahead of a black-skinned woman with a baby on her hip. The woman was crying. Gavi laid his hands gently on either side of her head, and after a few breaths, the woman grew calm. She looked at them, standing where the wall had once been. She still had tears on her face.

"Please come in," she said. "I'll prepare dinner for you."

Beside Isika, Jabari nodded. "We will come," he said. He turned to Isika and the others. "This part is important," he said, "so don't try to refuse. Gavi has healed her, but for her healing to be complete, she needs to offer hospitality. Because the wall hadn't been here long, the poison wasn't too strong, and we didn't need a more experienced healer. If the poison had been stronger, she could have gone crazy because we don't have a healer strong enough to heal the deepest wounds." He paused. "We have to leave many walls and come back when a strong healer is available."

He spoke kindly, as though he was happy to offer some knowledge like the new fruit Gavi had offered to them only a few hours before, as though there was any way under the four goddess's realms that Isika could understand the words coming out of his mouth. Almost none of what he had said made sense, but Isika still had a question.

"Why don't you just travel with an experienced healer, then?"

His face changed, and his eyes were sad. "We don't have enough healers for that anymore. The gift is given less, now that we don't have our queen. Gavi is an excellent healer, but he's still just a baby bird, right out of his nest."

Gavi was with them again, and he punched Jabari's shoulder lightly.

Jabari's words had only brought Isika more questions, but there wasn't time for them because they were walking to the woman's front door.

"We'll sleep here tonight," Jabari said, turning as they walked up the steps. "And continue in the morning. You three look exhausted."

Isika was surprised again. She didn't feel tired, but when she looked at Ibba, she saw her little sister yawning. Jabari and Gavi, meanwhile, after walking half the day and breaking a sacred wall to the ground, looked the same as they had when they had woken in the morning.

"But how do you know? How did you know that the wall was small enough for you to break?" It was the only thing she could think to ask, though there were about seventy-six more things she needed to know desperately.

"I just know. This is my kind of magic. I'm a protector, it's my gift. Gavi has a bit of protection in him as well, though he is mainly gifted with healing."

Isika stopped and looked at Gavi, who smiled at her and nodded his head. He crinkled his eyes and gestured that she should enter the house.

They entered the house together to find a clean, well-swept space, which, though small, had a kitchen with bright windows. They sat on mats on the floor and accepted bowls of spicy stew. Isika ate hers so quickly she hardly tasted it, then helped with washing up the dishes. Her last feeling before she fell asleep on her sleeping mat was irritation that Jabari knew so much more than she did. She would force him to explain in the morning.

CHAPTER 11

The next day, Isika jumped up as soon as her eyes flew open. Sun streamed through the open doorway and windows of the small cottage. She felt incredible. She stretched out her arms and legs, staring at them as though they belonged to someone else. She had so much energy, she thought she could spring out the door and straight into the sky. She looked around the cottage. There was no sign of Jabari or Gavi in the little room, but Ben and Ibba were fast asleep under their blankets. Their host was baking something over the fire, and the baby lay watching Isika from a blanket beside his mother.

"Good morning," Isika said, crossing the room to stand beside the woman.

The woman looked up from the dough she was rolling. "Good morning," she said. "Did you sleep well?"

"I did," Isika told her. The woman's eyes were brighter than they had been the day before. She hummed a song as she made the bread. The baby cooed from his blanket, and Isika held her arms out to him. "Can I hold him?" she asked.

"Of course," the woman said, smiling at Isika. She looked directly into Isika's eyes, the way Jabari and Gavi did. It still felt strange and exhilarating, all at once.

Isika brought the baby's little head to her face and breathed in his smell. He reminded her of Kital as a baby, with his nut-brown skin and tiny, grasping hands. When she thought of Kital, her heart gave a pang, and once again, it was sharp, like a blade. It was as sharp as the energy Isika felt, as strong as the joy she felt at the beauty of the sunny morning. All of her senses were heightened, and all at once, her need to see Kital became unbearable. She gave the baby a kiss on his lovely head, then carefully placed him back on the blanket. He watched her with serious eyes as she turned to find the others.

"Time to go!" she said. Her voice was loud, and Benayeem and Ibba sat up and looked at her sleepily. "Wake up, you two," she said. "We need to get moving."

Outside, Gavi was packing the kitchen bag with food, and Jabari was looking over his arrows, checking each shaft and settling them back in the quiver he usually wore slung over his shoulder.

"You're finally up," Gavi said, smiling.

"Well, how long have you two been up?" Isika asked, annoyed.

"Since the moon was still in the sky," Jabari said.

Isika crossed her arms and frowned at him. He smiled in

response, inspecting another arrow carefully before putting it in the quiver.

"Do you ever use that?" Isika asked, distracted by the soft clink of the arrow settling with the others.

"When I need to hunt," he said. He nodded toward Gavi. "It's rare when we're seeking, because people feed us, especially if we rid their houses of poison. Our kind host here has given us enough food for two more days."

"Well," Gavi said. "Maybe one, with the way these three eat."

Jabari laughed.

Isika narrowed her eyes. "Are you ready to go?" she asked. "I'm worried about my baby brother. He's probably terrified."

"Oh, we're ready," Jabari said. "We were waiting for you, sleepyheads." He grinned, and Gavi laughed as Isika reached out, without thinking, and pushed Jabari, who nearly toppled over and fell off the porch.

For a moment, Isika stood frozen, shocked at herself. What an intrusion on his person, and he was her elder! But then the sound of Gavi's laughter reached her, and Isika couldn't help joining in when she saw the look on Jabari's face as he regained his balance. She was startled by the pleasure that spread through her. She was becoming a new person, someone who was strong, someone who laughed loudly and pushed boys who teased her. One thing was sure; she was never going to be able to return to life as a Worker.

. . .

THEY LEFT the house with their hands full of biscuits to eat while they walked. The warm biscuits were made of toasted grain, honey, and cinnamon. They smelled glorious and tasted better, melting in Isika's mouth. She was still adjusting to eating so many times a day, but the taste of the food in this land! The idea that food could be plentiful and taste so good was new to her. She could get used to it.

She was trying to find the courage to demand the answers she wanted from Jabari, but she didn't have to, because he came to her first. He fell into step beside her.

"I think you and I should walk together today," he said. "I can see you have burning questions for me. They look like they'll shoot out of your skull if you don't ask them soon, and I, for one, don't want any people explosions on this journey."

Heat rushed into Isika's face. It annoyed her that Jabari could read her like that. But he was right, and this morning was so different. First, she felt as though she could run all day, and second, her thoughts were ordered in nice rows in her brain. Instead of having a tangle of unknowing in her mind, she knew the questions she wanted to ask, and even the order to ask them. It would be stupid not to take him up on his offer.

Behind them, Gavi walked with Benayeem and Ibba on either side of him, three abreast on the wide path. Ibba skipped and waved her arms on every other step, while Ben had a grin on his face from something Gavi had said. Honestly, Isika barely recognized her family. They were far from the overworked, hungry, grief-stricken people they had been two days ago.

The Othra had rejoined them. The huge birds flew overhead, landing in branches, singing to one another, then launching out of the trees in a storm of leaves and feathers. It seemed they could barely stay still. The leader, the one called Nirral, was the largest of the birds, over half as tall as Isika, and he had the most colors glimmering in his black feathers. The one called Efir was smaller than Nirral, and when sunlight hit her at a certain angle, she was mainly red and purple, though she still looked black in regular daylight. Isika had never heard the third speak. She seemed older somehow, with shades of deep blue glittering from her black feathers as she flew. Of the three, she sang the most, lighting on branches just before the travelers, trilling open notes into the forest.

"Who are they?" Isika asked, pointing at the birds. It wasn't necessarily the most important of her many questions, but she had to start somewhere, and she knew this was the right place.

"The Othra?" Jabari asked. When she looked up at him, he was staring back at her, his face surprised. "You've never seen them before?"

Isika had to smile. "Of course not. Did you think we had Othra in the Worker village? You have to understand, I've never seen any of this. Not the plants, not the blue sea we can swim in, not the sacred walls being torn down like paper..." She felt defensive, suddenly, and scowled. "You're going to have to explain it all."

Jabari looked thoughtful. "I'm sorry, I see now. It's just that I've grown up with the Othra. I can't remember ever not knowing them. They are ancient and special. They're guardians of a sort, caretakers of all that we are charged to protect and heal. The big one is Nirral. I think he's been around for centuries. His mate is Efir. Efir's mother, Eemia, is even older." He frowned, his voice trailing off as he watched Eemia trilling a song from a high branch. "They don't usually spend this much time with us. They often watch from afar, but..."

"What?"

He shook his head, a frown on his face, and he was lost in his thoughts for a moment. "Sometimes they come when we need extra help, or when something important is happening. I've never seen them behave this way. I'm not sure if you saw, but they pretty much commanded me to take you to the city."

"Oh. You didn't want to?" She felt her shoulders stiffen.

He laughed. "Don't be so prickly. I just had never encountered a situation like... you... in my whole life. I didn't know what to do. It helped to have their approval. If nothing else, I can blame them if the elders are angry."

Isika bit her lip. He was right, she *was* being prickly. "Not used to thinking on your feet?" she asked, stealing a glance at him and trying to relax her shoulders.

Jabari's mouth dropped open. "Are you teasing me, Isika? You *do* have a sense of humor. I wondered if you even knew what a joke was."

She smiled and changed the subject. "Are there more Othra? And why do I feel the way I do? Stronger every day? Do you know?"

"There are others, yes. But not many of them take notice

of us. They stay in their mountains and do whatever it is that they do. These three have always been part of life in the city. And as for your other question..."

He trailed off, lost in thought again. Isika watched his face until she tripped over a tree root, making up her mind to pay more attention to her feet. It was a while before Jabari spoke again.

"Well, it's to be expected," he said. "The same thing happens to the rescued ones. The poison is washing out of your body, and as it does, you begin to feel better. I'm a little confused because it usually takes a lot longer for the poison to leave. You've been out of the Worker village two days?"

Isika felt as though they had been away a month, but as she thought it through, she realized he was right. Yesterday they had met Gavi and Jabari in the morning. The day before, they had rowed after Kital. Yes, it had been two days.

She nodded slowly. "What do you mean by poison? Why do you use that word so often?"

"The poison is from the Great Waste: demon magic trying to destroy the world. It appears in many ways, but one way is in the growth of the walls. The poison is so strong that those within the walls can't see that they are poisonous. They keep others outside of their walls more and more until the walls form their identity." He glanced at her. "Some even believe the walls are sacred."

Isika blinked at him. He had just described their way of life and named it poison, demon magic. His face was full of pity. He looked away, tilting his head. She really looked at him, noting how straight he stood when he walked, his wide shoulders, the sweep of his jaw up to his ear. She frowned and looked back at the ground. She didn't want to stumble again.

"We need each other, Isika," he said gently. "Mugunta, the Great Waste, wants us to die separately, to be suspicious of each other, to demand money for normal services for one another, to rob us of love. Why do you think your people cast their own children away? It's because of poison."

"They cast them away because of the demands of the goddesses," she said slowly.

"The goddesses are manifestations of Mugunta, our name for the Great Waste," he said, that anger back in his voice. "They are made of the poison, they are demons. No one should ever cast away something as precious as a child."

She shook her head to clear it.

"Who is Mugunta? What do you mean, the Great Waste?"

"Mugunta is the cause of a baby crying in the night with no one to hear, a man without a home, people who live close to one another with no kindness between them. Mugunta and the Great Waste eat the hearts of people, they feed on fear and suspicion. They hate the Shaper for his beauty. They are disharmony and greed. They are the beginning of evil, those who eat light and spit out blood. And they do it through poison because people rebel against force."

Isika was stunned. Jabari paused, then went on. "You honor the walls. Where do they come from?" he asked.

"They—they just appear. The walls are gifts from the goddesses."

"To separate you and keep people out of each other's homes."

"Yes. A family's ground is sacred," Isika said, more firmly than she felt.

"And who tells you these rules, Isika? That you cannot look at one another or enter one another's houses?"

"The priest shows the way." Isika's voice was less certain as she spoke of the things she had always struggled with.

"Where does the priest hear about the way?"

"I—I don't know."

Jabari's voice was gentle. "The rules come from Mugunta. He has a thousand ways to spin hatred. The lies and tricks that keep people away from one another spill out of the evil that lives in the Great Waste. That evil is poison. And I think most of your rules come from one of Mugunta's most loyal servants, the Desert King."

Isika blinked. "Who?"

Jabari started to answer, then shook his head. "That's for another time."

Isika frowned at him, thinking over her life. Oddly, she wanted to protect the village she had run from, but she also couldn't understand why she had this protective instinct. She looked deeper. Something was prodding at her, making her uncomfortable with condemning the Workers as being lost to poison.

She saw it then. What she really wanted to protect was her mother's choice to live among the Workers. And she wanted to protect people like Jerutha, kind and good people. But being poisoned didn't mean that Jerutha wasn't kind and good, Isika realized as she worked through it. It only meant she was... poisoned.

Isika thought about how she had trouble learning to avoid eye contact, and how she had always thought people's eyes were so beautiful, even though she wasn't supposed to look into them. She realized that she believed Jabari. She believed that she had been poisoned and that the seekers needed to rid the land of poison. She wanted to go back to her village and do it right then.

"Why don't you come and tear down the walls of the Workers?" she asked. Jabari looked shocked.

"We can't do that! We tear down walls that have begun to grow in our own land, not in the lands of others."

"But they need you."

"They have to want help," he said. "Otherwise, it would begin a world of trouble; they would fight us, and there would be war."

She thought about that. The Workers certainly didn't seem like they wanted help, but that was because they didn't know they were poisoned. Surely if they knew they were being poisoned, they would want people to help them.

"Does the poison come quickly?" she asked. "Are you always... patrolling?"

"We call it seeking. It does come quickly. Maween is large, so we can only visit each place once a year, and we always have walls to tear down." He glanced at her, which she saw because she was looking up at him as he spoke. His eyes were serious, and he considered her for a moment. Isika tried to remember to pay attention to where her feet went.

Her pants flapped gently around her legs. She felt her new energy with every step. He went on speaking.

"We had a queen once," he said. "The elders say that when she was with us, the poison was so slow that the Maweel could take care of it themselves, and no seekers were needed. But she was stolen—kidnapped over thirty years ago. Ever since, we have to send the seekers to take down the walls. We still look for her." His voice changed. "It's why I became a seeker; I have taken a vow to find her myself."

Isika glanced at him, surprised by the passion in his voice. His fists were clenched.

"Why was the poison slow when the queen was with your people?" she asked.

"It was in my grandparent's time. My father was ten years old when the queen was taken. But that's a question I shouldn't answer. You'll have to ask one of the elders when we get to the city."

Isika wanted to protest, but when she looked at him, she saw his set face and kept quiet. They walked in silence for some time. The jungle was thick on either side of them, exploding with plants that waved in the slightest breeze, and bursts of sound when small birds sang into the day.

"You've mentioned the elders a few times," she said finally. "Who are they?"

"They watch over the Maweel. There are many elders, but four main people, who used to advise the queen. Now they run the land."

With a flurry of air and leaves, Nirral swooped down and

brushed Jabari on the head with the feathers of one wing. Jabari jumped.

"What?" he asked, coming to a halt because Nirral landed on the ground directly in front of him.

"You know, young one," the bird said. "Sing."

CHAPTER 12

The two female Othra landed and stood beside the larger male bird. Nirral spoke again, the words reverberating in the space between the travelers as well as inside of them. "You know the answer to her question, young Jabari," he said. "You must sing her the song."

As Nirral spoke, calm descended on Isika, and she heard a strain of haunting music. She looked up, but nothing was there. The sky was empty and blue.

"I can't sing it," Jabari said, shifting his feet and looking uncomfortable.

"You can," Gavi said, reaching out to punch Jabari lightly. They all stood in a messy semicircle around the Othra. "Sing, choir boy."

Jabari glared at him. He rubbed at the short, tight curls on the back of his head. Efir clattered and growled, spreading her wings to their full span, and Jabari sighed.

"Fine," he said. "But you had all better find a seat, because it's long."

They settled themselves on the ground, leaning against tree trunks beside the path. Ibba sat against Isika's knees, and Isika reached out and stroked her sister's hair. Ibba squeezed her hand in return. Jabari stood before them, straight and tall. The sun scattered the shadows of leaves over his skin. He was handsome. The afternoon was hot and humid, and Isika thought sleepily that the Maweel could make him their king if they were missing someone to rule them.

Nirral began a long haunting call, exactly like the music Isika had heard moments before. The other birds joined in. The hairs stood up on the backs of Isika's arms, but she still wasn't prepared for what happened when Jabari began to sing. He stood with his eyes closed and sang to them. His voice was beautiful, lovelier than any voice Isika had ever heard. But the song was a lament. It brought tears to Isika's eyes.

BLACK AS BELOVED NIGHT, eyes like stars,
    Her smile the sudden glimpse of
    a crescent moon.
    A line to the Uncreated One,
    a thread into heaven's heart,
    tied to the whirling sky,
    the planets, the stars, the mountain peaks.
    Protected by her love
    the Shaper's hand among us

light all around us
we were brought in and encircled
loved and surrounded

From her belly sprung
 a child of light and promise
 a child strong from the first.
 Their love the sun rising,
 the sight of them love itself
 but hearts break and the Great Waste
 moved against us.
 Thieves, they wanted her,
 they took our queen
 she was gone and her baby with her
 we wailed to the heavens,
 but the grasp of Mugunta was strong,
 the Great Waste didn't give her up to us.
 Still, we search,
 Still, we search
 Still, we search.

As Jabari was singing, Isika closed her eyes. Images began to flash through her mind until she was immersed in unfamiliar scenes. She saw the queen, crowned, tall, and austere, in robes of deepest red, a baby in her arms. She heard the queen singing a song to her baby. Then, a crack in the earth, a dead tree, black against the sky, men on horseback, swirling dust, the crown falling to the ground, a great shriek. She saw a dark-skinned king with a thin silver circlet on his head, falling with an arrow to the chest. The dead tree again.

When she came back to her surroundings, she found that she was crying. She quickly wiped her face with the back of one hand, feeling as though her heart was broken. She couldn't understand the strange emotions coursing through her. Why did she feel so desperate over a song?

Jabari and Gavi were frowning at her. Isika frowned back at them, then looked at Ben, who raised his eyebrows and shook his head.

"What?" she said.

"How do you know it?" Jabari asked.

"How do I know what?"

"You were singing the song," he said. "You sang it with me. Where have you learned it?"

Isika didn't know what to say. She hadn't known she was singing, so lost in the swirl of images around her, and she *didn't* know the song. She had never heard it before now, in Jabari's soaring voice. She shook her head. "I don't know," she said. "I don't know any of this." She stood, feeling shaky, needing to escape watching eyes. She wanted to get away from the deep sorrow she still felt after hearing the song. "I need to run," she said. "We're going straight on this path, right? Let me go ahead, I'll run for a while and then stop to let you catch up."

Jabari shook his head, glancing at Gavi. "I don't think

that's a good idea," he started to say, but he stopped at a sudden clicking from Nirral.

"Let her go," Nirral said, "we will follow the young one to watch her." The feeling he sent with his words was impossibly kind, and Isika blinked back tears and started to run.

As she ran, rather than growing tired, she gained more strength. The path seemed to help her spring forward, and the trees rushed by, the thick forest trilling with birdsong on either side. She felt angry and sad, even a little hurt from the look on Jabari's face when he had demanded to know how she knew the song. Isika didn't know how she knew. How was she supposed to know anything? This wasn't her land, she was a stranger here. He was supposed to be the one with all the understanding. The Othra had called him to guide the three of them. She had not asked for any of this.

She grew angrier, shrugging off the memory of Jabari answering her questions so patiently. Instead, she focused on the look on his face, laughing at her because she didn't know the ways of this land. He was nothing like the beautiful queen she had seen as he sang. Fresh despair nearly overcame her as she again saw the queen taken, and she ran faster, as though she could outrun it. *It was a different day,* she told herself. *It was a long time ago.* The sun was bright, the sky was blue, and she wasn't tired. Slowly, her mind began to calm as her feet took her along even faster.

The landscape changed abruptly, and Isika slowed her pace. She had come to the end of the vast forest. The path broke out at the top of a long slope, leading into what looked like farmland. The view was breathtaking; green and golden fields stretching out on either side of the road into blue hills on one side and the line of the sky on the other. In the distance, a small farm nestled between two fields, surrounded by cows.

Something pulled at Isika the way the tree had tugged her, back at the beach. She shivered and surged forward, her legs flying, the wind rushing past her. The air and the sky fed her energy, the road beneath her feet sent her flying. She ran faster than she had ever run before. Dimly, she could sense the Othra flying high overhead, calling to her. Still, she ran. She ran until she reached the farm and recognized where the sharp tug was coming from.

Around the house stood a thick wall, much taller than the one Jabari and Gavi had torn down. For a moment, Isika stood still, contemplating the wall with wide eyes, recognizing that she was possibly out of her depth. But the tug inside her was sharp and impossible to ignore. As she looked at the wall, a deep rage filled her, a swirling, seething feeling that came from somewhere deep within. It rushed over her until her eyes and toes tingled with fierce anger.

She attacked the wall, grabbing it with her hands, pulling at it until it crumbled and disintegrated beneath her fingers. Again and again, Isika pulled stones away, ripping the wall to pieces. It changed to dust before her eyes, and before long, the house was exposed to the road. She kept on—she didn't know for how—until it was nearly gone. As she reached the far side and pulled the final part of the wall to pieces, she heard shouts.

Dimly she recognized Jabari beside her as she pulled the

last piece of the wall down. He was screaming, with Gavi, Ibba, and Ben behind him. Ibba was crying. At first, Isika saw them dreamily, as though through water. Gavi grabbed large handfuls of his hair and looked around wildly. Isika slowly came out of her trance of destruction and began to understand what Jabari was saying.

"The wall was too big! They'll die! What are you doing, you stupid girl? What kind of demon magic possessed you?"

He rushed toward the house and pushed the door open without waiting for an answer from within. Isika followed, leaping over toy-strewn steps. Inside was madness. A man lay twitching and groaning on the bed while his wife screamed and hit her head against the wall. Two small children sat staring into nothing. Isika was horrified. This was the poison sickness Jabari had spoken of? It was horrifying.

She watched as Jabari went to the man and lay a hand on his head. Gavi followed and did the same with the woman, but nothing changed for either of them, and they continued to groan and scream. Jabari turned to Isika, his face twisted with rage and sadness, tears running down his cheeks.

"Do you see now, Isika? This is what poison madness is. When the wall is that far advanced, you can't take it away without a skilled healer. The people feel unprotected. They go mad inside."

Isika barely heard him. She felt another pull, a fizzing inside her chest. This time, instead of rage, it was exquisite warmth, like being filled by hot tea or climbing into a bath on a cold day. It felt like her mother singing to her.

"Let me try," she said.

CHAPTER 13

"o," Jabari spat. "Just leave them alone."

But Isika pushed past him and laid her hands on the man's head, imitating what Jabari had done. Some of the warmth inside her flowed toward him, and she smelled roses in the air. The man stopped writhing and groaning. He smiled, stretched, and looked up at her with deep brown eyes. He touched her face with one long, dusky hand. Then he closed his eyes and slept.

She went to the woman, and this time Jabari didn't say anything to stop her. Isika was only dimly aware of her companions. The woman calmed as Isika's hands touched her, and she stopped pounding her head against the wall. This time the fragrance of a freshly peeled orange filled the room, something Isika knew because oranges were a rare treat in the Worker village. The woman slumped into Isika's arms, and Isika lay her gently down on the bed, where she curled like a scroll bug. Next, Isika walked to the children and touched each of them on the head. They didn't fall asleep the way their parents had. Life flashed back into their eyes, and they laughed, the sound ringing out and the smell of mint filling the air. They began to play with a small toy, passing it back and forth between them.

Isika stood, gripping a chair with shaking fingers to balance herself. She was exhausted.

Ben, Ibba, and Gavi stared at her. Jabari was lost in thought, gazing at the man who slept with his face smooth and untroubled. Ibba smiled at Isika. She scrubbed at the tears on her face with her fists, then sat on the floor to play with the two little children; a boy and a girl. Isika watched as Ibba showed them how to set up a small ramp so the ball would fly up when they pushed it. She felt as though she could sleep for a month. She walked to stand beside her brother, leaning her head on his shoulder. He put one hand up to touch her face. Jabari looked at Isika, then, his face still thoughtful. He lifted his hand and rubbed at the crown of his head absently. Isika had a question, though her voice was weak when she spoke.

"Why aren't the children more concerned about their parents?" she asked. "Why do they just... play?"

Jabari's eyes snapped into focus, and she sensed that he wasn't frowning at her, but beyond her. He looked at the kids playing on the floor. They couldn't have been more than two or three years old.

"They're recovering from the poison, like their parents," he said. "They are still confused in their minds, though they will recover. The parents rest their confusion by sleeping, the children by playing. It's a mercy, for the parents won't wake for a while, and I wouldn't want to be a babysitter for distraught children."

Gavi grinned. "A puppet show, like that one time?" he asked, and Jabari smiled and shook his head.

"What?" Ben said. "I want to hear about this."

Gavi's eyes glowed, but a look from Jabari, he shook his head. "I'll tell you some other time. Just some fun from another seeking mission, when the parents didn't wake for around twelve hours." He laughed, then nodded to Jabari, and the two of them stretched the woman out on her simple bed, woven strings stretched across a wood frame. Gavi placed a bedsheet over her.

"We'll stay until one of them wakes," Jabari said. He gently touched the woman's head one more time, and she sighed in her sleep.

"I'll warm some broth," Gavi said, patting the metal container that he always carried over one shoulder. "They'll be hungry."

Isika lifted her head from her Ben's shoulder and looked at him. He gave her a gentle smile.

"What did you go and do, Isika?" he asked, and she laughed, but it turned into tears. She put her head back on his shoulder, and he reached up again and patted at her hair.

She felt restless and sick, pulled from the inside again, but she was too weary to follow the tugging. Ben squeezed her shoulder and said, "You should sit, don't you think?"

The pull was becoming stronger. It was so strong Isika

was sure she would vomit if she tried to ignore it. She shook her head.

"I'm going to get some air," she said, her voice faint. The tugging was definitely coming from outside.

Jabari pulled out a game of painted stones and tiles, barely looking up as she passed.

"Ben!" she heard him call behind her. "Come. I'll teach you while Gavi is playing nurse."

"Playing?" Gavi said. "Tell me that the next time you need a nurse for a splinter in your foot." Isika smiled.

The air outside the little house was warm and sweet. A light breeze caressed her face. She looked at the new view from the house that had no walls. She was the one who had torn them down, and yet she wondered at a people who had so few defenses. The tugging oriented itself and pulsed through her. It was coming from a large tree that stood beside the barn. She sighed with relief. Not another wall, then. She smiled and walked into the field next to the house, following a path to the tree.

This one wasn't snake-limbed, but a large, towering tree with strong limbs and small leaves. The bark was smooth against Isika's cheek as she leaned into it. Warm, solid feelings of safety coursed through her. She sighed and allowed her body to go limp. The air hummed with light and color. She closed her eyes and let all the fear and tension drain out of every part of her. The tugging continued, though she wanted to stay in that spot forever, and she sighed again and began to climb.

As soon as her feet left the ground, the tree's hum

increased and flowed through her. Light and peace surrounded her, and as she reached a wide branch, she lay back on it, stretching her whole body out. She looked at her crossed ankles and her feet, dark against the light bark of the tree. Closing her eyes, she felt the exhaustion drain out of her muscles and bones.

The deep, deep understanding of the tree surrounded her. There were lights behind her eyes, and though her eyes were closed, Isika could see the form of the tree, outlined in what looked like stars. She sensed a great warmth from the sky beyond the stars. It was nothing like the lidless stare of the goddesses in the temple or the slight warmth of a hug from Jerutha. It was more like the Othra, but bigger, deeper, and it went on forever.

Isika didn't know how long she lay there. Shapes moved, and scenes came to her again. A man on a wall in the desert, shouting and sending a charge of horses; a thin woman walking in the desert with small children trailing after, a child on her shoulders; a man with kind eyes and markings of paint on his face; the girl in the street again. She saw Kital in a boat, surrounded by the huge jumping fish, and her eyes flew open. Kital!

She lay still for a moment, reluctant to leave the tree, but soon, longing for her brother overcame her. She climbed down and walked back to the house through the field.

The light had changed. It was late afternoon; Isika had been gone a long time. Everyone had gathered in the front yard. Benayeem had his hand shading his eyes, looking in her direction. He saw her first and grinned, his smile appearing and disappearing in his face in a flash of white teeth. The man and woman of the house stood on the porch with Jabari, nodding as he spoke to them. Isika saw that they looked well. The woman wore a simple tunic over wide pants. She had wrapped a scarf around her head, and as Isika approached, she held out her hands. Isika took them, looking into the woman's brown eyes. She had freckles scattered on her dark cheeks. She was young, maybe in her mid-twenties, and she smiled at Isika with kind eyes.

"Thank you," she said, and behind her, Jabari scowled. He whistled and wandered over to his pack, heaving it onto his back in a smooth motion. Isika ignored him, or tried to, as she smiled back into the woman's eyes.

"I'd like to come back and visit you one day," she said.

"You will be welcome if you do, Protector," the woman said. Isika nodded.

The couple thanked them again and again as they left, pressing small brown rolls of bread into their hands for the road. Isika accepted gladly—she was ravenous, though it didn't seem possible that she could be hungry again. She had eaten more in these two days than she had in the whole week before, yet her stomach roared for food. She nibbled at the loaf as she walked, and felt the rich bread, full of nuts and seeds, take the edge off her hunger.

THE TENSION in the air was something you could touch, Ben thought. He tried in vain to shrug the discomfort off. They walked without much talking. Ibba jumped from stone to stone on the grassy sides of the road, oblivious. Gavi sang a song to himself, something about eating at the end of a long day, and Ben couldn't help smiling as he listened, though worry gripped his stomach.

The situation at the house had nearly overcome Ben. First, there had been the sickening waves of wrongness and terrible music coming from the house at a distance, followed by the thunder crashes of wild joy he heard in the air as Isika pulled the walls down.

Watching her then, understanding breaking over him, he was shocked by what he heard. When Jabari shouted at Isika, Ben wasn't alarmed—he knew in his core that his sister was doing the right thing. Then, while she healed the family, waves of song had echoed around the room, though Ben was the only one who could hear it. The music had made him tremble, and determination to protect his sister filled him. She had taken the wrongness and sickening sound out of the house, she had destroyed it. The song of joy had come after she had torn the walls down. The doom bells had ceased—she had restored the center of things.

Isika could make a place transform from torment to peace. For the first time in his memory, Ben felt hope, a way out that wasn't running or hiding. If he kept Isika safe, she could make things right, and in the meantime, she could keep Ben from going crazy.

After about an hour of walking, the little group stopped beside a well to refill their water flasks. They were surrounded by fields of grain, swaying in the afternoon light. The sky was very blue.

For the first time since they left the house, Jabari turned to Isika and spoke.

"That was incredibly foolish," he said.

"It turned out well," she responded. Her words were clipped and hard. Jabari's eyes darkened.

"It might not have," he said. "Don't go ahead again. Stay with the rest of us. You need guidance."

She stiffened and pulled her head up so she was tall and imposing, as much as she could be, anyway, when Jabari was half a head taller than her.

"I'm not promising you anything," she said. "I'm not a child, that you can tell me where to go or who with."

"Really? Then stop acting like a child. Don't you get it? You could have killed them!"

They stared at one another, and the hairs on Ben's arms stood on end. He didn't know what to do.

"Do you think Isika is a Healer?" Ibba asked in her little high-pitched voice. They turned to look at her as she shifted from foot to foot, biting the fingers on one hand. Ben stepped closer to her and took her other hand in his own. She looked up at him and stopped biting her fingers.

Ben had noticed that they often forgot how young Ibba was. She was only seven years old, walking all day, watching them pull down walls. And here she was, in the middle of a stand-off, trying to make peace. Ibba had been listening, the way she often did when Ben least expected it.

"Yeah, Jabari," Isika said. "Am I a healer?"

Ben cringed at the derisive tone in his sister's voice. She didn't need to be so disagreeable. But he knew she was used to being rejected and put down. She had grown a tough shell to deflect hurt. Rejection was the main thing they had known since their mother had died. And she *had* healed those people. Ben took a step forward.

Jabari's nostrils flared.

"No," he said shortly. "You have none of the characteristics of a healer." He gestured at Ibba. "Ibba does. She's probably a healer." His face softened when he looked at her, and he smiled. "She's kind, thoughtful, she listens, she makes others feel better. Those are the distinctions of a healer." He looked back at Isika, and his face hardened. "You're loud, and you don't listen."

Heat rose into Ben's face, and he took three giant steps until he was standing beside his sister, glaring at Jabari, who looked back at him, surprised.

"You know nothing about her," he said. His voice was low and menacing. He was furious. He pulled his staff from where it was tied on his shoulder and turned it to point at Jabari, conscious only of anger rising in him, hotter and hotter. His jaw felt locked in place.

Isika's face was appalled. She put one hand over the staff, but Ben's arm didn't waver.

Jabari stared, his brows coming together into a sharp frown. "What are you doing, little brother? Are you trying to start a fight on my land? Do you think you could beat someone older and stronger than you?"

Gavi stirred. "Jabari."

"Gavi, these sweet puppies have no respect."

Gavi cleared his throat. "Friends, we're leading you

through our lands," he said. "We want you to listen to those who know more about the ways of Maween." He glanced at Jabari. "By those who know more, I mean Jabari and me, but especially Jabari."

Ben felt a twinge of shame, but the anger didn't recede. "*I* want him to take it back. We *have* shown you respect. I don't want Jabari to say untrue things about my sister. She listens well, and you know nothing of us or our lives, where we've been or what we've been through. We haven't spent our lives traveling around, eating rich food, and breaking weak walls. You may know these lands, Jabari, but you can't talk about what you don't know. Take it back."

Jabari lifted his chin. "I may not know everything about her life, but I know she didn't listen to my warning about healing, and she leaped into a situation she knows *nothing* about. That makes her the most arrogant girl I've ever met." He turned to Isika. "You let that woman call you Protector when you've been in this land for two days!"

Isika flinched, but she stood straighter, and a familiar look came over her face. It was the look she got when their father insulted or beat her. Ben watched as his sister shoved the hurt far behind her eyes and made her face like stone. His heart hurt to see her that way, and his fury grew. She had done right! Ben knew it. He had seen in, perceived it in the dancing, joyous song around her. And now, because of pride in his own gift, this boy, Jabari, had stolen her happiness. Far above, the Othra flapped their distress, circling.

"Is that what's bothering you?" Isika asked. "Did she use a special word that you didn't like?" Her voice was like sharp steel. "I didn't ask her to call me that. You can have your beloved title. I don't want it."

Jabari was furious. Ben could hear anger boiling in him, and for a moment, he worried that Jabari would actually hit Isika. But he only spoke.

"You could acknowledge that we picked you up when you were discarded on the shore, that we're helping you get to your brother in Azariyah. Instead, you race ahead and play at magic like a little girl dressing up in her mother's clothes. You know nothing about what you're doing, you just leave us to clean up your mess."

"Don't talk about my mother," Isika said, her voice shaking. "And you couldn't clean up my mess. I had to."

She took a step back, her head still high. She looked at Ben, and he heard it, the droning sadness deep inside her. Her pain made him feel helpless. She looked as though she was climbing back into misery, hiding from hurt. "You know what?" she said. "We don't need them to get to this city of theirs. We'll go on our own. I know we'll find it."

"How will you find it?" Jabari asked, contempt radiating off him.

"Really, Isika, how will you find it?" Gavi asked. He looked angry and distressed, as well. "Do you know the way? Have you been here before? How did you tear down those walls back there? I don't understand."

Isika shook her head. "I'm not answering any more of your questions. We'll go our own way, and I never want to see either of you again."

Jabari laughed a short, angry laugh. "Fine then," he said.

"Have fun, children." He turned and walked straight into a field of grain. Gavi gave them one last look, smiling sadly at Ibba before disappearing into the tall, waving stalks. Overhead, the Othra gave three long, mournful cries and flew off in the opposite direction.

Ibba dissolved into tears and sat down on the path, sobbing into her hands as if her heart would break. Ben crouched to comfort her, his anger dissipating until all he felt was a deep, sickening gong in his stomach, beating a single rhythm. *Wrong, wrong, wrong.*

CHAPTER 14

*J*abari swung at stalks of wheat with savage strokes, making a path through the grain mindlessly until Gavi put a hand on his shoulder, and he stopped, head down.

"Sorry," he said.

"It's okay. Just remember this farmer didn't do anything to you." Gavi turned and held his hand out. The stalks of wheat straightened and healed.

Jabari growled, then turned and kept walking, this time taking care to slip between the rows of grain. His anger rolled out like a path in front of him, directing him so that he saw nothing but Isika's stoic face as she mocked his gift and his title. She had torn those tall walls down without care for anything! Not a thought for the people they protected, for the rules themselves, for the ones who took the risk of leading them through Maween. She didn't know anything about the other dangers that came from the Great Waste. If she thought walls were the worst of it, she was in for a nasty surprise. And then what kind of protector would she be? She wasn't even a protector! She was a visitor.

And her brother! Holding a weapon against a friend was poison. The poison-landers were tramping through his land, bringing their demon magic with them, and he, foolishly, had left them to wreak havoc on defenseless farms and forests. He let out another frustrated groan, shaking his head. Behind him, Gavi was silent. He knew Jabari well and was wise to wait.

They came to the end of the field and walked onto another road, parallel to the one they had been following before they left the others. Gavi fell into step beside him.

"Well?" Jabari said.

"Well, what?"

"I'm waiting for point one in the thousand ways I'm wrong."

Gavi smiled and whistled a verse of their favorite dancing song. Jabari looked at his brother. Gavi's face was the most familiar sight in Jabari's life. The two of them were like twins —the same age—and had grown up side by side, inseparable. Jabari's family had taken Gavi in when he was just two years old and newly rescued. Their parents thought it would be good for Jabari to have a brother, maybe to challenge him, since Jabari was already showing signs of being wild and strong-willed. And it was true that Gavi often calmed him. His gifts for nourishing and healing were an excellent counterbalance to Jabari's protection. Jabari hadn't been spouting book knowledge when he had listed the attributes of a Healer. He had been describing his brother. But Healer though he may be, Gavi hadn't come into his full strength yet. The tall walls required the healing of a mighty, deeply experienced Healer.

But Isika had done it! How had she done it? Jabari growled again.

"How did she do it?"

Gavi shook his head. "I don't know."

"Honestly, Gavi, it would take someone seasoned for a dozen years to do that kind of healing. She's been here for two days!"

"True. I'm confused too. But," Gavi said, and then he paused.

Jabari braced himself for one of his brother's insights, knowing it would be right and knowing he didn't want it.

After a silence, Gavi continued. "Why does it make you so angry, Yab?" Jabari knew Gavi used his special name for Jabari to soften the question. When Gavi had first come out of the sea, he was too young to pronounce Jabari's name and had called him Yabari, which he shortened to Yab.

Jabari took a deep breath as the nickname worked its effect, reminding Jabari of who he was—a boy with a brother, a father, a mother, a community. Gavi went on.

"And you, Yab, of all people! Going on about rules like that? My ears nearly fell off my head, hearing you."

Jabari couldn't keep a smile back. Gavi slung an arm around his shoulders. Jabari smiled at his brother and whistled the chorus of the song Gavi had been whistling. Gavi sang a few snatches of it, and things were well between them again.

But why *did* Isika make him so angry? And why had he lectured her about rules like that? He, who was always in trouble with his parents for ignoring rules. All he knew was as he looked at the poison-landers, especially Isika, so unknowingly beautiful and pitifully thin, the need for rules became a clamor in his head. He finally understood his father. And that made him angry again because he really didn't want to be like his killjoy father. He wanted to be himself; that was all he had ever wanted. He glanced at Gavi and found his brother watching him.

"You're not like him, you know," Gavi said, as though he was reading Jabari's mind, but he wouldn't have to; he knew Jabari so well. "Not that there's anything wrong with being him, I love him as much as you do, but you're nothing like him. You're you, Yab."

Jabari nodded and stiffened his back. That was the sting that made him angrier than anything else, how Isika had turned him into his father. How did she have that power over him?

"It's just that it's like she's playing. She doesn't know that we study this, that we have years of practice before we're trusted to come out here on our own. She could undo all of that! Right away! Who does she think she is?"

"I have a better question for you," Gavi said. He paused for a moment, looking up at the sky. "Forget who she *thinks* she is. Who *is* she?" He stopped, gazing upward while Jabari stopped in his tracks as well, staring at his brother. Gavi, whose hair always stuck straight up from his head. Gavi, who, though he was as tall as Jabari, was slightly stockier and could always win in a wrestling match. Gavi who didn't love wrestling as much as he loved eating.

Who was she? That was the real question. Jabari had been puzzling over it since they had met the tall girl who glowed from within.

"But I don't think we have time to puzzle it out now," Gavi said. "Because we've got company, and they're not going to be happy with us."

The words were barely out of his mouth before he flinched and covered his face. Strong claws gripped Jabari's shoulders, and he yelped as he was plucked off the ground and swiftly lifted into the air.

BEN AND ISIKA walked in the direction they had been traveling before the others left. The fields were gold on either side of them. Ibba trailed behind, casting hopeful glances behind her, still sniffling from time to time, though she wasn't crying anymore.

Ben pushed down on his jungle of music, blocking some of the sounds, which were conflicting and confusing. Drums of doom beside hopeful tendrils. He glanced at Isika, wondering if she would know what the music was all about. He didn't know how to bring it up with her. *Do you have anything like music living inside you, or threatening to burst out of people you know?* He shook his head and kicked at a stone on the path.

Behind them, Ibba was calmer. She sang softly to herself as they walked along the path, fields stretching into the distance on either side. It sounded like a song Gavi had been teaching her, but she hummed her way through the sections she didn't know. The day still held its heat, and they paused occasionally to rest under the great trees.

"Thank you for what you said back there," Isika said to Ben during one of their rests.

He looked at her. "What he said was untrue. You've always been a great listener. You do talk a lot, though, and sometimes without knowing what you're talking about."

"Okay, okay, Benny, you don't have to ruin it," she said, laughing and taking a drink of water from her flask.

"But he said some true things, Isika. We're new here, and we should respect their ways."

She scowled at him, wiping water off her chin with one hand. She shook her shoulders like she was shaking his words away, lifting her chin.

"He's a good person. You could trust him more, you know," he said.

"Wait. How do you know *that?* How can you tell after only two days?" She jumped up and changed the subject. "Let's keep walking. Come Ibba!"

Ibba ran to join them from where she had been watching a group of butterflies clustered around a flowering bush. They turned onto the road again. Ben walked quickly to keep up with Isika and thought about what he would say.

"I can just tell. I always can. I know it inside somehow." *The song is beautiful and strong when Jabari speaks.* "I've always known which vegetable stalls had owners who were more likely to lie about the weight of the tomatoes, or put a stone in with the wheat." *I heard the horrible, terrifying drums when I went to those stalls.* "I hated the temple always because I knew the goddesses were unjust." *There, the sounds were so horrible, drums and shrieks and even crying.* "You can't know," and his voice broke a little, but he steadied it quickly, "how relieved I am to be away from the darkness in that temple."

Isika looked at him. "You do look better," she said. "You aren't so hunched anymore. It makes you look younger. In a good way," she said when he frowned at her. "You used to look like an old man in a teenager's body. Now you look your age." He narrowed his eyes. "Or maybe a little older. Fourteen, maybe fifteen."

He laughed and swiped playfully at her, but she darted away from him. He walked with his arms swinging, thinking of how he used to try to escape the voices in him by slipping from place to place, never letting them start up because he didn't stay anywhere long enough for them to settle.

"I wonder if your knowledge is a gift," Isika said, startling him. "Jabari told me about some of the gifts."

It frustrated Ben. He could have asked Jabari about the gifts if Isika hadn't sent him away.

"I did say too much, didn't I?" she asked him, her voice hesitant. "But he doesn't understand. I'm not just trying to play dress up. I keep feeling this call, and I'm trying to follow it because if I ignore it, I feel sick. I'm only going from one thing to the next, and I'm not trying to make anyone angry. The call came really strongly before I pulled that wall down. I couldn't help myself."

"You've felt it at other times?" he asked. He was conscious of Ibba beside them now, listening intently.

"Not much in the village. Not so strong anyway. But since we came to this land, yes."

"From things other than walls?"

"Yes, from trees."

"Like the trees were talking to you?" Ibba asked, and Isika jumped.

"Whoa, I didn't see you there," she said. "How long have you been listening?"

"I listen to everything," she said. Ben looked at her. She reached her hand out and touched a stalk of grain beside her, and he smiled at how little she still was. But she listened to everything.

"Not talking to me," Isika said. "Calling me. Without words." Ibba looked up at her and then met Ben's eyes. She nodded, thinking it over, then raced ahead to look into a hole in a tree.

Ben thought over the idea that his madness could be a gift. What a terrible gift, if all it ever did was confuse him and make him want to hide. But that wasn't all it had done, was it? Back there by the well, it made him decide to protect Isika. But... "I wish I hadn't raised my staff," he said.

Isika nodded. "You probably didn't need to. But I was proud of you, anyway. You're very different from the brother

I grew up with." She looked back at the road behind them, then forward again. "So, do you know where we're going?"

"To the city?"

"But do we ever turn? Is it straight ahead on this road?"

They looked at each other with dismay. Isika sighed. "I wish I had held my temper," she said.

"Don't be hard on yourself. It wasn't just temper. He hurt you."

She gave him a grateful look and reached out to rub the top of his head. He shoved her away lightly and squeezed her shoulder, enjoying her company. It was easier to be with Isika when she wasn't overworked, and even days of walking seemed like little compared to the work at home. He frowned. Ibba had run so far ahead that she was a speck in the distance.

"Ibba!" he shouted. "Wait!" She didn't hear him. They walked faster to catch up.

It happened so quickly, they weren't sure at first what it was. As Ibba skipped along ahead of them, there was a sudden rush of air, and an enormous snake launched itself from the grain field at their sister, coiling around her immediately, nearly obliterating her small body. Isika screamed, and Ben started running, sprinting with all his might toward his little, Isika just behind him.

CHAPTER 15

ounds of danger shrieked inside him. The snake was gigantic, its body a deep red color, the same width as Ibba's body. Ibba clawed at the snake, her eyes wide with fear, but it only tightened around her, pinning one of her arms to her body.

"Isika!" she screamed. Ben reached her first and pulled at the heavy coils of the snake, beating it with his staff and scratching at its scales. Isika was right behind him, and at her touch, the snake froze for a moment, then continued its slow crushing of their sister. Isika was gasping and crying, and Ben felt like throwing up, shaken by the deep evil he sensed. This wasn't an ordinary snake.

There was a sudden fluttering, and the three Othra dropped to the ground in front of Ibba and the snake. Tears of relief came to Ben's eyes when he saw them, but though they flapped their wings and pushed at the snake with their claws, it didn't release his sister. She was unconscious now, from lack of breath or fear, Ben didn't know which.

"Jabari and Gavi will be here soon," Efir said, her voice strained from the effort of beating at the snake with her wings, and sure enough, the grain swayed like the passage of another snake as the two older boys crashed through it. After a moment, Jabari and Gavi broke onto the road, their eyes widening in shock as they saw what was happening.

"Gavi!" Jabari shouted, and Gavi leaped to Ibba's head, whispering to her. "Stand back," Jabari said to Ben and Isika, and they obeyed, Ben weak with relief. He wondered what was taking Jabari so long until Jabari suddenly jumped at the snake and grabbed its head with both hands. The snake tried to bite him, but he held its jaw tight, the muscles in his arms straining. He reached back swiftly and pulled an arrow out of his quiver, then, with one smooth arc, he plunged it into the snake's eye. The snake jerked back as steaming black blood fountained out of its head, covering Jabari. The snake collapsed and then, to Ben's shock, evaporated. Gavi sat on the ground beside Ibba and laid both hands on her head. He sang to her, something with words about the grass needing the sun to return and dry the dew off it, and as he sang, she smiled, and Gavi stroked the tendrils of hair that had escaped her braids, smoothing them off her face. He bent and kissed her forehead, then stood with her in his arms. She was tiny compared to him.

"She'll be fine," he said. "He injected a lot of fear into her, but he didn't stop her heart."

Just the words "stop her heart" made the earth wobble

under Ben's feet. He reached for his sister, and Gavi gently placed her in his arms. Ben closed his eyes and laid his forehead against hers. The heavy jarring drums inside him were silent, and a single, sweet song curled around his ribcage. He breathed relief and joy. He, too, could sense that Ibba would be fine.

He looked up. Isika stood next to him, arms wrapped around her stomach, staring at Ibba's face. He saw the streaks that tears had made on his older sister's cheeks, and he moved closer to her. Isika reached out and grasped Ibba's hand. A breeze whipped at Ben's clothes, and he looked up to see the Othra flying closer, flapping their great wings. They landed nearly on top of Ben and Isika, and Ben heard something new coming from them. It wasn't fearful or twisted, like the drums of doom, but it was strong and not entirely comfortable—a warning. Ben waited for them to speak, not sure that he wanted to know what they would say.

Nirral gazed at Benayeem, and Isika took a step closer to him.

"In the great lands of Maween, it is forbidden to raise a weapon to a friend," Nirral said, "and these are undoubtedly your friends, though they can be blind, even stupid at times."

Behind Nirral, Isika saw Jabari scowl, and she nearly giggled, shocked at the lightness of her heart.

"Jabari is still very young, and he does not see that you three are essential in the great story of our world. He cannot see far, for he has the gift of protection, and he thinks only of protecting the land from impulsive people."

Isika felt heat come into her face at being described as impulsive at the same time that Jabari said, "I can hear you, you know. I'm standing right here." This time a giggle did escape her.

She quickly made her face serious when Efir began to speak. Her melodic voice was more gentle than Nirral's, making Isika feel a thousand times worse and better.

"Unlike these children, we see far, and we can tell there is more than impulse drawing you, young one." She looked at Isika. "Your gifts are great. We have convinced Jabari to return to help you." She paused, and the air filled with warm humor. "It took some pressure to convince him." The Othra were laughing, and Gavi pressed his lips together to keep from smiling. Jabari rolled his eyes. Isika was shocked to see that the Othra could laugh. Was nothing serious in this land? Even the wisest of creatures acted like children. Isika was accustomed to gloom. Her face ached from the unfamiliar amount of smiling she had done in the last two days.

"You will make peace," Nirral said. "And then you will continue on to find your brother."

There was silence. Ben spoke first.

"I'm sorry for raising my staff," he said, heaving a great sigh. He looked down at Ibba, who lay in his arms with her eyes closed. "Thank you with all my heart for saving my sister. We were angry, but we weren't ready to be alone."

Jabari looked up. "I forgive you. And I am sorry for saying unkind words." He turned and winked at Isika. "I came back because I can't have you tearing through my land," he said to her, "breaking things down with no one to help you."

She bristled, then settled as Efir opened her wings the slightest bit. It appeared that she wasn't going to get much more of an apology than that. But she knew she had been impulsive, no matter her reasons, and she nodded. When he reached out to grasp her hand with both of his, she frowned slightly—it was unfamiliar to her—but she followed suit and closed her hands around his. She felt a shock of connection when their hands met, and she pulled back and looked at Gavi rather than meet Jabari's eyes. Gavi held his hands out to Isika as Jabari moved on to Ben. Gavi's hands felt happily normal, with no spark, and Isika smiled at him. He did a little step dance and tugged on one of her braids.

"I'm glad we're all back together, like tea and sugar," he said.

"I'm glad too," Isika said in a loud whisper. "But don't tell him." She pointed at Jabari. Gavi grinned, and at the sight of his smile, Isika's shoulders relaxed. Just then, she heard Ibba's soft voice.

"I'm thirsty," Ibba said, her eyes open, and Isika jumped to give her a drink of water. Ben set the little girl down on her feet and waited until she was steady before he let her go.

"How do you feel?" Ben asked.

"I feel okay," she said, gazing at Jabari and Gavi with big eyes. She smiled and jumped up and down, before running to Jabari, who picked her up and swung her around. She was so small that she looked like she weighed nothing when he picked her up.

"You came back!" she said breathlessly when he put her down. She ran to throw her arms around Gavi's waist. "You came back!"

Jabari met Isika's eyes then and smiled a small smile. He nodded at her, correctly interpreting what she was feeling. "Let's go find your brother," he said.

THEY WALKED until the sun had set, and there was almost no light left, then put their mats beside a great tree in a field. Gavi laid out three meat pies, and Isika's mouth fell open.

"The woman at that last house gave them to me this morning," he said. "She told me to save them for dinner. They might be a little banged up, but seekers can't be choosers." He pressed at one of the pies to make it round again, but it broke apart, and he grimaced. "Er, guess that one's ours, Yab," he said.

"I'll share with you," Ibba said. "I don't eat much."

"And I eat a lot," Gavi said. "So that makes us a perfect pair."

Jabari, Ben, and Isika shared the remaining two pies, each of them taking bites until there was nothing left but crumbs. Isika sighed with contentment, then remembered something. She narrowed her eyes at Jabari.

"Did he just call you Yab?" she asked.

Jabari flinched. "Yes. It's a sort of nickname."

"Does everyone call you Yab?"

"No," he said, shooting Gavi a warning look as Gavi

laughed quietly to himself. "Only Gavi. Because he's annoying."

"You love me," Gavi said, and winked at Ibba. She smiled up at him, and the happiness in her face was almost more than Isika could bear. There were too many things warring in Isika; happiness, contentment, worry, fear. Her eyes brightened when Gavi pulled out of flask of tea, though. She pushed worry down. They would find Kital, and he would not believe himself abandoned for long.

"How do you know each other?" she asked. They seemed so different.

Jabari and Gavi exchanged glances. "We went to school together," Jabari said, finally. "And somehow, I got stuck with him as a seeking partner." Gavi only shook his head, grinning and refusing to rise to the bait. It didn't really satisfy Isika's curiosity about them, but Jabari didn't go into it more. What was school like for the Maweel? she wondered.

Their camp was close to a small creek. Isika took Ibba, and the two of them bathed as well as they could, ducking in and out of the cold water, then pulling their dusty clothes back on. Isika took the braids out of her sister's hair and smoothed the curls down with water, braiding it again. She did the same with her own hair, then wiped some dried mud off Ibba's shirt and looked into her eyes. Ibba looked back at her, biting her fingers.

"I love being with our new friends," Ibba whispered, "but I'm worried that we won't find Kital."

"Shhh," Isika said to her. "Don't worry, love, of course, we will. Does Jabari seem like someone who can't find even the smallest thing that he wants to find?"

Ibba thought it over, then shook her head, blinking tears out of her eyes. She smiled, her dimple flashing, before skipping off to the others, pausing to touch each of the trees she passed. Isika watched her, wondering absently if her little sister felt anything in the trees. She didn't know how to ask, so she merely followed Ibba and lay beside her, falling asleep immediately.

WHEN ISIKA AWOKE in the pink light of the morning, she saw that Gavi had laid a fire and was boiling water. He scooped several large spoonfuls of coffee into the water, then strained it through a cloth into five small metal cups. Isika took one and lifted it to her nose, sighing. "How many amazing things do you have in that bag?" she asked. "Lemons, tea, now coffee?"

Gavi laughed. "I panic if I think I won't have hot drinks nearby," he said. "Jabari's always going through my bag before we set off, trying to get rid of things I want to bring, but he's always happy to have them in the end."

Isika hadn't known how happy good food, and the expectation of good food, could make her. To wake up knowing she would eat, that the hollow feeling would go away! It was incredible.

They started out soon after eating. Breaking camp was becoming routine as they each found a job and did it quickly.

They walked for most of the day, hiking along the road with endless fields on either side of them, first grain, then tall tomato plants, then berry bushes. They saw other farms in the distance, but none of them called to Isika, and she couldn't see any walls. She was glad. She didn't know whether she'd be able to ignore the tugging, and she wanted to respect the seekers and their work in Maween.

Sometime in the late afternoon, Jabari fell into step beside Isika. They walked in silence while Isika tried to stop feeling so awkward beside him. She looked down at his hands, swinging by his sides. He walked with long strides, his shoulders back, somehow relaxed and focused at the same time. He rolled when he walked, like a large cat. His walk was distinctive. She felt that she would know who he was from a long way off. She looked away when he glanced at her, embarrassed to be paying so much attention to him.

Isika thought about what she knew she needed to say to get rid of the awkwardness between them. Finally, she forced it past her lips despite the churning in her stomach. She longed for some of the feeling of well-being that the Othra spread, but they were nowhere to be seen. Come to think of it, she hadn't seen them since the night before. She cleared her throat.

"I wanted to say thank you," she began, "for taking us in and helping us find our way. I don't know what we would have done without you. Nothing, I guess. We probably would have wandered in circles until we died."

Jabari laughed, a rich, surprising sound. "Somehow, I doubt that."

But Isika had broken the ice, and the conversation flowed.

"How did the Othra convince you to come back to us?" she asked.

Jabari smiled. "Do you really want to know?"

"Of course."

"Nirral picked me up with his talons and put me in a tree, higher than I've ever climbed," he said. "He wouldn't let me down until I promised to return. Even then, he left me there for a while, I suppose, to teach me a lesson."

"You're kidding me."

"No, I'm telling the truth," he said, and he showed her the talon marks in his shirt.

"Did it hurt?"

"Only a little," he said, and shrugged. "The Othra are ancient and wonderful, but dangerous, and they're harder on me than they are on most people."

"Why?"

He shrugged. "They know I'm excellent at everything, so they have to push me."

Behind them, Gavi made a sound like he was choking, and Jabari grinned to let her know he was teasing. Isika wondered, though, why would they be harder on him? Did they think he was arrogant as well, or was there something in him they felt they needed to push?

The road left the fields and became lined with trees. These were trees that Isika had never seen before, and as she peered up to see them better, Jabari reached out and broke a piece of fruit off one of the branches above them.

"Try it," he said, pulling the fruit in half and offering a

piece to her. "It's called *reengu*, or traveler's fruit because it grows on the trees we plant along the roads."

The fruit was very bright pink and oblong. Isika lifted it to her mouth and took a small bite. Juice ran down her hand and arm to her elbow. The reengu fruit tasted bright and soft, like melon, but with some spice. Gavi picked one for Ibba, and Ben jumped up and plucked his own off a branch. They ate as many as they could fit into their stomachs, and when they finished, they were bright pink from the fruit's juice, but refreshed. Gavi poured water into their hands so they could wash.

They walked on. Jabari whistled a song for some time, and when he stopped, Isika saw from the corner of her eye that he was looking at her silently. She waited.

"I was thinking," he said, finally, "that I haven't heard anything about how you came to be with the poison-landers."

CHAPTER 16

*J*abari's deliberately light tone puzzled Isika. He hadn't asked such a strange question; he knew that Workers were usually white-skinned, so it was natural to wonder how they got to the village. Why was he being so careful about asking it?

"We came from the desert," she said, "when I was seven years old, and my mother was pregnant with Ibba. We walked in the desert for many months, looking for somewhere to live, I think. My mother was very tired of walking, and she always had to carry our sister."

Jabari did a double-take. "Your sister? Wait, you said your mother was pregnant with Ibba—you have another sister? Where is she?"

"She... she was sent out four years ago." Knowing how angry he became when they talked about the sending, Isika was reluctant to say the words. "My mother died soon after. I think she died of grief. She couldn't eat or sleep anymore."

"I'm sorry," he murmured. He frowned. "But Kital was sent out, too. Is it normal that another child would be sent out? I understood that each family only gives one child over."

She shook her head, a lump in her throat. "No, it's not normal." She looked at him. He was staring at the horizon with a thoughtful look on his face. She wanted to ask him about Aria, whether they had ever found another dark-skinned outcast girl—the question was right there, but she couldn't get the words out.

She would ask him later. Maybe it was a bad sign that he hadn't mentioned Aria right away. Maybe there were sent ones who didn't make it into the arms of the Maweel. They walked in silence for a while.

Heavy tree branches curved overhead, forming a canopy over the path. It was cool in this forest, and small birds flitted from branch to branch. The sun filtered through in places, shining a brilliant light on certain flowers or leaves. Isika thought, as she often did, that she should have offered herself to be sent out instead of Aria. But who would have cared for Kital when her mother died? Was it right that Isika had stayed behind? She often found herself in this despairing thought loop, especially before she went to sleep at night. She heaved a painful breath. Jabari broke the silence.

"Who did you live with when you were in the desert?"

Isika put her chin up and blinked hard to keep the tears back. Her throat hurt with old sorrows. "We lived with only our mother. We moved from place to place, sleeping in a tent that our mother carried. I remember... when we first left the city and went to the desert, there was a man. But he didn't stay long—perhaps he was only helping us leave. I think the desert weakened my mother. She was never very strong again."

"There was somewhere before the desert?" Jabari put a hand on her shoulder for a moment, maybe seeing her sadness over the memories. The sudden warmth of his hand only made tears seem closer. Isika took a deep breath.

"A place with tall walls. I don't remember much from that place. We left at night, and for a while, we ran. My mother would never speak of it." *And neither would Ben*, she thought, but she didn't tell Jabari. Ben had the right to keep his secrets from whoever he wanted, though Isika wished he would share them with her.

Jabari looped his fingers through the straps of the pack he carried. "And in the poison-lander village? Who did you live with?"

Isika gazed at the horizon. "Our stepfather. The man we call our father. His name is Nirloth. He's the priest of the village."

"Really?"

Isika looked at Jabari and saw she had shocked him. It was so similar to the villagers' reaction to Nirloth's marriage, a marriage to a black woman with four children at her skirts, that Isika smiled bitterly.

"I didn't know poison-lander priests married," Jabari went on.

"Of course they do," she said. "How else would they bear heirs to be priests? Nirloth married our mother when she came out of the desert. After she died, we children lived alone with him for two years, before he married another woman, Jerutha." She sighed. "It was Jerutha's idea that we take the boat and find Kital. I hated leaving her. She's a good person."

Jabari looked away, and Isika thought that maybe he couldn't quite believe that any poison-landers were good. He was blind, then, she thought. And how many more questions could he have? She was growing weary of her memories. But he had more to ask.

"Do you remember your mother?" he asked, and she looked at him incredulously.

"Of course! She died when I was ten!"

"What was she like?" He seemed untouched by her scorn.

Isika walked for a while without talking, wondering which of the precious memories of her mother she could entrust to this boy. Through the canopy of treetops, she saw that the sky was very blue. Beside them, the leaves shook in a sudden breeze. Isika put one hand to her throat and breathed in. Jabari had told her much that she needed to know. She could offer a few memories of her mother.

"Our mother sang a lot," she said. "She seemed to always be singing, even when we walked in the desert for months, and she was exhausted. She loved us. By the time we left the desert, she was very thin, though she was near giving birth to Ibba. I remember how happy she was to spot the walls of the village. It was the first time I saw her cry. She fell to the earth and put her face on the ground and cried. Then we went into the village, and Nirloth took us into his home."

For a moment, the forest turned into the dusty brown of the plains around the walled village, as Isika remembered.

"I'll always be grateful to him for that," she said. "After Ibba was born, our mother grew a little stronger, and she planted vegetables, making a kitchen garden. She sang to us in the cool of the day, when evening had fallen. But she was broken and tired, like a flower after it has been cut out of the garden."

Tears came then, and Jabari lifted a hand to squeeze her shoulder. When she had wiped her tears away, she went on. "When my father decided to give Aria over, my mother wept and raged until Kital came out of her belly a month early. Two weeks later, she died. She couldn't eat or sleep; she just lay on her bed and stared into the dark. She would barely speak." Isika's voice broke. Jabari squeezed her shoulder. She could sense him looking at her, but she fixed her gaze on the farthest point she could see and went on. She hadn't spoken of her mother like this for so long.

"Our mother was powerful. She was kind, and her words carried gentleness, even in a place where few people, including my father, had kind words for anyone."

Jabari nodded and gave her shoulder a final squeeze, then took his hand away. She was sorry when it was gone. He strode beside her with long steps, furrowing his brow.

He looked at her. "And your father?" he asked. "From birth? Do you know anything about him?"

She brushed the last of the tears off her face with the backs of her hands.

"Nothing. I know only Nirloth." She was quiet, reaching

out to touch trees gently as she passed them. Little waves of happiness came off them as her fingertips touched the bark, and she straightened her shoulders.

Jabari was quiet too, and they walked in silence for some time. "I'm sorry, Isika," he said finally. "You have had a very hard life."

Isika thought about that. "Yes," she said. "I suppose I have." She smiled at him, and he crinkled his eyes at her in return. It seemed they had found a little understanding of one another.

They walked in silence for some time, and Isika wondered just how much more walking they would do that day, when Jabari suddenly turned to face the others, walking backward just as easily as he walked forward. He raised his hands in the air. "Time to focus!" he exclaimed. Gavi groaned. "Yes, it's true, Gavi, it's our favorite time. Time to cross rivers!" He said it as though he was announcing something exciting and fun. Isika didn't see any rivers, not even in the distance. She hid a smile as she looked at him. He slowed to a halt, and they stood in a group, gazing down at the road as though a river would just appear.

"How do we cross rivers?" she asked.

From behind them, Gavi spoke, his voice glum. "We swim. It's cold, and it takes forever."

Jabari closed his eyes and held out his hands. "It's wonderful," he said, his voice fervent, and Isika looked from one to the other, wondering who she should believe.

~

THEY CAMPED for the night because Gavi flat out refused to cross a river with no food or rest.

"This is only the first of many," he said, busy at the fire. At Ben's blank look, he explained. "At the land where the rivers empty into the ocean, they spread out like a fan, and we'll have to cross many of them. We're at the deltas."

Jabari brought Gavi a rabbit, using his bow for the first time. Ben looked on, envious, as Jabari strode back into the camp with the dead rabbit by its ears. He had yet to pull out his own bow, and his hands itched to prove what a good shot he was, but he was nervous about overstepping himself. No one had asked him to hunt. Gavi roasted the rabbit over the fire, adding herbs from his pack. He heated water and made more lemon tea.

"We swim all the rivers?" Ben asked. He pulled his sandals off and rubbed at his sore feet.

"No," Gavi said, grimacing. He turned the rabbit slowly on the spit. "Thank the Shaper. We cross some by boat."

They ate, falling onto their mats after scrubbing their metal plates and cups in a nearby creek. Ben was asleep almost instantly.

"It will be mid-morning when we reach the first river," Jabari announced as they walked the next morning. "We have a lot of ground to cover today, so let's move quickly."

The landscape was changing again. It was still green and lush, but they walked in a different kind of forest, with tall, straight trees that rustled with leaves as tall as people. There were wide gaps between the trees, planted in rows, like an orchard, though Ben didn't see any fruit. The trunks were a golden yellow, the branches hung with silvery leaves. They were impressive. Ben had the idea of a great expanse, well-ordered and lovely.

"What kind of trees are they?" Ben asked Gavi as they stopped at a well in the orchard.

"Hoona," he said. "We used them to build homes and furniture."

"You build homes with wood?" Ben said, surprised.

Gavi swallowed and wiped his mouth with the back of his hand. "Only the beams," he said. "We build our homes with earth, usually."

Ben took a turn drinking, curious to see this city with homes built of earth and wood. The homes in his village were made of stone. He had never seen wood used in a house structure.

Later, they passed under trees with leaves that curved upward.

"Watch," Gavi told Ben, and he paused under a leaf and waited with his mouth open and aimed at the sky. After a moment, the leaf tipped and released a stream of liquid into his mouth.

"What?" Ben said, stunned.

"How did you do that?" Ibba asked in her squeaky voice.

"Look at them," Gavi said. "They release nectar every few minutes or so."

Ben looked around and saw trees all over the grove tipping their leaves and releasing streams of clear liquid. If you walked under the trees, you'd be wet in minutes.

"I want to try!" Ibba said.

"You can, Little One. Stand underneath and wait. The nectar is good for you. It gives strength." Gavi smacked his lips. "Tastes good, too."

Ben thought he could use a little strength, so he turned his face up under a leaf, feeling silly. He waited for a long time, and when the nectar came, it poured straight down his neck and into his shirt. Gavi laughed.

"That must have been refreshing," he said. "Wait just... here," he directed Ben by the shoulders. "Right at the corner, so it goes straight into your mouth. Go to a leaf that looks heavy in the center, where the nectar is collecting from the tree's heart. That's how you know it's ready to drop."

Ibba stood a few feet away. She got a mouthful of nectar, and Ben saw her eyes widen with delight. Just beyond, Jabari was showing Isika how to hold her face to drink the nectar. Ben looked around and found a leaf that looked heavy and full. He tipped his head back the way Gavi had told him to and waited. He flinched as he saw the leaf tip, ready to be soaked again, but this time it poured straight into his mouth. The flavor was like mint or lemon, but even more refreshing. He tingled to his toes and headed to another leaf to wait for more.

"Careful," Gavi warned. "One or two is okay, but you don't want to drink too much."

The second leaf was warming, and Ben felt the soreness leaving his muscles.

Isika bounded over to them. "Okay!" she said. "Why don't we run the next few miles, get closer to Kital?"

Jabari and Gavi burst out laughing. "Can you imagine

what one more would do to her?" Gavi asked Ben, and Ben widened his eyes and shook his head.

"Don't drink more, Isika," he said, though he looked longingly back at the nectar leaves as they left them behind and traipsed back to the road.

THEY SWAM THE FIRST RIVER, stripping to their underclothes in the sunshine of the morning. It wasn't swimming, exactly, more wading through water up to their armpits. The water was cold but not frigid. Ben's mind settled into a low hum, with no imminent threats nearby. He was at peace with his mind and body, and the water was gentle on him. As they crossed, they carried their packs on their heads. Jabari gave his bag to Gavi and carried Ibba on his shoulders, leading the way across the wide river.

Ben walked with Gavi, since the older boy was a bit slower, encumbered by two packs. He was also breathing heavily, and Ben shot a glance at him when he heard Gavi's breath hitch in his throat. The water was up to his collarbone.

"Are you all right?" he asked, reaching a hand out to steady Gavi.

Gavi gave a stiff nod and frowned in concentration as he regained his balance. In a few minutes, they reached the shore and joined the others lying on the bank, drying in the sun.

"I'm afraid of water," Gavi said to Ben, finally, his breath slowly going back to normal. Ben raised his eyebrows.

"You?" he said, reaching under himself to retrieve a rock digging into his back. "I wouldn't imagine that anything could make you afraid." He looked at the tall, broad-shouldered, almost-man beside him, with hair like a wheat field bleached in the sun. Gavi shrugged.

"Nothing does," he said, then glanced at Ben. "Except water."

Ben waited for an explanation, enjoying the feeling of the sun on him. In a moment, Gavi offered a slight one. "My father thinks it comes from being outcast. Many of us are afraid of water." Ben looked at him sharply. It made sense, he guessed, if they remembered being adrift in boats, even asleep. Or maybe they remembered being told they would be sacrificed in a boat. Perhaps that was enough to start a fear that lasted.

Jabari called that they needed to keep moving. Ben stood and pulled his pack on without dressing again. They walked in their underclothes, ready for the next river.

Ben worried that Kital would be afraid of water. He had a question for Gavi.

"Your father?" he asked.

Gavi nodded. "My adopted father. We all get new parents, you know. All the outcast ones."

CHAPTER 17

"Just over the next hill," Jabari called.

As Isika arrived at the hill's summit, the view stretched out around her. She could see squares of yellow grain stitched together, and tall forests in the distance. Off to their left was a village of small homes with no walls separating them. Just before them, a wide swathe of water ran westward, crossing their path. Isika strained her eyes, but she couldn't see the expanse of the sea. They had walked a long way inland, and the sea was far away.

She had dreamed about Kital the night before, and she found herself thinking about him all day as they walked, remembered his tiny body next to hers at night. As she sleepily fed him out of a glass jar with a rubber nipple tied to the top, Isika had poured all her love into the little baby. All while grieving for her mother. She remembered bathing him as an infant. At first, she was terrified that she would drown him, but then he smiled and played in the water as he grew older. He loved the water and begged to spend time at the shore.

Once, when Kital was about three years old, they visited Jerutha's mother, and Kital had asked Isika if they could swim in the sea beyond her door.

"No, of course not!" she had said, shivering at the sight of the black, choppy waters.

As they approached the green river, Isika wished she could introduce him to the warm, pleasant water of Maween, or show him new fruit. She pulled her shoulders in, feeling miserable. Nothing was whole without him. Isika felt like she was missing a part of herself.

Isika walked faster. Kital was only four years old. She hoped the Maweel rescuers were treating him with kindness. But of course, they would be used to two-year-olds... they would know how to care for young ones. Suddenly Isika thought of Aria, sent out in the tiny boat that was nearly too small to hold her. She shoved the thought back to the recesses of her mind. Hope too painful for words tried to surface, but Isika pushed and pushed until she had stopped herself from thinking about her lost sister.

As they drew close to the river, Isika saw that it was much broader than it had appeared in the distance, with small islands in the center. She turned to Jabari, her eyes wide.

"We have to swim this?"

She had loved swimming the last river—the water was beautiful, full of warmth and the flowing strength of a hundred little forest springs. She still felt invigorated from the swim. This river was three times as wide, though.

He shook his head, smiling. "This one we cross in a boat," he said. "It's the largest of the delta rivers." He went on when she didn't understand. "The mother river is called the Erial, the great river of Maween. Erial fans into many rivers as she makes her way to the sea at the deltas. Our city is built far upstream, on the feet of the Sister mountains, where Erial begins her journey."

Isika frowned. "So why don't we walk beside the river and cross where it is smaller?" she asked. The river's swift current looked dangerous.

Jabari shook his head. "Too slow," he said. "The road we follow leads straight to the city. Following the river would be a rough trail, and eventually, we would reach canyons that are difficult to travel. That way would take many more days than the road we are now on."

Isika nodded and took a deep breath. She would go the way that brought her to Kital the fastest.

They climbed down the hill to a dock where several small round boats were tied. Gavi reached down to loosen one while Jabari pulled an oar out of a nearby tree. The boat had bright paintings of water animals looped around its sides, with a sort of oily sealant over them. Isika leaned closer to look at the pictures. It was not a longboat like the ones the rescuers had used to take Kital. This boat was completely round—a deep bowl that sat in the water.

"Whose boat is it?" she asked, curious.

Jabari glanced at her from where he was inspecting the oar, running his hand along it.

"It's mine," he said. Isika supposed that made sense. It would always be tied to the dock on the side of the river where he needed it. "It's a coracle," he added. "The people of this village are craftsmen of this type of boat."

"Jabari has a thing for collecting boats," Gavi said, his voice dry. "He likes to gather a variety, so he can endanger his life in many different ways."

Jabari held the boat close to the dock while they clambered inside, rocking back and forth as they tried to settle in without tipping. They sat on blocks set into the bottom of the boat. Gavi was deathly white, and his jaw was clenched. Jabari had a wild, happy look on his face. His eyes flashed.

"Hold on!" he called out. He leaned his head back and laughed an exhilarated laugh, then plunged his oar in the water. Isika widened her eyes at Ben, and he smiled and shook his head.

"Enough with the theatrics," Gavi said, his voice weak. "Let's get through the river and onto the sweet, sturdy land."

The boat spun wildly as it set out, sitting very low in the water. "How many people can this boat carry?" Isika asked, her stomach plunging.

"Shhhh," Jabari said. "I'm concentrating."

Gavi shut his eyes. He was gray now, and his lips moved silently. Ibba slipped her small hand into his, and he immediately looked a little better, his eyes flying open.

"Wow, Ibba. That's quite a gift." He shook his head,

smiling slightly. "The three of you are the strangest poison-landers I've ever met. Thanks, little one, that feels better."

Isika was barely listening. She concentrated on the water that surrounded them—cool, smooth, and full of life. Its energy reached her as the swift waters curved around their little bowl, and as she closed her eyes, she could see the river as a young stream, making its way down the mountains, moving through villages. She saw cows bathing in its shallows as it passed lazily through the fields, gathering speed until it roared to meet the ocean.

She opened her eyes. A group of the large, fish-like sea animals encircled the boat, gliding through the water with ease. One leapt out of the air and flipped, splashing Isika, then several more followed his example. Isika caught her breath. Beside her, Ibba stared at the water animals with round eyes. They swam and jumped, curving in the air like the wind itself, their shapes mimicking the river's rounded currents.

Jabari laughed again, the sound of it long and loud and clear in the air. He shifted from laughter to singing a wild song Isika had never heard before, paddling all the while. The sky was very blue, the animals pink against it.

Jabari finished his song.

"My father told me that the naia are the most joyful of creatures because they have the clearest memory of the Shaper. They spend their days dancing their memories," he said.

Isika's heart ached at the sight of them. "Naia," she breathed, and the word clicked into place as though she had always known it. She felt that she wanted something, badly, something she could barely remember. "We have stories of something like this called the dolfina, but I thought they were just fairy tales," she said.

Jabari nodded. "Some people call them by that name. We call them naia, the friends of the sea."

Isika held her hand out to one of the naia, and he swam over to her and nudged her hand with his rubbery nose.

Welcome, she heard him say clearly in her mind, and she gasped. The naia left his nose in her hand until, as one, they turned and swam downstream, jumping one after the other, their bodies rising and disappearing in waves. Isika watched until they were too far to see, and still, she could feel their peaceful spirits.

Jabari guided the coracle to the shore and held it fast while the others cautiously climbed out of the boat. Isika's knees wobbled. Jabari carefully tied the boat to the dock there. After a moment of stretching and some strengthening tea from Gavi's flask, they continued on their way, Isika giving the wide river one last longing glance before she followed the others.

THEY SWAM the next river when the sun was beginning to slant toward the western sky. The water was warm and clear, and when they reached the far bank, they lay in the afternoon sun for a while, but then Isika sat up and said, "Let's keep going. We can dry as we walk."

Jabari nodded, and they walked in their underclothes. Isika marveled at herself, walking with two boys she knew only slightly, legs and arms and face warm in the sun. Isika, who a few days ago, had been averting her eyes because eye contact was impolite.

She walked with Gavi as Jabari, Ben, and Ibba walked on ahead, Ibba's head swiveling from one tall boy to the other as she chatted away. She looked like a small sparrow, hopping every few steps.

"Do you remember life in the Worker village?" Isika asked Gavi.

He glanced at her. He was very tall, at least a head and a half taller than her, and she was not short. "Also," she couldn't help adding. "You're very tall for a Worker." He smiled at that.

"It's remarkable what good food will do," he said. Then his face grew serious. "No," he said. "I don't remember. They cast me out when I was two years old. Sometimes I think I can remember shapes, or smells, or sounds, but I don't remember my parents. I don't remember their faces or the sounds of their voices. I wish I could, sometimes. But other times, I'm glad that I can't. Some of the other Rescued remember well, and it's hard for them; remembering people they loved who cast them away."

Isika felt a flash of alarm. Until they found Kital, he would be like that, remembering his brother and sisters but knowing they had allowed him to be cast away. They needed to get to him, and soon. Isika couldn't bear the thought of her little brother believing that they hadn't wanted him. And, as it had every moment of the last four years, the memory of Aria threatened to overwhelm Isika, but Isika pushed it away, again, again, again. She was so used to pushing away grief that she didn't know how to allow hope to enter her heart. It felt too painful to contemplate. Isika looked at Gavi for a moment, wondering if she should ask him about her sister, but she couldn't get the words out, although she opened her mouth to speak. Her heart was hot with pain. She focused on the trees around them, the way the branches met overhead and the blue, blue sky beyond.

Jabari, Ibba, and Benayeem were just out of sight around a curve in the road, heading toward the fourth river. After this, there would be two more, but Jabari had told them they were small and not anything to worry about. Isika wasn't worried anyway; so far, she had loved the rivers, even the biggest.

Jabari's shout rang out in the stillness of the afternoon. "Gavi!" They could hear the alarm in his voice clearly, sharp as a knife. "Come quick!"

Gavi broke into a run, and Isika started after him, struggling to keep up with the tall boy's long stride. They ran around the bend in the road, straight to the bank of the next river, where Jabari and the others stood gazing into the water.

As soon as Isika saw the river, she knew something was very wrong. It didn't feel alive at al—dark gray, the waters flowing slowly and painfully, as though they were captive to something horrible. In some places, the water was utterly still. Pools grew a thick white scum on their surface. The whole place reeked of rot. Isika felt compelled to go toward the water to touch it, but as she moved, Jabari cried out, "Stop!"

He looked relieved when she listened to him.

"If I get you to the city alive, Isika, it will be a miracle. This water has been poisoned. Its touch is fatal."

They stood and stared at the river. It was painful to look at—a dead body of water.

"What can we do?" Isika asked. "We have to cross."

"Gavi, we need to try a healing," Jabari said. Gavi drew in a breath.

"What?" Isika asked, looking up at Jabari. "What's the problem?" She looked at Gavi and saw that once again, his face was white.

"We can do it," Jabari said, his face set and determined. And after a moment, Gavi nodded, but he looked afraid. "You three need to back up, come on, we're not joking about this."

Then, like a nightmare, it happened. Jabari reached for a staff from his pack. Ibba moved closer to see it, ignoring Jabari's instructions. Ben started forward quickly to pull her back, but his right foot slipped on the wet grass at the bank, or perhaps the river itself pulled him in. He reached out for something to catch hold of, but his hands flailed in empty air, and he fell, slipping over the bank and into the poisoned water.

CHAPTER 18

*J*abari and Gavi shouted, and Ibba screamed as they saw Ben go over the edge. Isika threw herself on the bank and clutched at her brother's reaching hand. She saw the exact moment the water touched Ben. His eyes went wide with horror, and then they stared blankly, as though the water had killed him instantly. Isika held onto his hand with all her strength.

"Pull me back," she called to the others, and she felt strong hands on her legs, hauling her away from the river's edge. She and Ben inched up the bank until they were both on the dry ground, Isika still holding onto Ben's one dry hand. He was frozen, stuck in the same crumpled pose. She stood, horrified at the brown sludge that covered him.

"What do we do?" she cried, looking at Jabari and Gavi. Tears were flowing unchecked out of Gavi's eyes, and Jabari's face crumpled.

"There's..." he was silent for a moment, then went on.

"There's nothing, Isika. We can't heal that. Only one of the strongest elders could do it, and by the time we reach them, it will be too late."

But Isika wasn't paying attention anymore, because the tugging inside had become very strong, and her anguish at what they were saying was overcome by a strong desire to touch him.

She moved quickly, and right before she grabbed him, she heard Jabari shout, "Isika! No!" But he was far too late because her brother was in her arms. Her heart was full of every single thing they had been through together: walking in the desert hand in hand back when they were small, imagining things in the garden at their house, sending their mother out in the funeral boat, staring dead-eyed at the walls when they were so overcome by grief they couldn't do anything else. She thought of the way their eyes would meet when Ibba or Kital said something ridiculous, the way Ben's bowed head looked from behind when he trudged out to the temple in the early mornings. Now she knew his whole being had cried out against being in the temple. A sudden rage filled her as she held him. This was Benayeem's time. He couldn't die now, just as he was breaking into a better life.

She leaned close and laid her forehead on his. The poison, murky with despair, drained out of him and filled Isika, but instead of killing her, it met the fire in her heart and fizzled. The poison met the strength of the trees moving through her and vanished like steam. Isika knew then that her brother would be fine.

She dropped him and stood as an even stronger pull

tugged at her. Ben's eyes opened, and he sat up, but she saw it as though from a great distance, occupied with the need that screamed at her from the river. She turned her back on the others bending over Ben, and dove into the river in one straight, clean dive, like a water bird. Some small part of her protested that she had never done this before, that she shouldn't know how to shape her body to cut the water, but it was drowned out by the thudding purpose in her blood.

The poison of the river was much more malicious than what she had felt in Ben's body. It pressed against her, urgent in its despair, and she felt it clouding her mind. It was malevolent, desiring to suck the ability to think or move right out of her. Isika forced her hands in front of her face with the strength of a tree that withstands the rain, and pushed them back through the water to her sides. She swam like a fish or a strong water bird. The water glowed where she touched it, and she felt the poison loosen its grip. Just before her lungs gave out, she broke through the surface, inhaled sharply, and dove back below.

This time, she felt life stir in the water. The water creatures were waking from their poisoned sleep, and they helped her. She pushed her arms through the water again, and small, brilliant lights sparked along her arms, outlining her in light. The poison vanished; the water rushed back to life. Now the water fed energy back into her, but Isika was exhausted. She had taken the poison into herself to pull it out of the river, and she had extinguished it. Her body slowed and stopped swimming entirely, turning to look up at the river's surface, thinking, *Come on, Isika, swim up there.* But she had no strength left, and she could only drift along with the current.

She watched the light playing across the surface, which seemed very far away. Her lungs felt as though they would burst with the need for air. She couldn't move her arms, couldn't swim. Her mind was light and strange, sad, and resigned. A dark shadow crossed the sunlit surface above her head, and a giant shape crashed into the water. She saw an underwater version of Jabari reach down and grab her, just before everything went black.

JABARI LOOKED up from Ben and knew Isika was going to jump two seconds before she leapt. He lunged for her, but he was too late, and he watched her dive perfectly, her body cutting the water like a knife. Fear and anger flooded into his body, shaking him from head to foot. He waited for her to freeze as she hit the water, the way Ben had. Then he gasped. He saw her swimming under the murky water, and where she swam, gold lights flashed behind her, clearing the water.

Slowly the river shifted from dull gray-brown to a light tea color. Isika surfaced and took a breath, then dove again. Jabari was speechless. He sat down to take off his boots, glancing back at the river repeatedly as he did so. He couldn't lose her in the water. The lights coming off her now were gold, blue, and green. The water started to move properly, like a real river, with sunlight glinting off it in flashes that blinded him. The river was whole again. But Isika didn't surface, and Ibba was crying.

"Don't cry, little one," Jabari heard Gavi say. "She'll be okay. Look, Jabari is going to get her."

Jabari ran and jumped off the riverbank, tucking his body into a dive as he aimed at the spot he had last seen Isika. He broke through the water and was shocked at its purity, like new water, freshly born from the mountains.

There! She drifted near the bottom of the river, dragged in an undercurrent. Her eyes met his, and he saw sudden hope in them as he reached for her. He grasped her arms and pulled, but now her eyes were closed, and she was limp. Jabari put one arm around Isika and under her arms to hold on as he swam to the surface. She hardly weighed anything. He broke into the air and swam as quickly as he could to the bank. Isika was so thin, like a child, he thought, though she was fourteen. Fourteen! How could a fourteen-year-old poison-lander heal a poisoned river? And how had she done it without a cleansing fire or a staff? She had used only her body. Jabari had never heard of such a thing.

He reached the bank, and Gavi leaned over the edge to pull her up, quickly placing his hands just under her collarbone. She coughed as Gavi sent healing into her, willing the water out of her lungs. She vomited water onto the bank, then curled onto her side and was still. Ibba threw herself at her sister as Jabari wearily climbed out of the water. Gavi let the sobbing little girl hold onto Isika tightly. He put a gentle hand on Ibba's shoulder.

"Don't worry, little one. She'll be fine. She's just very, very tired."

But Gavi looked up at Jabari then, and Jabari saw the worry in his brother's eyes. Jabari went to Isika and took her hands in his. They were cold, freezing, though the day was still sunny and the water hadn't been that cold.

"Let's get her warm," Gavi said.

Together he and Jabari lifted Isika from the soggy riverbank. Jabari scanned the area for a good place to camp while they waited for Isika to recover. His eyes landed on a smooth, flat grove, a little way upstream, with several tall trees encircling a small clearing, guarding it against the wind.

"There," he said. "Ibba, stay with Ben until we get back to help him." With two of them carrying Isika, she seemed to weigh even less. Gavi frowned as he tried to avoid rocks.

"Not feeding children is despicable," he said.

"Just give them a while in the city, and they'll soon be strong enough."

"That's the thing, though," Gavi said. "They're strong. Frail but strong. I can't imagine what they would be like if they were stronger. It's almost scary to think of it."

Jabari looked down at Isika as they reached the clearing and laid her down under a river tree.

"She will make a good ally," he said. He was still unsure, hoping that she would become an ally, nervous because she would be a terrible enemy. If she did whatever she felt like doing, what would keep her from falling into the traps of the Great Waste? Jabari thought that he understood his parents' emphasis on rules and training for the first time. And then he hated the feeling.

Gavi pulled a blanket from his pack and spread it on the ground, then they carefully picked Isika up again and laid her gently on the soft blanket, wrapping it tightly around her with a sheet on top for good measure. Jabari gently moved her braids out from under her head and tucked the blanket around her face. Like this, so still and seemingly small, it was impossible not to want to protect her.

"How did she do it?" Gavi said.

Jabari shrugged, looking at his brother helplessly. "I was hoping you would know."

"I have never seen such a thing before, as you well know," Gavi said. "I worry for her, it's as though she drank the poison to drag it out of the river. She's freezing and in shock. Where are the Othra?" They turned to go back to Ibba and Ben and help them to the new camp space, and Gavi continued to mutter. "Why didn't they come when their precious children were in danger?"

"No one knows why the Othra do what they do. They don't feel the need to explain it to us."

"What about you, Yab? Are you going to explain to these poison-landers? Are you going to tell them who we are?"

It was the Othra who had told Jabari to keep their identities a secret, but he knew it was also a way for him to keep control as he warily led them through his land with little influence over what Isika did. She was too powerful and impulsive to contain, as they had seen again today. What she had done so far had been benign, but she was like a wild young eagle trying her talons out. She wasn't safe, and he didn't want to tell her all his secrets.

"They'll find out soon enough," he said.

"But they'll be walking into it blindly," Gavi replied, his face downcast. He kept his voice low as they drew closer to Ben and Ibba.

"I won't hold you back from telling them if you want to. But you'll have to deal with Nirral afterward."

"No," Gavi whispered. "I'll follow the Othra's sense of it. But I think we know Isika well enough by now to know that she is going to be very angry."

CHAPTER 19

When Isika woke, she found that she was curled at the base of a tree, dressed in the tunic and pants Jabari had loaned her. They were clean and dry. She blinked. The sky was dark. Through the branches of the tree above her, she saw the round, full moon. Somewhere nearby, a fire crackled, and she heard the murmuring voices of the others. Isika stayed where she was, enjoying the feeling of warm sleepiness. She reached one hand out to touch the tree, which was tall and silver, with papery bark. She felt its deep energy humming through her—this one different from the other trees. This tree felt like a long drink of water, and all at once, Isika realized that she smelled food, and she was ravenous.

She sat up and saw her brother and sister sitting with Gavi and Jabari around a fire, not far away. She stood, shaky for a moment, but stronger once she stood for a few breaths, regaining her balance. No one saw her approaching, and she startled Jabari when he finally looked up.

"Isika!"

Jabari leapt up and lunged toward her, crushing her in a hug. Isika was shocked by this but didn't have much time to think about it before she was passed into Gavi's arms. Then she came face to face with Benayeem. They looked at each other for a long time. His eyes were dark and serious in his face, wide-set in that Benayeem way, like no other person in the world. He smiled at Isika, and she felt a sense of wonder as she looked at him. There was so much more to him than she had ever seen, more than had been permitted to exist. She wondered what he would become.

"Thank you, sister," he whispered.

Ibba clung to Isika's waist, the little girl's head buried in Isika's stomach. Isika put her arms around her little sister and squeezed, then sat on the ground and pulled Ibba into her lap. She sat back and looked at the four of them, and they looked back at her. They had strange expressions on their faces. If she had to guess, she would say they looked at her with fear...or awe.

"What?" she demanded, and Gavi laughed.

"She's still Isika," he said to the others. "I'm relieved."

"I don't get it," Isika said. "What's so funny?"

"It's not funny at all," Jabari said, his face earnest. "It's just that we haven't seen anyone ever do what you did. I don't even really know *what* you did. It looked like you took the poison out of that river with your *body*." He grinned. "That's not something that people do, and especially not fourteen-year-old people."

Isika frowned and stared at the fire. Somehow she didn't want to talk about what had happened under the water. She couldn't explain it any more than Jabari could, and it was like a dream from long ago, like something she shouldn't pick up and try to figure out, something she should leave in its proper place.

"How long was I asleep?" she asked.

Jabari and Ben exchanged a look. "Two days," her brother said.

She sprang to her feet. "What? What are we doing, then? We need to go now!"

Gavi laughed and shook his head, and Jabari grinned. "We're not leaving in the dark," Jabari said, "so settle down."

"Why didn't you wake me?"

He raised his eyebrows. "What makes you think we didn't try?"

Slowly, she sank back down to the ground, and Gavi passed her a metal plate mounded with roasted fish, hot from the fire. It was delicious, but she thought she might cry over the lost time.

"We're close now," Jabari reassured her, looking at her over the fire between them.

The light danced on his face and Gavi's face, and Isika felt a sudden swelling of connection. Everyone looked more beautiful in the firelight. There was conflict within her. She wanted to get to Kital, but she didn't want to break up the new circle of friends. As much as she sometimes longed to wipe the superior look off Jabari's face, he had become a true friend to her. She remembered his eyes just before he grabbed her shoulders and pulled her out of the river. She smiled, and he smiled back, almost as though he knew what she was thinking.

"Are we close to the city?" Ibba asked in her high voice.

She was picking at the bones of her fish, getting every tiny morsel off, the way they were used to eating if they ever got something as special as fish, which was rare. Eating fish was for rich Workers.

"Yes, close to the city," Jabari said.

"What's it like?" Ibba asked. She looked up from her fish bones, her eyes wide.

"What do you think it will be like?" Gavi asked her.

"I have no idea," she said, shaking her head so her braids swung. "I've never been to a city." She frowned. "I can't even imagine. Actually, what exactly *is* a city again?"

They all laughed and laughed until Ibba's turned into wobbling lips, and Isika stopped laughing and pulled her close.

"A city is like a huge village," Isika told her. "But I don't know what this one will be like either. The only city I remember was in the desert before we left. It had walls, big ones, all the way around it. This city has no walls, right?"

Jabari and Gavi shook their heads firmly. "No," Gavi said. "Definitely no walls."

～

In the morning, Gavi made coffee and heated leftover fish. Isika paced while she ate; she was so impatient to get going.

"Come ON!" she said to Jabari as he washed his face in the river water for what seemed like far too long.

"You know we have one more stop on the way, right?" he asked as he fell into step beside Isika.

"No, we don't. You're kidding," Isika replied.

"We do! But it will only take a minute, don't worry. We'll be in Azariyah by tomorrow evening."

"A minute? Really?"

"Well, a few minutes." Jabari swung his staff and tapped a few nearby rocks with it as he walked.

"Where are we stopping?" Ben asked from behind them, and they waited a beat so he could catch up to them.

"To swim in Lake Ayo," Jabari said. He caught the skeptical looks she and Ben gave each other. "No, seriously. You'll love it. We can't come so close to the lake without stopping."

"What's worth it?" Gavi called from where he was walking with Ibba.

"Lake Ayo," Jabari called back to him.

"Oh yes, it's worth it," he said, nodding with energy. Isika sighed.

They reached the lake when the sun was high in the sky and left the road to walk through a large stand of the same silver trees that had been near the river. The trees were so ethereal that Isika caught her breath, but she was annoyed at the delay.

"It's already been a few minutes," she grumbled as they walked.

"Isika, calm down," Jabari said. He turned around and looked at her. "You could trust me, you know. This has been a long journey, and we can all use some rest. Do it for Ibba if no one else."

He looked hurt. Isika realized he was trying to do a nice thing for them, and though impatience seethed inside her, she decided to hold it in.

"Sorry. Let's go on," she said, trying out a new, soft voice.

Behind her, Ben laughed. "Nice, Isika. But now you don't even sound like you."

They came out of the trees to a wide shore, covered with rocks. Before them, a lake gleamed like pure silver in the sunshine. The water was perfectly calm, reflecting the trees with their white trunks and purple leaves like a mirror.

Ibba gave a little gasp. "It's so beautiful," she said.

Isika's heart beat faster. "It is," she breathed.

"Wait till you get in!" Gavi said. He tore his clothes off until he was dancing around in only in a pair of shorts. "Last one in the water has to clean the cooking pots after lunch!" he cried, running down the beach toward the water. He splashed in until he was deep enough to dive under. Isika watched him in shock.

"But he's afraid of water," she said to Jabari.

"Not this water," Jabari said. He smiled at Isika. "Some of our neighbors call this the Lake of Healing. They swim on its other shore."

Isika wanted to ask about these neighbors, but she didn't want to wash the cooking pots, and she wanted to try swimming in water that could override Gavi's fear. She stripped down to her underclothes in no time, racing toward the lake. She glanced back and saw Jabari lagging on purpose, allowing Ibba to reach the water before he did. She grinned.

In the last few days, Isika had swum in the sea, and she had waded through rivers, and both times she had felt the life and energy of the living things within. This water was different. The feeling Isika had was that the water itself was alive, friendly, and loving. She sighed as she let her whole body sink into it, opening her eyes in the clear water to see the smooth stones at the bottom. Exhaustion and worry melted away. The boys floated for a while, then wrestled each other into the deep part of the water until Isika had to swim over to them and take Ben's side, splashing Jabari in the face until he let go of her brother. Ben slung his arm around her and laughed at Jabari's startled look.

"I'm afraid of the two of you together," Jabari said, his eyes glinting.

"What about me?" Ibba asked from Gavi's shoulders. "Are you afraid of me?"

"You are the most terrifying of all," Jabari answered, and she nodded proudly.

"That's right," she said.

AFTER, they sat on the beach in peace as Gavi sliced a loaf of bread he had bought earlier. "When there aren't walls to tear down, we have to buy our food," he had told them as he ducked into the shop. "We're always glad when there are no walls, though."

He had bread and a little cheese, and the reddest, most luscious tomatoes that Isika had ever eaten. She narrowed her eyes at him. "There aren't any cooking pots," she said.

He pretended to look surprised. "I guess I miscalculated," he said.

"It's too bad," she said. "I was looking forward to watching Jabari wash them."

Jabari looked up, his food already half gone. "I'm sure you'll get your wish. Gavi nearly always makes me wash up—except when there are people who leap in ahead of everyone and wash without taking turns."

Isika was mildly shocked. She had been teasing, but with his words, she realized that she had assumed that cleaning was her responsibility because she was a girl.

"Well," she said. "Now that I know, I'm never washing another plate."

She stopped talking to eat. After swimming, Isika was hungry with a perfect, roaring hunger that sharpened the incredible taste of the tomatoes. Around her, the others ate silently as well. They sat in a cluster on the rocky shore, faces turned toward the lake's peaceful expanse.

"Why are there so many beautiful things here?" Isika asked when she finished her food, waving her hand at the lake before them.

Jabari sat with one knee up, his arm looped around it. His eyes grew thoughtful as he looked at the lake, then at her.

"Beauty is a gift from the Shaper. The Maweel have been charged to take care of the gifts, and to enjoy them." He shrugged. "So we do. We try, anyway."

"What else are you supposed to do?" Ben asked. "And how do you know?"

Jabari leaned over and picked up a smooth, white stone. He closed his long, dark brown hand around it, then opened it and looked at the stone, tossing it up and catching it. Isika kept her eyes on his hands, waiting for the answer.

"The ways have been part of the Maweel for thousands of years, told by Nenyi to Kings and Queens through generations. Now we work with the memory of what we know and what we can see."

"Who is Nenyi?" Isika asked. "I've heard you speak of the Uncreated One, but I don't understand who that is."

"Nenyi is the Uncreated One, the Life-giver, Mother and Father to the world. He gave the Maweel the tasks of removing poison, healing the land and its people, doing right, enjoying the gifts, rescuing those who need us, and always fighting Mugunta and the Great Waste. We rescue the outcast because these ways are in our bones, imprinted in us. Azariyah, our city, is a home for many who were once cast out from their own homes. And we have allies against the Great Waste at the shore of the sea. The Hadem; people who are white like Gavi, who hold back the Great Waste with all their might, though they have a different way."

"There are others who look like Gavi?" Ben asked. "Not Workers?"

Jabari looked surprised. "Of course. Throughout the great lands, until the sea itself, there are many kinds of people, stretching as far as we can imagine. There are people across the ocean, as well. We don't have as many allies as we would like, because the Great Waste is mighty. But the Hadem are some of our oldest friends. They hold the sea people back, the ones who steal our children, selling them to other kingdoms." He sighed. "Another of Mugunta's works."

Isika's eyes were wide. Jabari's words stirred her heart, like the shape of a story she had once known. She looked at Jabari and Benayeem sitting side by side and thought they could be brothers or cousins. They both had high foreheads and dark skin. Benayeem's skin was a shade or two lighter than Jabari's. Ben's eyes were wide-set like Jabari's. Jabari's cheekbones were higher and more pronounced, his lips fuller, his jaw firmer. He was taller, but Benayeem hadn't finished growing yet.

"Do you think we could have come from the Maweel long ago?" Isika asked. Ibba and Benayeem looked at her. Jabari stared at the stone in his hand.

"It seems possible," he said.

THAT NIGHT they camped for the last time. Jabari said they would reach Azariyah by the next evening. Ben lay awake under the stars, torn about the thought of arriving in the city. He liked this companionship, the friendships they had made here. He liked the peace of the wilderness, the music inside him quieted with the breezes of many leaves. Ben knew the clamor would rise again in a city, the bells gonging the wrongness of tiny things. The noises were a compass, he was finally coming to understand, his own body the instrument that rang out when wrong things were done or when the whole world rejoiced with rightness. It was overwhelming. Sometimes the things he perceived were so powerful they kept him from thinking clearly. Ben didn't know how to control the sounds he heard. Maybe there would be someone in the city who could help, he thought, as he traced the brilliant stars with his eyes. All around the fire, the others breathed softly, none of them awake or troubled.

He must have dozed because when the horrible ringing began, he jolted awake. He sat up, looking for the source of the noise, but realized quickly that it was inside him. Gongs clashed in jarring discord, *wrong, wrong, wrong*. Ben cowered in the darkness. He wanted to slip away from the source of whatever the dissonance was, like he had in his village, turning and running, head bent against the horrible noise until he found a cool, dark place. He looked around wildly for a way to run, then stopped himself.

This was a warning. Something was wrong. Ben needed to calm himself and find out what it was. He took deep breaths, searching for the source of the clamoring. He found it and turned to where his sister slept behind him. Isika. Figures crept from the shadows toward her, one with a cloth in his hand, stretching for her face.

"No!" Ben shouted, using all his strength. "Wake up, Isika!"

CHAPTER 20

"Jabari!" Ben shouted, and as one, he and Jabari were on their feet.

Jabari grabbed his bow, but Ben ran empty-handed toward Isika. She sat sleepily as the man above her hesitated. When Ben was two steps away, a spear whistled through the air from behind him, not from Jabari but Gavi. The spear went wide, missing the man, but giving a clear message, and the man backed up a step. Isika blinked at him.

"Hyder?" she said. Then her eyes landed on the second shape, just beyond the light of the fire. "Jak?" She scrambled up off the ground and held her blanket out in front of her. "What are you doing here?"

"Poison-landers," Jabari breathed, his face hard. "Why do you trespass in Maween?"

"We don't want to do you harm," Hyder said. He was a short, broad-shouldered man, very like his son, Jak, the boy from the village who had bullied Ben all his life. "Nirloth, the priest of our village, sent us to retrieve these way-breakers and bring them back for punishment. It's the only way to get out from under the wrath of the goddesses."

"How did you find us?" Isika cried.

"The goddesses give help to their priests, or didn't you know that?" Hyder sneered. "They want you, so they came to Nirloth to tell where you could be found."

Ben froze, shocked. Not retrieved as children, but as criminals. Not because his father wanted them, but as more sacrifices to appease the endless hunger of the goddesses. His head spun with the pitch of the horrible music, telling him how wrong it was.

"No," he said. He stood very tall and looked at his former bully and the man who was the bully's father, the coward who had tried to take them in the night. In the shadows, more men moved. Of course, there would be more. Two men were not enough to take three children over the miles they had crossed. "We won't go."

"You can't escape the goddess, Fate, boy," Hyder said. He smiled without humor. "She will never let you go."

Ben remembered the ugly, blank stare of the goddess in the temple. He remembered wiping the dust off her head, bird droppings off her hands. Ben had given her fresh flower petals, dabbed perfume on her feet. He had burned incense for her, rung the bells to wake her.

"I know Fate," he said. "Better than you. We won't go with you." He sensed Gavi and Jabari, alert and aware beside him. Ibba sat on the ground near the fire, her eyes wide with fear. Isika still stood with her blanket held out in front of her, her head bowed. How many men were in the shadows?

"Capture them," Hyder growled, and then many things happened at once. As Hyder lunged toward Isika, she threw the blanket she held into his face, and Ben tackled him. Jak lunged at Ibba, and she screamed. By the time he had her by the shoulders, Gavi was there. He delivered a swift kick to the back of the boy's knees, and Jak fell. Gavi sent another swift kick to his head that toppled him. Ibba jumped back as he fell, looking up at Gavi, hands over her mouth.

Ben didn't hear what she said, though, because he felt someone behind him. He turned. It was a large man, a stone smith from his village. The man looked stunned by what was happening but determined to capture Ben. Ben evaded his large hands and ducked under him to leap away. Jabari took Ben's place and punched the man twice in the face, rapidly, and the man backed away, a hand to his bleeding nose. Two more men lay on the ground near Jabari, holding their faces. These men weren't fighters—they were Workers.

Hyder had extricated himself from the blanket, and he held up a hand.

"Enough!" he roared. "We were not instructed to fight, only to bring the way-breakers home. We weren't aware that your new companions were your guards, Isika. Or should I say, Honored Isika?" His voice dripped with sarcasm. Isika flinched.

"We're not going to fight to take you, we don't have the skills these boys have. But Isika, Benayeem, I appeal to you as daughter and son of the temple you serve. Come and receive your punishment. Take the curse from our village and onto yourselves where it belongs."

Ben squared his shoulders and stared back at Hyder. He knew the answer he needed to give, without any whispering doubt. The man's spirit was full of sincerity, but beyond, in the minds of the goddesses, Ben heard evil. Beside Hyder, though, Isika drooped, curling on herself. He knew she was crying. Benayeem knew he needed to give the answer in his heart, because she might falter now, within reach of the poison of shame.

"No," he said. "We will never go back with you. Your goddesses will never have us now. They have no part of us."

Hyder stared back at Ben, and hatred broke over his face.

"Very well," he said. "I see the way Workers are repaid when they take garbage from the roadside. Nirloth is a fool, and your mother was evil to deceive him."

Beside Ben, Isika flinched. Ben put a hand on his sister's arm to keep her from speaking, sure that she would offer to go back if she did.

Hyder turned, gesturing to the others, who slowly picked themselves up and limped away. Just before they left the clearing, Hyder turned to Jabari.

"We have known of your lands and ignored you. You can count us as enemies now. Never assume that your borders are safe. We're not fighters, but the goddesses are good teachers."

Jabari's eyes flashed, but the men disappeared into the night. Isika collapsed on the ground with her head in her hands. Slowly, the drums in Ben's heart ceased their clamor, and his body returned to stillness. He helped the quiet come back by gazing at the stars, vaguely aware of Ibba beside Isika, stroking their older sister's back as she cried. The stars were lovely and pure in the sky, in the right places. Calm filled Ben. Jabari and Gavi quietly sorted blankets and picked up pots that had fallen over in the scuffle. As the cold purity of the stars soothed him, Ben felt that he was the ruler of himself for the first time. He smiled at the sky.

I⊤ was mid-afternoon the next day when they came to the first houses in the city. Isika was heartbroken by last night's argument. She couldn't help thinking of people like Jerutha and her unborn baby, people who were good and true, even if they were poisoned, people who would bear the brunt of the punishment for Isika's wrong.

Isika had been ready to turn and go with the men from the Worker village. She didn't know how Ben had found the courage to deny them, but she was glad for it because they were still on their way to Kital. The fight had left her feeling nervous and sad, and as they came to the outskirts of the city, her stomach seemed to be filled with small restless creatures fluttering against her ribs.

The sight of the first homes calmed her; they were pleasant and ordinary. The houses were short and wide, with flat roofs where laundry hung in colorful lines. People came out of their homes as the little group passed, shouting greet- ings to Jabari and Gavi, looking at Isika and her siblings with curiosity. As they walked farther into the city, the path beneath them became a real road, paved with wide stones. Many different kinds of trees lined the road, and the houses got closer together as the travelers traipsed farther into the city.

Isika took a longer look at one house. It was made of earth painted a bright white, with intricate holes cut into mud work edging the flat roof. Three girls sat on a wide porch with cups in their hands. Two of the girls were black, their hair done in what looked like hundreds of tiny braids, and one was white, with freckles and straight brown hair that was braided as well, though with fewer braids. All three girls had beads in their hair. Flowers climbed the walls of the house, and a vegetable garden grew in the yard before the house.

Isika stopped walking to look. The plants were a riot of color; tomatoes, orange flowers, and beans tangled in and around each other, and Isika sighed as she thought of her mother in the garden. At a word from a tall woman leaning against the doorway, one of the children ran to the garden. She picked a few tomatoes and held them out to Isika.

Isika laughed and shook her head, but the girl continued to hold them out to her expectantly, so she took the handful of tomatoes, giving them to Gavi when she caught up to the others.

"That was kind," she said, "but I didn't mean for her to give them to me. I only wanted to look."

"It is our way," he said. "She had plenty to share."

The buildings grew taller as they came into the city, some stacked two floors high. Ibba's eyes were round as she skipped along beside Jabari. There were children everywhere.

"There's no school today," Gavi said when Isika commented on it, "so they're free to roam."

"They can go wherever they want?"

"Yes, of course. If they tell their parents."

Isika had grown used to how much Gavi and Jabari looked into her eyes, but she was taken aback by all the eyes she met as they walked along the wide road. She was the girl who had always wanted to stare into people's faces, but the sheer number of eyes that looked into hers overwhelmed her. She reminded herself that eyes couldn't steal anything from her, couldn't really see her soul.

Isika's feelings had been mixed as she eased into the new way, old fears rising in her suddenly and without warning. She took a deep breath and held her head up. She had nothing to fear from meeting people's eyes. They were only parts of the face after all.

Stone pots of flowers and fragrant herbs were clustered around some of the houses. Everywhere Isika looked, the only walls were the walls of the buildings themselves, with nothing protecting the gardens. Sometimes there were short fences, spindly things that a child could step over. Most of the doors were flung open. People sat together outside, on porches or their front steps, eating and talking. Flowering trees lined the streets. Isika had never seen a place so lovely, so welcoming. She felt a longing that threatened to bring her to tears. She wanted to belong to this place, but she was a stranger here, a poison-lander.

She saw many people who must have been rescued, white-skinned like Gavi and the people of the Worker village.

And she saw children who looked like they came from other places entirely, with light brown skin and deep-set eyes, strong brows and long bones, or long eyes and high cheek-bones. The people were dazzling in their sheer numbers and differences; they wore colorful clothing of many shades; reds, blues, greens. Some people wore sashes or scarves wrapped around their heads, and Isika saw long robes and dresses, or simple pants and tunics like the clothes she wore. It was beautiful but overwhelming, and Isika felt her heart speeding up as she grew apprehensive.

A strong breeze whipped at the edges of her tunic, and Isika looked up and caught her breath. The Othra. They had returned. Isika waved at them, her heart full of happiness at seeing the familiar birds. Nirral soared down and touched his talons to her shoulder for just a moment, not quite landing on her but flapping his wings near her face, surrounding her with warmth and peace. The night's sadness and some of her nervousness disappeared. The Othra followed the travelers, flying overhead, and people came out of their houses to lay food down for them. The birds descended and ate bright fruits and bread, then lifted in a storm of wings, their feathers flashing all colors.

Ahead, a building rose above the others. Isika drew a breath. It was large and imposing and lovely, sculpted out of brilliant white stone. It looked as though it had grown from the earth, with tall towers reaching toward the sky, a bell on top of the tallest spire. Gently pointed bulbs crowned some of the towers, and holes were cut out of the walls' upper edges, with curves and flourishes like the ones Isika had seen on the homes in the city. The building had a long, wide doorway in its center, and from there fell back into walls with windows and towers on either side.

Ibba breathed a small sigh and slipped her hand into Isika's. "It's beautiful," the little girl said. "Are we going there?"

Jabari nodded. "That's the palace where the elders live. They'll know how to find Kital."

They reached the beautiful palace more quickly than Isika had expected. Her heart pounded in anticipation of seeing her brother, and her hands trembled. The palace was even lovelier as they drew near; its walls were stippled with the texture of many carvings, making it look like a living thing. Bright flowers spilled out the open windows of clear glass, and ponds filled with colorful fish flanked the steps they climbed. Two guards stood at the door, swords sheathed by their sides. Isika glanced at the swords, feeling weaponless and a little afraid, but the guards smiled at Jabari and Gavi, bowed to them, and then motioned them through. Isika frowned, a tendril of doubt sneaking into her mind.

"Why did they bow?" Benayeem asked as he and Isika passed the guards. Isika shook her head.

"I don't know," she said.

As soon as she stepped into the palace, Isika felt it sigh. She stopped, shocked. The building itself seemed to hum and settle. She looked around at the others, but no one else appeared to notice, so she shrugged it off. They walked through a hall that had lofty, airy ceilings and murals covering the walls. Isika wanted to stop and look at every panel, every picture, but Jabari strode toward a large pair of open doors at the end of the hallway. And Isika was fine with going quickly because her heart ached with longing for Kital. She would find time to look at these paintings later. At the doorway, Gavi glanced at them once, an apology in his eyes. Then, as Isika's heart sped up again, he and Jabari walked through.

CHAPTER 21

*I*t wasn't long before Isika understood Gavi's look. The huge doors opened up to a long room flanked with pillars made of the same white stone as the rest of the building. The tops of the pillars disappeared into the ceiling, far above where Isika stood. Her first impression of the room was light and color. Tall, arched windows lined the walls, fabric and tapestries hung from every available surface. The afternoon light streamed through the windows, illuminating a large table on a raised platform at the farthest end of the room. Two men and two women stood around the table, animatedly discussing something in front of them. Both men and one of the women had rich black skin. The second woman was white.

All four wore long, colorful robes, with embroidery that sparkled in the light from the windows. The scene was rich and beautiful, and Isika drew in her shoulders, transfixed and nervous at the same time. The people looked up as Isika and the others came nearer. One of the men, who wore a thin silver circlet around his head, turned to them with his hands outstretched.

"Jabari! Gavi! Welcome back, sons of my heart!"

Both Jabari and Gavi put hands over their hearts and bowed from the waist.

"Our hearts have come home, Father and Mother, Elders of our land," they said.

The man grinned and walked down the steps to clasp Jabari in a firm hug, then he moved to Gavi and hugged him. The other three people walked to join in, leaving their papers on the table behind them.

"Wait," Ben said to Isika. "Did he mean sons as in figurative sons or real sons?"

Isika shook her head, frowning. She felt heavy and confused. This must be the regent, and if Jabari and Gavi were his sons, well, they were like princes, weren't they? And brothers! They had never said they were brothers!

She looked at Benayeem and Ibba, and they stared back at her, wide-eyed. She felt sick to her stomach, as though the room had turned upside down. The camaraderie of the last days evaporated in the rich, scented air of the palace. The tall, elegant people finished with hugging and kissing the two boys. Isika felt shabby and dirty in her traveling clothes. When Gavi looked at her, she glared at him. He came close.

"Jabari didn't want to tell you," he said. "I had to respect that."

"So you thought you'd spring it on us now?" she hissed at him.

Jabari spoke to the robed people, who stared at Isika and her siblings with curiosity. The one who had called Jabari and Gavi sons opened his mouth to say something, but just then, the Othra swooped into the large room, bringing breezes of peace with them. Isika had never been with the Othra in a closed space, and as they flew past the guards and through the columns, she was full of wonder at the way feelings of wellbeing reflected off every surface. She straightened her back as Nirral and Efir settled at her feet and Eemia landed a foot or two ahead of Benayeem. Jabari's father shifted from foot to foot, and the other man, who hadn't yet spoken, lifted his head to look directly in Isika's eyes.

"Jabari, what is this?" Jabari's father asked.

It was Isika who answered. "Sir," she said, "We are looking for our brother. Jabari and Gavi have brought us to find him."

Jabari shot her a look. She narrowed her eyes at him. He cleared his throat.

"These three are poison-landers," Jabari said. The woman with black skin gasped. Isika noticed that she also had a circlet on her head. Jabari went on.

"They followed an outcast," he said, his head up and his back very straight. "We led them through Maween so they could reunite with him in our city. I worried about taking poison-landers through our lands, but they," he swept a hand toward the Othra, "were very persuasive." He paused, watching the large birds, as though leaving room for them to speak, but the Othra were silent, besides a quiet whirring and clicking that came from Eemia. They looked at home in the large room, rather than out of place, and the jewel colors in their feathers flashed and changed continually.

"But they don't look like poison-landers," the second woman said. Her white skin was a stark contrast to the black skin of the tall, silver-haired man who stood beside her. He held a long staff in his right hand, made from wood that looked like the silverwood trees beside Lake Ayo. He had the darkest skin Isika had ever seen, with eyes that shone the reflective lights of the day-lit room. The woman who had spoken was breathtaking. She wore a long, green robe embroidered with silver flowers, and she had flowers in her hair, which was flame-colored and fell to her waist. She shook her head.

"But wait, they are tired. Come children, sit, it seems you have walked a long way."

The man with the staff guided them to a nook in one corner of the room. Low, wooden platforms were covered with colorful cushions, and these had even more pillows piled on them. Servants emerged from behind the pillars and placed cups of water and plates of fruit on a low table in front of them. The soft-footed servants startled Isika; she hadn't seen them before they moved. The cushions were soft, and as Isika sank into a mound of pillows, she felt her weariness threaten to push her farther into the seat. She could sleep for a year.

She pushed herself straight upright, willing herself

awake. Once she found Kital, she could sleep, but it was essential to concentrate, with her baby brother so close. Not far from the cushioned area, the Othra settled themselves on short pedestals and promptly went to sleep, tucking their heads under their wings.

As everyone found a place to sit, the first woman spoke again. "Please introduce your friends, Jabari," she said. Her circlet was thin and delicate on her forehead; it looked like a silver thread against her dark skin. Her robe was a deep orange color, also covered in intricate silver embroidery. Everything was gorgeous. Isika sank farther into the cushions.

"Yes, Mother. This is Isika, this is Benayeem, and this little one is Ibba," Jabari said, gesturing to each of them. Ibba stood up and gave a deep bow, and everyone laughed. She sat down, flustered, but Jabari's mother smiled and beckoned to her, and she settled Ibba close to her side, holding her hand.

"Welcome, young ones," said the man with the circlet. "We will have food, beds, and baths for you soon. But first, I'm afraid we must talk. I am Andar, regent, and high elder of this land. You have met my sons, and this is my wife, Laylit, second elder. This is Ivram, third elder and my advisor, and his wife Karah, fourth elder, first of the rescued ones in Maween."

Isika stared at Karah, then remembered she was in a palace, and there must be some response called for. She bowed her head in greeting and felt Ben doing the same beside her. Then she took a moment to really look at the elders.

Andar was perhaps an inch or two shorter than Jabari,

but he was elegant and gracious, with glowing black skin and short, tightly curled black hair. He radiated authority. His wife, Laylit, was smaller than him, short only by Maweel standards. In the Worker village, she would be considered a tall woman. She was the most beautiful woman Isika had ever seen, her skin a rich brown, with a high curving forehead and large brown eyes. The lines of her face looked as though an artist had drawn them, and her hair coiled around her head like a crown. Laylit watched Isika with a slight frown between her eyes, as though she was puzzled by something.

The man with the staff was extremely tall, with dark skin, gray hair, and long limbs, and his wife, Karah, was tall like him. Her red hair was loose, flowing around her, but Isika saw that pieces were braided into tiny plaits that shimmered with gold beads. Together, the four of them were impossibly beautiful. They shone in the room.

Isika tried to hide her dirty feet, jumping as Gavi elbowed her and winked. She gave him a small smile in return before she remembered that she was angry with him.

"So," Andar said. "Introductions are behind us. You followed your brother. We have never heard of this happening."

"That's because it has never happened before, sir," said Ben.

Andar sat back and looked at them. "But how did you come to live with the poison-landers?" he asked.

Isika sighed. So many questions when she simply wanted to know where her brother was. And Aria. She shoved back the tiny flame of hope with Aria's name on it. Isika told the story of her mother in the desert quickly, then asked, "Do you know where our brother is?" She couldn't quite keep the impatience out of her voice, and she saw the man called Ivram smile.

"Andar, the child is right. We have time for these questions later," he said. "Let's help these journeyers if we can. But, young one," he said to Isika, "we were just now conferring about a strange problem." He gestured toward the table, and the papers scattered over it, which Isika could now tell were maps. "The rescuers haven't returned, and we are wondering whether we should send someone for them. They should be back by now."

A strange, choked sound came from Jabari. Isika looked at him. It was the first time she had seen how fear looked on his strong face, and her stomach flipped with dread. She leapt to her feet, towering over everyone who remained seated.

"What? What do you mean?" she cried.

Gavi touched her leg. "Sit," he whispered, frowning toward the seated elders.

Isika sank onto her cushion, legs shaking, her face on fire, angry and embarrassed at whatever rule she had broken, despairing because she had believed she would hold Kital this very day. She had thought she would arrive in the city and simply open her arms up to Kital while he ran into them. Her hands shook, and she sat on them to make them stop.

"What do you mean they're not back?" Jabari repeated, and Isika felt worse when she heard the urgency in his voice.

"We don't understand either," Andar said. "What could

have held them up?" The elders gave each other troubled looks.

"How many rescuers?" Gavi asked.

"Four," Ivram said. He heaved a deep sigh. "Ivy was with them."

Gavi sat back with his head in his hands.

"Who is Ivy?" Isika whispered.

"Our daughter," Karah answered.

"Do you think—?" Jabari started, his face creased in a frown.

"Yes," his father said before Jabari had even finished his question.

"What? What?" Isika asked, looking at the faces before her. It was cruelly ironic; they sat here with kind people and beautiful things, fruit sliced on a plate before them, but Isika could not enjoy a single bit of it because of the fear that broke over her like a wave.

Andar looked at her, his face serious. He had the same wide-set eyes and strong jaw that Jabari had, but when Isika looked at Laylit, Jabari's mother, she could really see Jabari's face. Gavi, the former Worker child, sitting beside his brother, didn't look like either of his parents, and Isika briefly wondered what life was like for him as an adopted rescued one.

Andar spoke. "We have enemies we call the sea people, for we don't know their name and they have never told us, preferring to stick to shadows and betrayal rather than declare themselves. Our neighbors and allies, the Hadem, have told us that recently the sea people have been more powerful than usual. For every boat of Hadem that patrols the outer waters, there are three of the sea people's, working to break into our lands and steal our children. The Hadem can usually hold them back, but lately, they have been struggling. They brought us a report just last night," Isika saw Jabari sit up straighter, "that they have seen signs of boats that have landed on our shores, but that the boats had been burned."

Shock rippled through Isika, and this time she had no words. She sat and waited for it to sink in.

"What do they do with the children they steal?" Ben asked.

Andar looked into the distance. It was Ivram who answered. "They sell them," he said. "Sometimes the Desert King takes them as slaves or sacrifices, or sends them overseas to the far continent."

Isika slumped in her seat, staring at the cup of water she still hadn't sipped from. A memory of her brother came into her head, unbidden. After she had forgotten to speak the sacred words at the gate one too many times, Nirloth had punished her. She was holding a cold cloth to her face later when Kital—he couldn't have been more than three—came to her and placed his hands gently on each side of her face. He looked into her eyes and sang the words she had sung to him ever since he was born, the same song Isika's mother sang to her when she was alive. She remembered his gentle eyes and felt despair flood her. He was too small and vulnerable to survive slavery.

"What do we do?" Ben asked, his hands clenched into fists. "We need to find them."

"Do you know where the boats landed?" Gavi asked.

His father nodded. "The Hadem elders showed us on the map yesterday."

"Then let's go!" Isika exclaimed. She sat forward, her hands on her knees. The Othra fluttered on their perches, then were still.

"You must wait in the city, child," Laylit said, leaning forward, her eyes troubled. "We will send a group of rangers to find them—"

"Laylit," said Ivram, and the end of his staff glowed white. He closed his eyes and opened them again. "Forgive me. I believe they have a right to see their journey through. Isika and Benayeem will go with the rangers. The little one will stay here." Isika saw a look of relief cross Ibba's face before she frowned and looked like she would cry. Isika could see telltale signs of exhaustion in her sister. She had walked a long way for a little girl, but Ibba knew Kital better than any of them, and Isika knew her sister's heart longed for Kital.

"I would like the little one to stay with me," Laylit said. "Would you like that, darling?" Ibba looked at her, then nodded. She blinked back tears and snuggled back into Laylit's arms, eating a slice of orange. Isika didn't really like the idea of Ibba staying with a stranger, but she could see that her little sister seemed born to be a princess. She met Gavi's eyes, and they looked quickly away from each other, stifling smiles. It was impossible to stay angry at Gavi.

"We leave in the morning," Ivram said. "Get some rest."

Andar looked sharply at the man with the staff. "You too, brother?"

"I will go to search for my daughter," Ivram answered.

Isika wanted to protest that they should leave immediately, but she saw a steely look in Ivram's eyes and knew she was fortunate to be going at all, so she closed her mouth and crossed her arms, tucking her hands under her elbows. She finally leaned forward and drank the cold cup of water on the table, finishing it in one long swallow.

Everyone stood, and Isika saw Andar turn to Jabari.

"Traveling with these young ones was without incident?" he asked quietly.

"Oh, I wouldn't say that," Jabari said, glancing at Isika. "Some poison-landers came deep into our lands to pursue the young poison-landers. And there were... incidents." Heat blazed into Isika's face, and she turned away.

"Very well," Andar said. "You may give a full report later." Isika had no doubt that Jabari would tell all her misdeeds when she wasn't around. She tried to shrug it off, but it bothered her. For some reason, she wanted the elders to think well of her.

THEY BOWED their way out of the room, Jabari and Gavi promising to come back to give their parents a full account of the trip later in the evening. Isika turned on them as soon as they reached the hallway, her fists clenched. She wanted to punch them, but the door guards were watching, and she didn't know whether hitting an insufferable son of a regent was allowed in Azariyah.

"Why didn't you tell us you were brothers? Or that your father was the regent?" she demanded.

Jabari shook his head. "It doesn't matter in the outer reaches of the land. It only matters here, in the city."

"Well, you could have told us—I don't know—when we were approaching the city? A little warning would have been nice!"

Jabari looked at her, his face frustrated. "Would you have walked in there with us if you had known?"

She thought about it, "I don't know. Maybe." Actually, probably not. She would have expected trouble and might not have gone. The whole journey would have been different if she had known Gavi and Jabari were more than the young seekers they had claimed to be.

"The Othra told me not to tell you, if you must know my reasons. They said you would equate my power with the power of the poison-landers, that you wouldn't know it for what it really is, and that you would be afraid."

Isika whirled to face the Othra, who had followed them out of the great room, but they were gone. Gavi shook his head and touched her on the arm.

"You need to learn to trust, Isika. Not everything is a battle."

"How can I trust when people don't tell me the truth?" she asked, shaking with anger and exhaustion. She covered her face with her hands and took a deep breath, trying to understand. If anyone had been on her side, it was the Othra, but they had kept this from her. She reached out with a question inside her mind, and to her immense surprise, she felt a response from far away. She saw the perspective of the Othra as they circled the city, and she breathed in sharply as her gaze followed the city, nestled into a valley, one edge climbing a mountainside. The countryside spooled out to the east of the city. The mountain sheltered the buildings from the strong winds from the north. The deep comfort of Nirral touched her heart gently, and she was so surprised that her anger evaporated in a moment.

Isika had never seen through someone else's eyes before. She looked up at Jabari, stunned, and he took a step toward her, but just then, a scuffle broke out at the palace doors.

"Ibba!" Benayeem called. "Where are you going?"

Isika turned in time to see Ibba run through the vast doorway, leaping down the wide steps and into the street. Isika ran after her little sister. She had to watch her feet closely as she clattered down the unfamiliar stairs, but she looked up as she reached the bottom to see Ibba running after a cluster of kids. Isika chased her, stopping as Ibba paused, looking unsure.

"I thought I saw Kital," she said.

"You couldn't have," Isika said. "He's not here."

The group of children turned to look at them. There, in the center, was a tall girl with a bow, hair woven in hundreds of tiny braids that clung to her head and cascaded over her shoulders. She wore a sky-blue, sleeveless tunic over wide brown pants, and she had soft leather boots on her feet. But it was her face that stunned Isika. She looked exactly like Kital. She looked like Isika's mother.

"Aria!" Isika breathed, and then the world spun. Jabari caught up to her and caught her as she fell. Her last thought before she lost consciousness was that this didn't mean she wasn't still mad at him.

CHAPTER 22

"Bring water!" Isika heard Jabari call from what seemed like far away. Her head hurt, and as she came back to herself, she realized that she was lying on the ground, the top half of her curled up in Jabari's arms. She sat up immediately and pushed away from him, accepting a ceramic jar of water so she could hide her face in it, regain her composure, and calm her spinning head. Jabari stood and held a hand out for her. She took it and pulled herself to her feet without looking at him. Instead, she looked back at her lost sister, standing there surrounded by other young people. Aria looked back at Isika warily.

"Aria, it's good to see you," Jabari said.

The tall girl smiled at him, dimples creasing her face. "It is good to see you," she said. "Have your travels gone well?"

"Aria, don't you know me?" Isika asked. Aria frowned, confused.

"What are you talking about?" Jabari asked Isika. "How do you know Aria?"

"This is my sister," Isika told him, and just then, Gavi and Ben reached them, Ibba holding tight to Gavi's hand. Aria looked at Benayeem and then Ibba, and understanding broke over her face slowly, like the sun setting. Isika saw its heaviness hit her, and that's when she realized that Aria had put them away on a shelf outside of her mind. She had tried to forget them. This was a forceful reminder.

"Isika," Aria said, and her face crumpled. Isika walked over and took her sister in her arms. Aria was nearly as tall as she was. She laid her head on Isika's shoulder for a moment, then Benayeem joined them and put an arm around Aria, and Ibba threw her arms around Aria's legs. The four of them stood like that for a moment, and when Aria drew away, her face was shiny with tears.

She stared at each of them in turn, and Isika thought of how different they must look, four years after she had seen them last. Aria certainly looked different. She had been so small and thin when she was given over. Now she was strong and tall, muscles showing in the forearm that gripped her bow. Every year, Isika remembered Aria's birthday, aching again from her loss. Isika knew Aria was eleven years old, and she would be twelve in a few months.

"What... what are you doing here?" Aria asked. She looked confused and upset. A crowd had gathered, and the audience stretched to the nearby houses; dozens of people had moved to their porches or the street's edges to see what was going on.

"The Workers sent Kital out," Isika said. "We followed him."

"Kital?" she said, and Isika felt the blood leave her face again. She nearly fell. Aria didn't know who Kital was. She didn't know her brother existed; she had been sent away before he was born. The evil of what the Workers had done hit Isika in the gut like a fist.

"Oh, Aria," Ben said, beside her, and when she looked at him, his face was drawn and pinched. "He is our brother." Aria's face closed, and she turned away.

"I don't... I don't want..." Aria said, her voice rising. She lifted one arm and waved it, pushing at the air, pushing them away. "This is... what is this?" Her voice broke. She turned to Jabari. "They can't be here. They cast me out."

Isika's heart felt the way it might if Aria shot her in the chest with her bow.

"Aria—" she said. "Please, we love you."

Jabari took over. "This is a lot all at once. I think we need to meet later to talk, give Aria time to recover." He turned to Aria. "I'll find someone to tell your parents."

Her parents? She had parents? Isika didn't want to lose sight of her sister, even for a moment. She protested. "No, I—"

"Isika, just listen," Jabari said. "Unless you want to put on a play, or do a dance, it would be better to talk later." Isika looked up and saw the hundreds of people watching them intently. She nodded numbly, stunned by the events of the day. She watched as the group of children her sister was with closed back around her, and they walked away, whispering and huddling across the paving stones. Jabari started in the opposite direction with Gavi, Ibba, and Ben, and with one last look, Isika followed. She wanted to race after Aria to tell her NO! They were her family, not those strange people she was with. Didn't she know how much they had grieved for her? Didn't she know that it had taken their mother's life? But of course, she couldn't know. Isika walked without seeing anything. She didn't know where Jabari and Gavi were taking them, and she almost didn't care.

"I should have seen it," she heard Jabari murmur to Gavi. "We were all so stunned when we rescued Aria from the boats because she didn't look like a poison-lander. I should have known they were connected."

"I thought about it," Gavi said, squinting up at the canopy of branches that met over the road. "But I didn't want to say anything and raise false hope."

"You could have told me," Jabari grumbled. Gavi elbowed him, and Jabari stuck out a foot and tripped his brother. Gavi stumbled and came up grinning. Isika watched their affection for one another, but it didn't make her feel better. Her stomach hurt as she thought about the separation of her family. Fathers, mothers, siblings—everyone torn apart.

AFTER WALKING A SHORT DISTANCE, they turned onto a street that climbed the hill behind the palace. It was another stone walkway that turned into wide steps at points where it became steepest. Jabari turned in at a house that was plastered and painted a pale blue, the earth walls smooth and rippling along their surfaces, with square corners, holes cut into the earth for windows and along the top of the roof as decoration. Flowers lined the stone path to the front door, and as they approached, a couple around Jabari's parents' age walked out onto the porch to welcome the travelers. They had dark brown skin, the man with a beard and gray, grizzled hair. The woman was plump and lovely and wore a tunic and pants and an apron.

"This is Dawit and Teru," Jabari said. "And these are the young ones, Isika, Benayeem, and Ibba."

"Come in, come in!" the woman said. She showed them into a room with a high ceiling. The interior was white with flowers painted in bright colors along the tops of the walls and around the doorways. On one side of the room, a wooden table was set with a meal.

"I thought we would eat first, and then you can all bathe," the woman said. "We've sent our niece out to get you some clothes—she has a great eye for beauty," she told Isika, putting a hand on her arm, "I thought it was best. I haven't shopped for a young person in a while."

Isika looked at Jabari with wide eyes. "I'm sorry," she said. "What are we doing here?"

Jabari grimaced at Gavi. "I'm the worst at explaining things," he said, grinning. He took a breath. "This is your family." Isika's jaw dropped. "We give all the rescued ones a family," he went on. "Almost every couple in the city has taken in a rescued child. Ivram told us to put you here because Dawit and Teru have room for the three of you."

"But when did this happen?" Isika gasped. "How did you know?" She stared at the couple. "We don't even know how long we're going to be here."

Dawit laughed. "You must think we're mind readers. I'm a guard in the throne room. I approached Ivram immediately after you spoke with him, volunteering to take you three in. I passed you in the street in my hurry to tell my wife that you would arrive. She was over the moon. I know her well. She's been longing for family."

Isika stepped back to take a better look at the man who would so quickly agree to take care of them.

He spoke again. "The Desert King stole our son while he was seeking three years ago." He put a hand over his face for a moment. When he looked at them again, his eyes were damp. "We have room in our home for you, and you can stay as long as you are in the city."

Tears sprang to Isika's eyes. She was stunned. Was there an end to the surprises in Maween? This place was so far beyond her imagining that she felt she had entered another world, not just another city.

"But what about your mother?" she asked, turning to the boys. "She wanted to have Ibba stay with her."

Gavi and Jabari exchanged glances. "We can work that out. Ibba could stay at the palace while we are gone and come back here once we're all back," Jabari answered. "Or maybe Mama will change her mind when she learns you've already been placed with a family." Isika touched the top of Ibba's head lightly. She was nervous about leaving her, but she didn't want to bring her tiny sister into more danger. She pushed the question out of her mind.

At the table, there were chairs for all of them. They sat and ate the soup Teru had prepared for them. Isika was ravenous, and she ate quickly. The fish and potatoes of the morning were far away, a lifetime ago. Teru set a cold pitcher of fruit tea on the table and poured a cup for each of them. She had cups made of real glass, like the glass of window panes, and Isika picked one up and stared at it. Ibba leaned into her, tired and full. She gazed up at the glass Isika was holding and whispered something that Isika had to strain to hear.

"I didn't know there were so many beautiful things in the world," the little girl said, and Isika put an arm around her and squeezed. She felt the same way.

She looked around with more curiosity. They sat in a spacious, medium-sized room, and near them were open double doors. Through the doors, Isika saw a large courtyard sheltered by a lattice of wood overhead. Teru spotted Isika looking outside and suggested that they move outdoors.

They walked out with glasses of tea in their hands. In one corner, a shade cloth was tied to the wooden poles that criss-crossed overhead. Underneath, several swing chairs hung from the rafters. Isika sat in one, and it swayed gently back and forth. Plants in pots lined the courtyard walls, which transitioned into a garden filled with trees and flowers. It was the loveliest home Isika had ever seen. She looked at Ben, and he smiled at her. She smiled back, and they sat swinging in the chairs.

Isika was silent, barely keeping herself awake. Jabari, Gavi, and Teru kept the conversation going, discussing what they had found on their seeking journey and worrying over the rescuers not returning when they should.

"When do you leave?" Teru asked, her voice sharp. Isika looked up and saw worry creasing her face. Did she already care about them?

"We leave in the morning," Jabari said. "At first light." Teru sighed, then nodded, clapping her hands and standing.

"If that's the case, you need to be prepared for a journey," she said. "Baths and clothes."

"And we need to go and see Aria," Ibba added. She paused for a minute. "I wish she could stay here with us."

Teru glanced at Dawit. "She's settled with her new family, sweetheart. But you should see each other all the time if you can."

"Yes," Isika said. Her voice shook slightly, but she steadied it. She wished she was already sitting with Aria. "I still don't understand why we had to put off talking to her," she said to Jabari.

He looked at her from his seat on a large pillow. "It was a shock, Isika. No other family has ever come back before. Aria has been raised to believe that you were gone forever."

Isika frowned. "Come with me," Teru said to her. "You're first."

~

TERU LED Isika through the courtyard to a small room at the back of the house. Tiles covered the floor and walls. Isika blinked. She had never seen colors like these in a house before; purple, green, blue. On one side of the room, a fire crackled under a large steel cylinder, and in the center of the room, a deep cistern sank into the floor, lined with blue tiles. When Isika looked closer, she saw metal pipes coming from one side of the cistern. Teru turned a handle on the pipes, and steaming water flowed into the hole. Isika tried to keep her face still, but she wanted to shriek. Water that ran into the house? Was this what it meant to live in a city?

Teru filled the basin nearly to the top. Isika undressed, then stepped down into the bath and sank under the warm water. Teru moved around the room, humming, gathering things that she brought to the basin's edge. She handed Isika a thick piece of soap. Isika soaped her body, feeling like a baby in a pail, like Kital being bathed on the back porch of their house in the Worker village.

"Down you go," Teru said, lightly touching Isika's hair, and Isika submerged her head in the water to get all of her thick hair wet. Her hair had always been hard to manage, but she had kept it long regardless because her mother had liked it that way. It was tightly curled, wiry, and strong. Teru worked soap through it and rinsed it, then added oil, using a wide comb and her fingers to separate Isika's hair into sections and get all the tangles out. Tears came to Isika's eyes, both from the pulling on her scalp and the memory of her mother combing her hair this way when she was a small girl.

Teru finished with the comb and smoothed Isika's hair back from her forehead. She handed her a rough cloth.

"Give yourself a good scrub," she said. "I'll go see whether your clothes have arrived."

Isika used the cloth to scrub off days of grime that their brief swims in rivers and Lake Ayo hadn't been able to wash away. The soap smelled of oranges, and the citrus scent rose from the warm water. She rinsed herself under the water again, and when Teru bustled back into the room, Isika stepped into the bath sheet she held out for her.

"Here you are," Teru said. "My niece picked lovely things. I have travel clothes for tomorrow, but for your meeting with your sister, you should wear something nice."

Isika pulled a tunic over her head, this one a deep blue, shot through with silver thread. The pants were dark purple and reminded Isika of the Othra's wings. They felt like the softest clouds swirling around her as she walked the room, trying them out. She looked up and smiled at Teru, blinking back tears that pricked at her eyes.

"Thank you," she said, and Teru pulled her into a hug. The older woman smelled like flowers.

Teru dried Isika's hair and separated it into four braids; two fell down her back, and two swept away from her face and met at the crown of her head. Isika peered into the mirror Teru held out to her. She looked nothing like the girl who had lived with the Workers, wearing thick dresses and walking with her head down. Holding her arms over her head, the silky wide sleeves of her tunic falling down around her elbows, she turned in a circle. She looked beautiful, she thought, though there wasn't much that could be done for her face, the dark black of her eyebrows and the width of her mouth. But she grinned at herself in the mirror. She liked the new Isika.

When she went back into the courtyard, Jabari and Gavi were gone. Isika curled up on some cushions on the floor while Teru took care of the others, so contented and clean that she fell asleep.

CHAPTER 23

When Jabari arrived at Dawit's home to collect Isika and Ben, the house was silent. He stood in the doorway for a moment, peering in. Dusk was falling outside, but warm lamps shone in the room already, and he could make out the shapes of his three fellow travelers sleeping on cushions in the living space. He smiled.

"Teru Auntie," he called.

She came quickly, frowning at him. "They're sleeping, you'll wake them," she scolded.

"We have to wake them," he said. "Dinner at the palace."

"Surely, you can let them sleep."

He smiled. "Sorry. They can sleep after the incredible feast that's been put together for them."

Teru made a noise that sounded strikingly like the clicking and scolding of the Othra, and Jabari ducked. She shook her head as she gestured for him to come in, bustled over to the sleeping kids, and bent over one of them.

"It's time to go, Isika," she said. "Jabari is here to get you."

Isika sat up, looking sleepy, disoriented, and slightly grumpy. It was cute. Jabari grinned at her. She narrowed her eyes at him.

"Come on!" he said. "I'm waiting. Let's go sleepyheads!"

Isika stood slowly and brushed at her clothes. She looked radiant, brand new after such a long journey, her hair tied back in a way that emphasized the lovely lines of her face. For a moment, Jabari had to look away to catch his breath. He shook the feeling away, looking down at his own clothes. He had bathed and changed as well, and he now wore a white shirt that crossed diagonally over his chest and long black pants of stiff cloth. The palace barber had even visited, frowning at the state of his hair. Jabari was clean and trimmed and pressed, just like Isika. He stood a little taller.

Isika tried to wake Ibba, but the little girl muttered, frowned, and rolled over, refusing to get up. Teru's face was so fierce that Jabari finally told Isika to leave her to sleep. Benayeem stood and clasped hands with Jabari. He looked good as well, dressed in dark pants and a bright green shirt. His hair was dark and curly against his head.

"We clean up well," Jabari said. "If I hadn't seen just how many twigs you can get stuck in your hair, Benayeem, I might even be intimidated."

Ben stretched and grinned. He took his sister's arm, and they walked to the doorway together.

"Don't keep them out late," Teru said sternly.

"I'll try," Jabari said. "But they're animals at a party." Teru swiped at him, but he evaded her and ducked out the doorway into the dusky evening. He took another look at the siblings as they left the house. He shook his head.

"You look as though you'd always lived here," he said, striding down the path so that they had to walk quickly to keep up. "Who on earth are you? I'd love to know."

"I'd love to know for once where we're going," Isika grumbled, and he slowed down to look at her.

"Oh, that. There's been a change of plans," Jabari said. "My father has invited us all to eat at the palace, so we're meeting Aria there."

Isika stared at him.

"Do you really think the palace is a good place to talk with our sister for the first time in four years?"

"You already talked to her for the first time," Jabari said. "In front of a hundred strangers. But yes, I think it'll be okay. They'll give you a small table, curtained and out of the way. You'll have privacy to talk." He leaned closer. "I wrangled that for you with my palace connections."

"Great," Isika said. She was scowling at the ground.

"What?" Jabari asked, elbowing her. She turned the scowl on him, then it disappeared suddenly.

"Can you—" she hesitated. "Can you come with us? You know Aria. She'll feel better if you are there."

Jabari looked at her and caught a little glimpse of how hard this day had been. "Sure," he said, and he slackened his pace so they could walk in a more leisurely way. He reached out to pat her arm, and she shrugged him away.

Ben chuckled. "Just because she asked you for help

doesn't mean that she wants to need your help," he said, and Jabari laughed under his breath.

A smile flitted over Isika's face as well, so quickly, Jabari almost missed seeing it.

They reached the palace before long, just as it was truly becoming dark. The grand building was brilliant at night, with lamps in the corners chasing the darkness away, and lanterns flanking the steps into the entryway. Candles lined the wall alcoves and the stairway railings, casting flickering light onto the carved and painted walls. They walked to the dining hall, a vast room with twenty tables piled with food in the center. Cushions and low tables were placed along the walls, and people stood and conversed with one another, glasses in their hands, or sat on the cushions, eating and talking.

A servant approached and held out a tray of glasses filled with juice that sparkled red in the light. Jabari took two and handed one to Benayeem and one to Isika, and then took one for himself. He took a sip of the fermented berry tea. It was sweet, sour, and bubbly, and he finished the glass in one long drink.

"What is this?" Ben asked.

"Tea made from vera berries and fermented with the theto mushroom," he told them. They looked back at him blankly.

"Never mind. It's just a bubbly drink."

They had the look of stunned people. Jabari took another look at the room. Over one hundred men, women, and in some cases, children, walked around or sat on cushions. In the corner, musicians played flute and drum, and the room rang with light and sound from two hundred lamps and voices and laughter that bounced off the stone walls. Jabari could imagine that it was ever so slightly intimidating if one had never been to court before. He turned back to Isika and Benayeem.

"They're all just friends, sort of," he said. "But come this way, and we'll find Aria and your quiet corner."

He led them through the room, weaving between people in gorgeous clothes, to greet his parents and the other elders.

"Welcome," his mother said, Karah by her side. "Congratulations on your reunion. We have not seen one before, and we knew we had to invite you here to observe."

Jabari flinched. He loved his mom, but she could be so... courtly. He kissed her cheek and rounded his eyes at Isika. She smiled and bowed her head, then darted a quick glance at Jabari's mother and Karah. Jabari saw that they were dressed in robes covered in glittering stones. The whole room sparkled. Jabari took Isika's elbow and continued walking through the room with Ben walking on her other side. Jabari nodded and greeted people he knew along the way. He didn't love being at the palace the way he loved being in the wild seeking with Gavi, but he had grown up here, and it was as easy as breathing to him. Life in the palace was like a game.

He stopped near the back of the room and looked around for Aria. Beside him, Isika rubbed at her temples and closed her eyes.

There was Aria. She was only half a head shorter than Isika, but she looked child-like without her bow and quiver.

Her many braids were coiled around her head, and she wore a deep orange tunic.

"There you are, little sister," Jabari said, using the familiar way of addressing younger girls in Maween. "Greetings, Jabari," Aria said, bowing her head slightly. Her voice was soft and hoarse. She was still such a little girl in many ways, though she was in the place between two ages, neither young nor old. He felt sympathy for her and pity for the others, so he straightened and took charge.

"Reunions go better when we fill our bellies," he said. "I think we should eat."

They sat in an alcove in the corner, beside one of the low tables. Jabari sank into the cushions, taking a sip of another drink, this one a spiced tea. The spices warmed his stomach. A servant brought platters of food with flatbread and spicy meat, a plate of tomatoes, and a bowl of fruit. He did love the food in the palace. They ate, and Jabari watched Ben and Isika as they chewed slowly to savor the food, leaning toward each other to comment on what they were tasting.

"Good?" he asked.

"I've never tasted anything like it," Isika said.

"That doesn't tell me whether it's good or not!" he laughed.

"It's amazing," she said, narrowing her eyes at him. "But you don't need me to tell you that."

Aria wasn't eating much or meeting anyone's eyes. She cleared her throat after a while.

"So we have a brother named Kital?" she asked.

Isika nodded, her face immediately stricken. The lamp-light reflected in her eyes, which were very serious.

"And you followed him?" Aria asked.

"Yes, but he isn't here."

Aria looked at Jabari.

"The rescuers may have been attacked," he said, his words soft. "We leave tomorrow to find him."

Aria sat up straighter. "I want to go too."

"Aria..." Jabari said, his voice a warning. "It's not a good idea. You have your studies, and you're not ready for seeking."

"I want to go. He's my brother too," Aria said again. She held her head high when she said it, and her eyes were like flint. Jabari's shoulders sagged. These stubborn people; he could see Aria's resemblance to Isika now. It would be a journey filled with children, then, because Jabari knew that Ivram wouldn't deny Aria the right to find her brother. He shrugged.

"Take it up with Ivram," he said, and both Ben and Isika looked at him with wide eyes. He put his hands out, palms up. "I'm not in charge of this journey," he said. "I can't tell her whether she can come or not."

Isika looked like she was going to argue, but which way Jabari didn't know. She didn't say anything, though, and he watched her hands clench and unclench around the fabric in her lap a few times before she straightened them and smoothed her crumpled tunic.

They ate in silence for a while, then Aria had another question.

"How is our mother?"

Isika gasped, and Ben looked down at the ground. Jabari didn't know where to look. This was a lot harder than he had thought it would be. Isika leaned forward, getting closer to her sister. Jabari saw the physical resemblance between them when they were near each other. Something about their forehead and their eyes. Aria was lovelier, but Isika looked stronger and wilder, as though she belonged in a forest. Aria's eyes were guarded as Isika looked into them. Jabari felt horrible as he understood that Aria didn't like her sister, and maybe even felt hatred for her. Aria was the sibling who had been cast away.

"She died, Aria," Isika said, and Aria's guard slipped. Tears filled her eyes, and she lifted a hand to her face, sobbing. Isika reached across the table and caught her other hand, holding it tightly. "After you were given over, she never recovered. She died two weeks later."

Aria took deep breaths and blinked tears out of her eyes, dashing them away with the back of her hand. "Who took care of Kital?" she asked. "Father?"

"No," Isika said. "I did."

Aria had been looking at her plate, but at that, she glanced up at her sister, measuring. Jabari saw that she was really looking at Isika, her eyes still wet, taking in what Isika's life had been while Aria had been in Maween, learning new ways, gaining a new family who took care of her.

"It was hard," Isika said. "I missed you so much, I missed our mother so much I felt like I would die. But I had to take care of Kital all day and all night when he couldn't sleep. Father would yell at me to make him quiet, and sometimes I couldn't, and I had to walk the grounds with the street dogs." She glanced at Benayeem. "But I wouldn't change it, wouldn't give him to someone else. He was my baby."

Aria watched her with a serious look on her face, then stood abruptly. "I need to go. I'll see you in the morning." She walked away, paused, then turned back to them. "What will you do?" Her eyes were accusing. "When you find him, will you go home?"

"Back to Father?" Isika asked. "What do you mean?"

"No," Ben said. "We're staying here."

"You understand that we can't go back, right?" Isika asked Aria. The younger girl towered over the three of them on their cushions.

Jabari nodded. "The poison-landers would send them away again, little sister. Or worse."

Aria gave one short nod, then left, slipping through the crowd in the great room, a brief blur of orange, and Jabari didn't see her anymore. When he looked at Isika, he saw tears in her eyes, and he looked back down at his food, not hungry anymore.

THEY WALKED BACK through the great hall on their way out. Isika and Ben were drooping, and Jabari felt half-dead, ready for bed and sleep. He tried not to think about the fact that they would be leaving again at first light. As much as he loved seeking, he wouldn't mind a few more days of rest. Gavi caught up to them in the hall.

"How did it go with Aria?" he asked.

Jabari waved his hand in a way that meant just okay, and Gavi nodded.

"Where were you?" Jabari asked.

"With our parents, Yab, where do you think?"

"Is Mother fretting about us leaving tomorrow?"

"Again...what do you think?"

"Better you than me, you've always been better at taking the mother guilt." Gavi stuck a finger in Jabari's ribs, and Jabari shoved back, knocking him into Ben, who laughed and pushed Gavi away. It turned into a bit of a wrestling match, there in the palace hall, until Isika's voice broke through.

"Ben!" she called, her voice high and urgent. She had stopped somewhere behind them and was standing still, eyes riveted to one of the many murals that lined the halls of the palace. There were scenes of deer and birds and ships on seas, but Isika stood before the large portrait at the base of the tall staircase. She stood with her hand covering her mouth, and as they hurried back, she turned and stared at Jabari with frantic eyes.

"Who is this?" she asked.

Ivram walked toward them from the dining hall, where the feast was still in full swing. Jabari met the elder's eyes, then turned to face the portrait Isika was staring at. Jabari knew the painting as well as he knew his own face—he had seen it all his life. It was the image of a tall, thin woman with skin as black as night, her eyes like stars in the dark beauty of her face. An Othra sat on her shoulder, and her hand rested on the head of a tall, deer-like creature standing beside her.

She wore impressive robes in the painting, flowing like water, shot through with every color in the rainbow. But it was her face that Isika stared at.

"She was our queen," Jabari said, his voice soft.

Ivram reached them, his silverwood staff in hand, shining blue in the dim light of the corridor.

"This was painted just before Queen Azariyah was taken from us," Ivram said. "Why, what is the matter, child?"

Isika was shaking. "For a moment, I thought it was my mother. She has the very same face, here," she pointed at her own brow, "and here." She put her hands over the lower half of her face. "Do you see, Ben? She looks like Mother." Her words ended in a sob, and Ivram's staff flashed white in the dim hallway, nearly blinding Jabari.

Benayeem nodded slowly, his eyes fixed on the painting. Jabari and Gavi stood staring at the two of them, then Jabari cocked an eyebrow at Ivram.

"Uncle?" he said.

Ivram heaved a deep sigh. "I think it's possible," he said, "and even likely, that you are the grandchildren of our lost queen." His staff glowed bright white, energy crackling off of it. Jabari had known the words that would come from Ivram's mouth, and he heard them now with a sinking in his stomach, as though they had been written down many years before and handed to him here, to read at last, to know as truth. He shook his head. He had been searching for the queen for many years, and it couldn't be that Isika was the queen's grandchild. Isika wasn't right at all. Did it mean that the lost queen of the Maweel was dead?

Jabari heard the wings of the Othra as they drew near, and then he was shocked because he could hear Isika's voice in his head as she called to them.

Help me, she said, without speaking aloud.

Don't be distressed, child, Efir answered, and the words echoed in Jabari's mind. *We're here.*

CHAPTER 24

Somehow—amid the confusion and aftermath of Ivram's statement, the discussions with the regent and his wife and the other elders—Efir managed to impress on Karah that Isika and Ben needed rest.

After what felt like a blur of steps and whispers, they found themselves back in Dawit and Teru's house. Teru showed Isika to a room that had two beds, one with Ibba already sleeping in it. Isika crawled into Ibba's bed with her, leaving her own empty. The little girl smiled in her sleep, and Isika threw her arm around her and sank thankfully into oblivion.

IN THE MORNING, she woke smelling cinnamon and coffee. Ibba was gone. When Isika reached the kitchen, she found her little sister sitting on the stone cooking bench, chattering away to Teru, who was bending over the stove, clothed in a soft gray robe. Ibba's hair had been braided into dozens of tiny braids with bright stone beads threaded on the ends. When she shook her head, her hair clattered. She grinned at Isika.

"I wondered when you would wake up!" she said. "You slept forever!"

"I did?" Isika teased, reaching out to feel one of the beads and laying her hand softly on her sister's cheek. "We certainly couldn't wake you up yesterday evening."

Isika took a good look at Teru as the older woman turned and smiled at her. She was of medium height and a little plump, the kind of woman you could lean on while she stroked your hair, and she was beautiful, with high cheekbones and soft eyes. Isika sighed. She wanted to stay in this house and let this woman care for her.

"Come and eat, child," Teru said. "Then you can dress in your travel clothes. I hate that those elders are taking you away so soon, you had such a day yesterday, and no time to recover." Isika squared her shoulders. If she wasn't careful, she could let Teru's sympathy absorb every bit of her willpower. To face the day, Isika needed hard-faced strength. She sat in the nearest chair at the table, which was laid with the same bright ceramic plates she had seen yesterday. She picked up a plate and looked at it curiously. It didn't look anything like the rough clayware of the Workers at all.

"How do they make this so thin?" she asked.

Teru laughed and said, "When you get back, I'll bring you to the master potter's workshop, and you can see for yourself."

"They make these here in the city?"

"Yes, like everything else. The master potter is an old friend of mine from school days. I'll introduce you."

Teru bustled around the kitchen, gathering food. When she came to the table, Isika set the plate down so the older woman could lay several spiced pancakes and a pile of thin-sliced mushrooms on her plate. The mushrooms were fried lightly, rich and full of flavor. Isika ate quickly, piling wild fruit jam on her pancakes, nodding at Ben, who appeared from the back of the house, his eyes sleepy. He took a deep breath at the sight of the food on the table, then popped his eyes at Isika.

She knew how he felt. This was a big change, to say the least. They had gone from one meal of porridge a day to multiple meals of fresh, aromatic food. Isika could see a difference in herself and her siblings. They were stronger and more sure with their bodies. She hoped they were ready for whatever this journey would bring.

AFTER THEY ATE, Teru brought out Isika's new traveling clothes: another tunic and pair of wide-legged pants, but dark brown and made of a tougher material, with pockets in the tunic and orange embroidery on the collar and hems. After Isika put them on, Teru handed her a belt to buckle around her waist. It had several pockets as well. In one, Isika found a compass; in another, a knife. Then Teru handed her a tall pair of boots, like the ones Jabari had been wearing on their last journey. They were made of the softest leather, and Isika loved them immediately. She laced them over the wide pants, all the way to her knees, and afterward, she stood and looked at herself in the mirror while Teru rebraided her hair so that it wrapped around her head, no loose hair hanging. She looked like a warrior. All she needed was a bow or a sword. She walked out to find Benayeem with Dawit, dressed almost identically to her, except instead of a tunic, he wore a shirt. Teru handed Isika a scarf.

"This is a *ser*," she said. "It will come in handy. You can wrap it around your head if the sun is beating down on you," she showed her, "or use it as a towel, or wet it if you are too hot." Isika wrapped it loosely around her neck and looked at the kind older couple. Teru handed them each a bag of food. Isika glanced inside and found a water flask, bread, meat, and nuts.

"How can we thank you?" she asked the kind couple who had taken them in.

"By coming back so we can really begin our life together," she said. "Now, you three need to go. You're supposed to meet the others at the palace, and I dare not go because Ivram will receive a tongue-lashing like he has never had in his life if I get my sights on him."

Isika smiled and impulsively reached out to give the older woman a hug. She smelled like flowers and warm skin, a motherly smell a little like Isika's own mother.

She swallowed past a tight feeling in her throat. "What do we call you? I haven't even asked."

"You can call us Auntie and Uncle. Or Auntie Teru and Uncle Dawit if you want. But Auntie and Uncle will do."

Isika smiled and gave Auntie Teru's hands one last squeeze. "We will come back, Auntie. Come, Ibba," she said. "The regent wife is waiting for you." Ibba sat on a cushion on the floor, pulling a piece of string for a kitten to pounce on.

"I'm not coming," she announced. "I'm staying here with Auntie."

"No, you said that you would come and stay with Laylit," Isika said.

"Oh, but I changed my mind," she said. "And I'm staying here."

Isika felt like she was getting a glimpse of what it was like to work with herself. She looked at Auntie. Teru shrugged. Isika thought quickly. She didn't want to start the journey by dragging Ibba somewhere she didn't want to go. Surely the regent wife would understand and not want to uproot the little girl again.

"Okay," she said, "you can stay here. But behave."

Ibba waved from her place on the floor. Isika could tell it meant nothing to her that Isika had given her permission because Ibba hadn't planned to come in any case. Isika gave Ben a look, and he frowned back at her. He looked worried.

"I think we're going to see a side of Ibba we haven't seen before," Isika said.

"We're seeing new sides of all of us," he agreed, "but I'm a bit worried, Isika. The regent wife isn't going to like that."

Isika shrugged. "She'll have to accept it."

They waved their way out the door, and Isika looked back

at the little house on the side of the hill as they climbed down. Auntie Teru and Uncle Dawit stood in the doorway with their arms around each other, and Isika realized how hard this must be for them; their son had gone on a journey like this and had never come back. Isika gave a final wave, and her heart leapt to see them raise their hands in a wave of their own.

BEN COULD SEE a crowd waiting outside the palace as he and Isika drew near, walking down the steep path. The regent and his wife were there, as well as several other men and women dressed in the robes of elders. There were others in traveling clothes, and Ben assumed they were the rangers who would accompany them. Then there were Jabari and Gavi.

"Welcome, travelers," Andar said from the top of the palace steps, a smile on his face. He was tall and imposing, standing with his wife, who shone and glittered in the sun. Her robes were covered with tiny pieces of mirror, and they caught the morning light, flashing in their eyes.

But then Andar shifted his focus to Jabari. "Your boot is unlaced, son," he said. Suddenly the elders didn't seem as intimidating anymore.

Jabari glanced at his boot and frowned, quickly bending and tying it.

"As though I don't know how to take care of my boots

after all these long months in the wilderness," he grumbled to Gavi, who stood smirking beside him.

"Our friends look better than when we found them, eh, Yab?" Gavi said as Jabari straightened, and Jabari grinned.

"Look at that," he said. He reached out and clapped Ben on the shoulder and nodded at Isika. "Completely respectable travelers now, no longer running around in their underclothes."

Ben laughed, and even Isika smiled. Overhead, the trees shook in a light breeze, and the cool of the morning softened the sun that shone on them.

"Respectable or not, I don't know what rangers are," Ben said.

"They're like grownup seekers," Jabari said. "They do similar work, but on the more dangerous borders, and they have to fight to protect us sometimes."

Then Laylit spoke.

"Where is Ibba?" she asked, raising her voice to reach them from the steps.

Isika exchanged a glance with Ben.

"She didn't come," she said. "She wanted to stay with Auntie Teru."

Laylit stared at Isika, her gaze cold and her face upset.

"I requested that she stay with me," she began, but Andar put a hand on her arm.

"Yes, love," he said softly, "but she is a child, and she needs rest."

"Our sister became close to Auntie Teru quickly," Ben said,

surprising himself. "It was a long journey, and she is tired." He didn't feel anything wrong coming from Jabari's mother, beside a bit of pride, perhaps. As he reached to hear the music that came from Laylit, he heard sorrow, most of all. It made him want to be gentle with her, no matter how fierce her look was.

Laylit drew herself up. She gave them another look, and it held a challenge. There was a lot of tension in the group— Ben heard echoes of it everywhere. Much of it must have come from the night before, when Isika had recognized their queen, and Ivram had made the guess he did.

"Why is she behaving this way?" Isika whispered to him.

"Maybe she thinks you want to rule her country," Ben said, "now she knows your ancestor might be the queen." He was only half joking.

Isika snorted, crossing her arms. "She can have her country. I don't want to run any country. I just want to find my brother and get back to Auntie's to eat more of her jam."

Ben laughed, and a bit of his own tension eased. To get away from the eyes of the elders, he bent and retied his own laces, though they didn't need it. There was a little burst of activity at the edge of the group, and when he stood up, his other sister was there. Aria stood straight and tall, her silver-wood bow in her hand and a pack on her back. Her boots had buckles on them, and Ben stared at them, thinking of how expensive they must be. She had a scarf tied around her hair, and she was so surprising, standing there, real and taking up space in the world, in a way he had thought would never happen again. She was very much alive.

"You came," Isika said, hurrying to give her sister a hug.

"Of course," she said, stiffly hugging Isika back. "I told you I would."

Ben hugged Aria lightly, and Jabari and Gavi greeted her with their hands on their hearts in the custom of the Maweel. With the cluster of kids, Ivram, and four rangers, there were ten travelers. Andar held his hands out over them and spoke the travel blessing.

"Go well, with speed,
The road be smooth
The trees give their bounty
Your hearts thankful and brave
Come back to us quickly."

PART III

CHAPTER 25

They walked along the road that led out of the city, between people who waved from their houses and occasionally offered gifts. Ben found himself somewhere near the end of the line of travelers, Isika and Gavi behind him. And then Ivram was there, smiling at Ben, lines spreading from his eyes in fans that reached down his dark cheeks, his grizzled hair glowing in the morning light. Ben stared at the beautiful silverwood staff that Ivram always kept with him. It shone slightly, though it was harder to tell in the bright morning sun.

"I thought we could walk together for a time," Ivram said. "To talk."

Ben nodded, intimidated despite himself. The elder was so tall, his body bent slightly at the shoulders as he leaned his head to talk to Ben. His silver head matched the gorgeous staff, and the deep lines around his eyes told Ben that he was older than Ben had first thought.

"Of course, sir," Ben said.

"We call our elders Uncle and Aunt here," Ivram said.

"Even for someone like you?" Ben asked.

"Yes, for we are all sisters and brothers. To lord over someone is to break the bond between the Shaper and the shaped. Our regent should be the lowest among us."

It didn't seem that things were working out that way. Ben thought of Jabari and his quick anger at Isika, of Laylit, and her frustration at being defied by a child.

"Of course we are still human," Ivram said, as though he was reading Ben's mind. "We often need reminders. It's why we have each other. But do you have questions for me? This must be strange for you."

It came to Ben in a rush, what Ivram was offering. Ben didn't like to ask Jabari too many questions, afraid to show his ignorance. Ivram was offering to be an information source, and Ben's shyness fled.

Isika pushed forward and stepped onto Ben's other side.

"I have so many questions!" she said. "Can I walk with you and talk as well?"

"Of course," Ivram said. "We have room for another. Although you may find yourself walking in the trees at the narrower points in the path. Ask away."

They were silent for a moment, and Ben wondered if he would get the courage to ask about his strange inner music, the drums, and the way he could read the intentions of people. Isika spoke first.

"Jabari told us about the different gifts. So far, we know about healing and protecting."

"Justice, too," Ben interjected.

"What are the other gifts?" Isika went on.

"Good question," Ivram said. "I don't know that even we know all the possibilities of gifts and magic. We could be surprised." He looked up at the sky, squinting at one of the Othra, who wheeled high overhead.

He went on in his rich, deep voice. "There are some gifts we train and honor. Justice, or discerning, as you mentioned. That's a rare and very welcome one. It's great if there is a dispute over property lines, and a person can just sense where the line is supposed to be." He smiled. "Then protection—that's pulling down the walls and fighting all the other ways the poison reaches us. You saw that at work. Was it a little shocking to you?"

"That's an understatement," Isika said, popping her eyes at Ben.

Ivram chuckled under his breath. "I have wondered how it would look to a person from a Worker village. Let's see... healing—that's healing from poison but from heartbreak and sickness as well. Jabari said Ibba might have a gift for healing, and you too, Isika. Then there's gathering—growing the food we eat and bringing it in for the people and let's see... building. The building gift can be for anything, from larges things like homes to small things like the cups we use. It is the gift to speak to the things we make, so they perform what we need them to. Then there is the rarest gift—the life gift."

He breathed a deep sigh, smiling.

"People with the life gift can speak to animals and the land, and sometimes even learn how to break the normal rules of the earth and make nature follow their will, bringing the land itself back to health when it has been poisoned."

They stared at him.

"Jabari has the life gift as well as the protector gift," Ivram went on. "He is a very gifted young man, perhaps the most gifted that we have had among us in many years." Ben remembered Jabari with the Othra, the way they would speak to him without using words.

Up ahead, Jabari turned and looked smugly at them, wiggling his eyebrows.

"Even the dullest of ears can hear a compliment to itself," Ivram called. "Tell me, Jabari, what gifting traits did you see in Isika in your travels?"

Jabari frowned, then turned forward and kept walking. "She did magic," he called back to them, "but I didn't see strong traits of any one gift in her," he said.

Isika bristled. Ivram smiled at her, putting a hand on her shoulder.

"She may have the traits of all the gifts," he said. "And that's the rarest of all."

"The goddesses forbid the use of magic," Ben said, almost to himself.

"That's because using gift magic draws on love and connection to the rest of the Creation. Mugunta wants to keep us dependent on slow and useless sacrifices, on our own work. So the goddesses come flying out of the Great Waste to forbid the gifts, saying it is unholy. Fighting the work and lies of the demon magic is one of the biggest charges of Nenyi, the great Shaper."

"Who is he?"

"Nenyi is first and last. She always was and always will be. She is neither male nor female, person nor animal, star nor sea. She is father and mother. Her love goes on forever, like a great ocean, but larger."

Ivram paused and smiled at them, the lines around his eyes very deep. "She is."

Ben stared at the ground ahead of him as the words lit a fire within him, but Isika sighed.

"You've just called Nenyi 'she!' How can I understand if I don't know what he or she is?"

Ivram nodded. "We always want to make the Shaper smaller, to make him look like us, to imagine he makes the mistakes we do. Nenyi is neither and both. She is higher, greater, encompasses all, and is none. She is not something we have made. We have to learn to be comfortable with the mystery of the Uncreated One. We cannot contain the Life-giver." He went on.

"I was an advisor to the queen before she was taken from us. Things were very different then. Imagine knowing that everything is connected to everything else, that all goes back in a long line to the Uncreated One himself, that all will continue as it should. This is how it was before our queen was kidnapped. She was our strongest link to the Shaper, she was the conduit."

"How could she be kidnapped if she was so strong?" Isika asked.

Ivram was silent, and Ben looked at him in time to see a shadow cross his face.

"We don't know," he said. "But I believe our queen was betrayed. The deepest poison is betrayal, and our beloved queen was human, so betrayal would make her very weak. None of us can be as strong as we should be if others are using poison against us."

They walked in silence for a while, and Ben thought about the queen, wondering the ultimate question. Who was she to them? *Was she their grandmother? The singing mother their own mother had told them about?*

Ivram spoke again. "We are the saddest of people," he said, "and that is why we sing the sad songs and mourn. The poison breaks the world away from what it should be. But we are also the most joyful because we know how it can be. How it was, once."

"Restoration," Ben murmured.

"Yes," he said. "Exactly. But if I'm not mistaken, you have a question for me, young one." He looked at Ben.

Ben smiled. "Does your gift include mind-reading?" he asked.

"Only when the thoughts of the person are practically leaping out of their eyes," the elder said.

Ben smiled again, then his smile faded. How could he ask, especially with Isika walking beside him? He had never before put the things he wanted to say into words. But it was past time to know, to understand.

"All my life," he began, darting a look at Isika, who watched him, puzzled, "I have heard music, felt music, felt drums, seen colors somewhere inside myself. Drums of doom, I call them to myself. Strange, horrible music sometimes. And then sometimes, beautiful sounds and light and colors." His shoulders slumped. It sounded crazy, crazier than he had thought when he said it out loud. But he trudged on, committed now—maybe they would believe him insane, but there was nothing he could do about it.

"Lately, I have noticed that with the music, I can see into the thoughts of people. At home in the village, the songs were almost always songs of doom. But since we have been journeying, the music lets me know when something will be okay. Or what I should think or do. When Isika broke down the walls, I didn't sense anything wrong, there was no music telling me it was wrong. I heard beautiful sounds, so I knew I needed to stand with her. Or when," he spoke in a rush, determined to get it all out before anyone interrupted him, "the men came in the night to take us, I woke because of the drums that warned me."

He dared a glance at them. Isika was staring at him, and he quickly at the ground and went on. "I'm beginning to understand a little. But all my life, it has made me feel insane, like I might die. I had to hide, all the time, to keep from going crazy."

He waited for Ivram to speak. Isika spoke first. "You really have all of that going on inside you, all the time?"

He nodded, miserably, his shoulders hunched.

"It does sound like a lot, Benayeem," Ivram said. His deep voice had a warm, comforting tone to it, and Ben looked at his face. He didn't look horrified, only puzzled.

"Young one, I have heard of this only once before, and I need to confer with the Othra before I can give you an answer. But in the simplest terms, you seem to have a gift for Justice, which lets you discern the truth from falseness or right from wrong in a way that others have to guess at. I have this gift, and this is why I am an advisor. But the last time I have heard of it displaying itself this way, with your own body as the instrument for your discerning, is hundreds of years ago, in a time which is long past."

"Can you just tell me if I'm crazy?" Ben asked, feeling desperate.

Ivram smiled, and the creases around his eyes were very deep, his eyes very kind.

"You are certainly not crazy. Chosen, maybe, but not crazy. I can help you control this, young one."

It was comforting. Ben's shoulders relaxed. As he walked, he felt the light heart that came from a secret spoken aloud. He didn't need to hide anymore.

CHAPTER 26

*I*sika was thinking about Ben, stunned by his revelations of years of an inner life that was unknown to her, and she barely noticed they were getting close to the river until they rounded a curve in the path and suddenly there it was. Three canoes were on the riverbank.

She came to a halt beside Jabari.

"We're taking boats?" she asked.

He nodded. "To save time," he said. "We'll take the river nearly to the sea, then walk to the last place we knew they were, the boat marks that the Hadem told us about."

Two of the canoes carried three people, and the last one held four. Isika rode in the canoe that had four people; Jabari, Aria, Benayeem, and herself. The boat settled low in the water. Isika closed her eyes and dipped her hand in the river, feeling the sharp flame of life within. The river at its headwaters was very pure, cold, and clear, with nothing but fish and stones in it.

"Jabari," she asked as they started off, Ben with one paddle and Jabari with the other, "why didn't we take this river on our way to the city, if it's faster?"

Jabari smiled and shrugged. "We could have," he said. "But I was on seeking duty. And I felt that I needed to have a little more time to get to know you before we reached the city. You can't always rush things, little sister."

Isika felt a flash of anger. "Sometimes, you need to rush things," she said. "Such as when a little boy is in danger."

Jabari's face grew serious. "We didn't know then that he was in danger. And it's not nearly as fast to row upstream. It wouldn't have saved much time. Plus, your spindly arms couldn't have done it." He was teasing her again, just like that. She sat back in her seat, feeling a little better at his answer, but still desperately worried about her brother.

Aria was silent, gazing out over the water. Reeds lined the banks of the river, the silverwood trees were tall overhead. The sun shone through the trees, falling across the boats with dapples of light and shadow dancing across Jabari and Ben's arms as they paddled. Behind the silverwood trees were taller trees with feathery tops. Birds swooped over the water, chirping about food and sky. Isika turned her face up and tried to rid herself of the deep, hot lump of fear in her belly.

Kital was so small and vulnerable. Ivram had said that betrayal was the most dangerous poison. The Workers had betrayed each of the children they gave over. Maybe that was why Aria seemed to be so angry with them. Was it a poison that could ever be removed? Or did it remain and fester? Would Kital ever be the same? Or Aria?

Isika turned to her sister. "What is your gift?" she asked.

Aria gave her a cool, level look before answering. "Protection." After a moment, she added, "Most of the rescued are gifted in protection. Ivram believes it is because we were betrayed, and the longing for our own protection grows into a gift for protecting others." She looked out over the river again.

"Aria," Isika said, her voice low and intense. "You know I didn't send you away, right? I was only ten years old."

"You stood there," Aria answered. "You didn't come after me." Her face was hard and shuttered, a gated house. She chewed her lip, then reached to take the paddle from Benayeem, paddling with Jabari, her arms strong and quick. Her hair scarf was loose, and since her hands were busy, Isika retied it for her. Aria's shoulders remained rigid. Jabari glanced back, and Isika saw a flash of pity in his eyes.

Aria was right, though. Isika hadn't come after her. When Isika was ten years old, she hadn't even known it was a possibility, and even if she had, she wouldn't have left her mother. And if Isika had come after her sister, what would have happened to the newborn Kital? The futility of the past struck her silent, and she didn't speak again. Overhead the Othra flew, crossing paths with a flock of white birds.

Wait, child, be patient, Efir told her, and she took a breath, not yet used to hearing their voices from afar. She took the paddle from Jabari and rowed against the pain in her heart.

They were on the river for two more days, stopping at night to set up bedrolls and sleep. It was all very organized, with Gavi and one of the new rangers in charge of the food.

Between meals, Isika nibbled at the nuts Teru had given her. The bread was gone on the first day, and on the second, they relied on fish that the rangers caught, fruit from the trees, and Gavi's ever-present bag of potatoes. He roasted the potatoes in the coals of the fire, and they ate hot fish and potatoes with a little salt in the cool evenings, the wind on their cheeks cooling them after another day in the sun.

Resting under the stars, weak from the strain of sitting in the canoe all day, Isika was sleepy and content. But fear for Kital never left her, and sometimes it washed over her like a tide, threatening to overwhelm her.

On the third day, when the river was impossibly wide and drawing near to the sea, they rowed to the bank and pulled the boats up high, covering them with wide branches from the nearby trees, the ones with leaves as tall as a person. Isika adjusted her boots and looked up to see Aria doing the same, tightening one of her laces. She met Isika's eyes as she straightened, and for a moment, they looked at one another, then Aria turned back to Jabari and continued talking with him. Isika felt close to tears. Overhead the Othra fluttered. *Wait, child.*

The landscape was different. The trees grew sparser, and red rocks lined the path the rangers chose. In places, the boulders towered over their heads, and Isika felt prickles up her neck as she thought of all the possible hiding spots for waiting enemies. The rangers were on their guard, taking turns to run ahead and check the road ahead of the company. The red rocks were beautiful and strange, twisting in shapes that curled into the sky. Others were sheared away, with long flat faces. Often there were carvings in the walls of rock—pictures, and words that Isika couldn't quite make out.

They rounded a curve in the road, and ahead Jabari and a ranger stood searching the ground. Isika and the others soon caught up with them.

"This is it?" Ivram asked.

"I think we found it," Jabari said, nodding and scanning the ground.

"Found what?" Isika asked.

"The place where our rescuers were overtaken," he answered, pointing at various places on the ground. "There's a poisonous magic residue here, and the earth is churned up and kicked around. See...here. And here. So this is the story, they were already on the path back home when they were taken."

Isika saw what he meant. There were long stripes in the earth in places, as though something had been dragged through the dirt.

"Why didn't they row up the river?" she asked.

"The rescuers leave the longboats on the beach and walk back. It gives time for the rescued one to grow more comfortable with a small group, before entering a city full of thousands."

Isika saw a patch of color behind a rock, and she cried out, running to pick it up. It was one of the sending cloths that she had carefully placed around Kital's head in the small boat.

"This is Kital's!" she said.

Aria joined her. "His sending cloth," she said.

"I'm surprised the rescuers kept it," Isika said.

"They always do," she replied, her voice cool as usual. "As a reminder of what we came from, what we were saved from."

Isika looked at her. "I'm so sorry, Aria," she said, putting a hand on her sister's arm. Aria stared down at Isika's hand on her arm, then slowly reached up and covered it with her own. She gave Isika's hand a brief squeeze, then let go. Isika's heart leapt up. It was something.

"We go this way," Ivram said, indicating a narrow goat path that went up and over the rocks toward the sea. "The tracks lead back toward the water."

Isika walked behind her sister. Overhead, the Othra swept through the sky, and Eemia sang a brief song. Isika watched everyone lift their heads as they felt the comfort of the huge bird's music. She climbed quickly, passing rangers on the rocks. If they were going to find Kital around the next curve, she wanted to be at the very beginning of the company that found him.

There was an even smaller path that was parallel and went straight up instead of curving, and she walked along it, ignoring the teasing she heard behind her. She thought about how she would have climbed this path with the Workers, half-starved and exhausted, and she exulted in her new strength. She could have run straight up the hill, but she held herself back and simply walked. Behind her, the teasing changed to words of praise as Isika climbed up the faces of rocks with only shallow places for hands and feet. She seemed to know instinctively where to put her hands, and it seemed as though the rock helped her, giving her spaces for her feet to cling to, holding her up.

"Isika climbs like a young kid," Ivram yelled from the path below. "Wait, young one, I'll climb with you if you have the patience for an old goat."

Isika slowed reluctantly. She could have scaled a mountain, feeling the way she did. While she waited for Ivram to catch up with her, she looked at her hands. They looked like the same hands she had always had, but they could do so much more. Every day, she was stronger. She still had her hands held out in front of her when Ivram arrived.

"I don't understand what is happening to me," she told him.

CHAPTER 27

*I*vram and Isika walked side by side, slowly this time. To her right, Isika saw a ranger checking the nearby rocks. Overhead the Othra scanned the landscape as well.

Ivram seemed to know what she meant. "As far as I can tell," he said. "Your soul is returning to its proper home. You are becoming who you truly are, without shame or poison to hinder you. This seems to be your land, perhaps in a way that is deeper than any of us could know."

Isika looked at him and saw the questions of the queen's portrait in his eyes.

"Please tell me about your mother," he said. "What did she tell you about her life? About her mother?"

"She didn't tell us much," Isika said slowly. "I remember that her mother sang to her a lot and that she was very tall. But she died when my mother was only ten."

Out of the corner of her eye, Isika saw Ivram stop, and she turned to look at him. He held a hand to his face, and when he pulled his hand away, his eyes were wet. It struck Isika that maybe he had known the grandmother she had only ever heard about. He had been her friend.

"Go on," he said, his voice hoarse with tears.

"They lived in a city in the desert, the same place I remember living when I was very small, before Ibba was born." She paused, looking at the clear blue sky and the red of the rocks beneath them. "The walls in that city were very high. I don't think we could see outside the city."

"Did your mother seem to have any... abilities?" Ivram asked. Isika didn't have to slow down for him. He walked like a much younger man, without leaning on the staff he carried with him. Isika could see tear tracks on his cheeks.

"You mean like gifts?" Isika thought about it, then shook her head. "I don't remember anything. She seemed frail. But she had so many children, and I think she was still very young."

"She would have hardly over thirty when she died," Ivram murmured, and Isika looked at him, startled. "If indeed she was our queen's daughter, I was there the day she was born. She must have had you when she was only twenty years old. Living among poison, with so many children, it's no wonder she seemed frail."

Isika felt a painful flash of guilt for being one of the children who had weakened her mother.

"How did you come to leave that place?" Ivram asked, and

Isika blinked back the tears that threatened to come, pressing her forehead with her hands, trying to push away the ache of losing her mother.

"I think someone helped us. Someone my mother knew. The memory is fuzzy. There was a man, and we left at night. We walked and walked for months, and we finally found the Worker village. My mother was strong on that journey, pregnant with Ibba and carrying Aria most of the way, but she was exhausted by the end, and she never fully recovered."

Isika paused and took a breath. "When Aria was given over, grief took the rest of her strength. She talked about a different way sometimes, she told me that the Worker way was not the only way to live. I didn't really understand what she meant, and I think she couldn't tell me. Her name was Amani."

She looked at Ivram. Tears were openly streaming down his cheeks. "Was that your queen's baby's name?" she whispered.

"No," he said. "Her name was Azariyah, like her mother before her. Amani was her middle name. But it would have been giving away too much, to keep her royal name, the name of our beloved city. Her mother would have kept it hidden to protect her."

He stopped in the path, turned his face to the sky, and began to sing. Isika was growing used to Maweel people singing all the time, whenever they felt like it. Maybe it was too much, what Ivram felt, to simply think about, and he needed to sing to get the sadness out.

"Lost, we lost her.
All of heaven grieves
Take this sorrow
Oh, take this sorrow
Bring back our beloved
Lost, we lost her."

Ivram wiped at his face and reached for Isika's hand. "I am almost certain," he said. "I'm nearly sure that you are Queen Azariyah's granddaughter." The gem on the staff flashed white again, and overhead, the Othra gave three long cries that raised the hair on Isika's arms and made her skin tingle. Her face flushed with heat.

"Do you know what this means, child?" he asked. "You are her descendent. Our lost queen has come back to us."

Isika shivered. She knew what he said was true. It had been growing in her from the day they entered the city. But she didn't know how to be a queen, and she recoiled from the thought of ruling anything. She felt small and broken from days and years of serving as a Worker. She shook her head swiftly.

"I can't, Uncle. I—" Ivram stopped her and put a hand on her shoulder, squeezing gently.

"Don't think too much on it," he said. "We'll take it slowly. For now, let us find your little brother." He smiled. "We can't lose anyone else."

THAT NIGHT they camped in the shelter of a tall red rock. Isika climbed it as the others made the camp, and as she looked, her sight seemed to fly far past what she should have been able to make out. She saw the sea and three large boats in the distance, perhaps a half day's journey away.

"We will reach them tomorrow," she said when she came down from the rock. The others were sitting around the fire, and they looked at her, then at each other. Ivram bowed his gray head.

"Very well," he said, not questioning how she knew. "We will be ready."

He stared into the flames, his hands resting on the top of the silverwood staff. Aria and Jabari sat side by side, looking over their arrows, talking quietly together. Isika felt a twinge of jealousy as she looked at them, though she couldn't say for what. Perhaps for the way they seemed to belong there, to be natural together in a way she would never be. Aria's face when she looked at Jabari was so open, unlike when she looked at Isika and Ben and seemed to be keeping herself miles away.

"What will we do when we find them?" Isika asked. "We won't hurt anybody, will we?"

"Sometimes, we must fight," Ivram said, "though we don't love it and don't want to cause pain."

Isika couldn't stop thinking of herself as a Worker, toiling away in a system she hadn't known a way out of. The people who had stolen Kital—did they mean to be evil? She didn't know, and she fretted over the thought of hurting or killing anyone.

Nirral flew into the camp and settled on a rock next to Isika. Efir drifted down from a high place in the sky and joined him.

To her surprise, they spoke so that only Isika could hear. She could see by the blankness on the other's faces and the echoes in her own mind that she was the only one hearing their words.

You will need to be very careful, child, Nirral said. The sea people have laid a poison that will attack your mind and the minds of your companions, setting one against the other.

We tell you, Efir added, because as the World Whisperer, you will be the strongest against this poison.

Isika spoke back to them from deep inside herself, not using words that others could hear, but shaping the words with her mind.

World Whisperer?

Ask the elder, Efir said, when you are alone.

Nirral went on. The poison is potent. There is something terrifying, something beyond the sea people alone. This is strong evil of Mugunta's making. Be aware. Be careful. You may be the only one who can withstand it.

Isika wanted to ask more, but just then, Gavi spoke. "Are you talking to them, Isika? Nirral, is she talking to you?" Nirral and Efir took off in a flurry of wings.

Isika nodded briefly at him.

"Did you see that?" Gavi asked Ivram. "Isika can mind-speak with the Othra. Animal speech. That's a life gift." Jabari scowled at his brother across the fire.

"I saw it," Ivram replied. He smiled into the fire. "But

you're about to let those potatoes burn, so maybe you should stick to worrying about your own gift, son."

Gavi lunged at the potatoes, which were smoking at the edges, and the company finished their food quickly, turning in for the night. Isika's stomach was tight with fear over the Othra's warning. She felt as though the company was walking into a death trap. She was sure that she wouldn't be able to sleep, but somehow she drifted off.

When she awoke, the moon had set, and the sky was filled with diamonds. She wasn't sure what had awakened her until she heard whispers in the dark.

"I don't know, Uncle. How can we be sure?"

"I do know, young one. I'm as sure as I have ever been."

"It bothers me. I worry that it's poison—demon magic. Look where she came from!"

"Jabari, demon magic cannot commune with Othra. You know that as well as anybody."

"No demon magic that we have seen before. What if it's different now?"

"Go to sleep. You'll be tired enough tomorrow without wrestling over matters that have been set in their course from the beginning of time."

"But—"

"Sleep," Ivram said, and the command in his voice was so strong that Isika blinked under it. She lay in her bedroll, feeling as though Jabari had hit her in the stomach. He thought she had demon magic? Did she? Her ears burned, and tears ached behind her eyes, but she blinked hard, refusing to let them fall.

She thought of Jabari reaching to pull her out of the river, of him saying, "You pulled the poison from the river into you!" Why did he doubt her now? Was it because he was the regent's son? She thought of the cold eyes of his mother.

Isika wanted to be miles away from the camp, away from the hurt of his words. She lay there with her heart and thoughts racing until the stars dimmed, and the sun came up.

As soon as she could see the shape of the rocks, she sat up in her bedroll and thought for a minute, then stood and packed her things into her sack. She walked away from the circle of sleeping bodies near the dying fire and climbed a short ledge that wasn't too far from where they had slept. The rocks began to glow as the sun rose. She could see for miles. It was so beautiful it could have made her cry, but she didn't want any more tears. Today was the day. Perhaps the poison from the Great Waste would be enough to pull the company apart; perhaps they would all die trying to save her brother.

She opened her mouth and sang. She sang a song of beginnings, of the first time the sun had risen on the newly made earth. She sang a song of thanks to the Uncreated One, recognizing it as something her mother had sung she was a child, though the words hadn't made sense to her then. She hadn't known what the silverwood trees were, or the crystalline water of a deep lake. She hadn't known about the red rocks and the blue of a clear sky. She had grown up in the desert, then moved to the dimness of the plains. She was being born anew, along with the earth as the sun rose again. When she stopped singing and looked down at the camp, she saw her sister looking up at her. Aria held her hand to her lips for just a moment and held it up to Isika, an old gesture from their mother. Isika grabbed at the air in front of her and brought it to her chest in response.

*a*fter they had eaten a small breakfast of potatoes and fish from the night before, the company set out.

"Potatoes and fish," Ben muttered to Isika as they walked. She poked him in the ribs.

"Are you really complaining about eating the same thing two days in a row?" she teased.

He grinned at her. "I can't wait to find Kital and get back to Auntie's for more of her food," he said.

She smiled at him, agreeing. Their smiles faded as they looked at each other.

"We'll find him, Isika," he said.

Isika stuck with Ben on the path, their shoulders touching occasionally. She needed to be around someone who believed in her, someone who knew her as she had been; just Isika, a hardworking girl with a sad life, someone who took care of people around her, someone who was tired and frail, not a girl who could speak to animals and suck poison out of rivers.

For the briefest of moments, Isika longed for her space on the floor in the small house in the Worker village, for the comfort of gathering the losh wood in the mornings, for the one simple meal a day that only just kept them alive. Life had all become too much, and there wasn't any time to take it in.

They walked without talking. Isika could hear the low tones of murmured conversation around her, but nothing loud enough to understand. She saw Gavi's blond head up ahead, the same height as Ivram's grizzled head beside him.

Benayeem glanced at her and touched her arm.

"How did you do that?" he asked quietly. "Speak to the Othra with your mind?"

Isika smiled and wrinkled her nose. "How would I describe it?" she said. "It was like thinking, I guess, but with more push. And toward them." She thought about it, catching sight of his quiver on his back. "As though I could shape my thoughts into an arrow and shoot it."

Ben nodded. "But how did you know how to do that?"

She shook her head. "I don't know." She thought for a minute. "I think I would have enjoyed it more if they weren't offering such scary news."

He laughed. "I can tell that you're not saying something," he said, one eyebrow raised in Isika's direction.

"What is this new ability to read minds?" she asked, reaching over to squeeze her brother's arm. "And this music? These tones that you've never told me about?"

He lifted his arms and dropped them. "We didn't know anything like this existed, sister. I thought I was going mad. But don't change the subject. What are you not saying?"

"I don't think I want to say it," she said.

"There's something that you have to do, something that others can't do, isn't there?" Isika looked up from the path, startled.

"I knew it would be something like that. If it was about some danger to the rest of us, you'd tell us right away."

She shrugged. "I think it will be dangerous for everyone, but everyone is expecting danger. Nirral said that I might be the only one who can tackle this particular evil, as he called it." Her throat felt tight then, and she dropped her head, remembering Jabari's words of the night before. *Demon magic.*

Ben linked his arm through hers, and they walked that way for a while. His quiver bumped her elbow every few steps, but she didn't want to pull away.

"We have to find Kital," Ben said again. "He deserves a chance to live here too."

"Do you like it with the Maweel?" Isika asked, angling her head to look at his face.

"Of course I do!" he said. "You do too! Or you did. Right?"

"Yes, I do," she said, but she was thinking about Jabari again. Maybe even if she didn't go back to the Worker village, she could live somewhere else. She didn't want to live where people looked at her with suspicion. She had lived her whole life that way, and it didn't seem fair anymore.

The farther they walked, the angrier Isika felt toward Jabari. She had long conversations with him in her head, telling him what she thought of him. At one point, she was so focused on the imaginary conversation that she forgot to watch her feet and stumbled into Ben. She laughed and apologized, but he pulled away from her.

"Watch it!" he said, scowling at her.

She frowned back at him. "Sorry. You don't have to talk like that."

"I wouldn't if you weren't so clumsy," he said, his voice getting louder as he spoke. "Be careful!"

She gasped. "I'm not clumsy!"

"Tell that to all the dishes you broke back in our house, right before this brilliant plan of yours to find the brother who we still can't find," he responded, and he sped up, so he was walking ahead of her rather than beside her. She wanted to scream at him, but she bit her tongue and stared at the back of his head. What was happening? She looked around. Ivram, at the head of the company, was shaking his head and thumping his staff on the ground.

"Coming unprepared to meet an enemy camp is unacceptable," he shouted. "We don't have enough for lunch for all these people. Have you ever tried boarding enemy ships on an empty stomach?"

"And what about the fact that we have no boats?" Gavi yelled back. "Have you thought of just how long it will take the rangers to retrieve our boats from upriver? Or did you expect us to run along the water's surface like insects?"

"You know nothing of war or battle plans!" Ivram shouted, halting in his steps, so the ranger behind him stumbled into him.

"So this is war, now? I thought it was a rescue party!"

At the back of the company, Aria yelled for Jabari to just leave her alone already. Isika rubbed at her forehead with her hands.

"Stop!" she shouted. Everyone turned to look at her with scowls on their faces. "This is the poison the Othra warned me of," she said, her voice ringing out in the silence. "We must be almost there. We have to stop arguing and be on our guard."

Ivram pinched the bridge of his nose, frowning, then he smiled a thin smile.

"Just now, I wanted to tell you to stop thinking you know more than an elder. This truly is dangerous poison."

"I was going to say the same thing," Jabari said, his fists clenched at his sides. "And I might still say it. Are you so much better than everyone around you, Isika?" He sneered. "You are new as a baby bird, there's no way your knowledge can be so advanced—it doesn't work that way. Unless, of course, your knowledge comes from demon magic."

Ben growled. "Don't talk to her that way," he said, advancing on Jabari with his own fists clenched.

"Oh, great deserts," Isika said, tugging her brother back toward her. "Listen to yourselves." She scanned the air for signs of the Othra, wishing for peace, but the sky was clear and empty. She looked at Ivram, pleading for his help with her eyes. He raised a hand.

"Okay, Isika is right. I'm now giving orders. Walk forward, carefully, and guard yourself against ill-temper toward your friends around you. We are very nearly there."

They walked again, this time mostly in silence besides an occasional, "Watch it," hissed in annoyed tones.

Isika fought deep doubt in herself. Did she have demon magic? The question repeated over and over inside her spinning head. How could she have magic from the Uncreated One when she had spent her life in the temples of the goddesses? She barely saw the path in front of her, but at some point, her eyes widened. The rocky path grew more damp, saturated with sea spray. They were drawing near to the great ocean.

She was just about to pull on Ivram's shirt to warn him when one of the rangers waved frantically for them to halt. They were in a narrow place between two sets of rocks, damp with spray, and just through the rock formations was a cove. The rocks continued into the sea in giant, intricate shapes.

At first, Isika was so distracted by the lacy, towering cliffs that she didn't see what everyone else was muttering about. But then she pulled up beside Gavi and saw what they pointed at. She felt sick—as though she would lose her breakfast—and put a hand over her mouth.

The sea was stone-still, a putrid, slimy green, with bubbles occasionally burping to the surface, yellowish foam gathered in heaps. In the distance, past the towering rocks, Isika could see two ships, spinning slowly, impossibly, as no ship can ever move, one clockwise and the other counter-clockwise, an endless whirling. It was horrifying, and it made her sick to look at them, but still, she stared, trying to discern whether Kital was on one of the ships. Of course, she could feel nothing.

One of the rangers broke away from the company and ran to the water, ignoring the screams that followed him. He waded into the scummy water, and it happened instantaneously. As soon as his feet touched the water, he fell heavily, his eyes open and staring. Gavi and another ranger ran to pull him by his shoulders, heaving him onto dry sand. The company gathered around the man. Another ranger stepped forward and bent over him, touching her palm to his face. She shuddered.

"I can heal him," she whispered. "But it will take all my strength. No one else can go in."

Jabari's breath hissed out between his teeth. "Uncle, what is this?"

Ivram's brow furrowed as he looked out toward the ships that spun at the mouth of the cove. "I've never seen anything like it," he said. "It looks as though the sea people are caught in it as much as we are."

The healer yelped. "He's dead," she said, her voice frantic. "It happened so quickly, I don't know how—like he was pulled beneath my reach." There was a stir as the other rangers rushed to kneel by the dead ranger. Ivram bent and checked the man's pulse, then bowed his head. Jabari jumped to his feet, shaking his head.

"It's no use," he said. "We need to give this mission up. There's nothing we can do."

Isika clenched her fists, shaking. "We can't give up! They have our people. You don't want to give up! What's wrong with you? Poison is making you talk like that." She felt the poison working on her so that even as she said it, she doubted herself.

"We don't know that they have Kital," Jabari said. "Or the others, for that matter. How can we ever tell, with this horrible water between us?"

"The Othra told me Kital was here," she answered, her chin thrust out at him.

"But we couldn't hear that, could we? Convenient of you to be so bold about something none of the rest of us could hear." She stared at him, telling herself it was only poison. She couldn't blame him for the unkind words.

"Ask them, Jabari. You can ask them."

"They aren't here, are they?" he said. "They've disappeared as usual." Isika stared at him. Surely he wasn't doubting the Othra's intentions now! She looked around. Every face was turned toward her, and she saw that no one believed her with a full heart, not even Ivram or Ben. Worse, their faces were shadowed and discouraged, as though they had all aged years since they arrived on this horrible rocky beach. Tears silently streamed down Aria's cheeks. Ivram's staff looked like nothing more than a stick in the gray light.

"We have to try, right?" Isika asked him, but even as she said the words, she felt a wave of the strongest longing, to turn back and go home to Auntie, to sleep on those beautiful cushions and drink a cup of hot tea, to forget it all.

"First, we must sing our songs of loss and mourn our brother," Ivram said. "And then we can talk, but I fear that there is nothing more that we can do, child. This poison is stronger than any I have ever seen in all my years. I don't even know what it is."

WHILE THE OTHERS piled stones around the dead ranger's body, Isika sat on the beach to think. Before her, the boats spun in a sickening dance. Behind her, the Maweel sang the deep, mournful funeral songs.

There was some kind of cloud over her mind, and she rubbed at her forehead to clear it.

Brother. Kital beside her, curled next to her at night, sleeping, just a tiny baby without a mother. Kital touching her face after she had been beaten, Kital chasing the chickens in the yard when he was a toddler, falling over every few steps. She thought of him tied up and struggling on one of those boats, and a deep rage boiled up in her.

She pushed at her mind, trying to send it out over the sea, to see as far as she could into the murky green water, searching for any form of life, searching the gray skies, and after a moment, she gasped.

Efir, she said. *Can you hear me?*

Yes, child. Of course. What do you need?

Can you show me what you see?

It was as though Isika was sky-borne, drifting on a warm wind above the murky waters. She could see the boats from above, see the grim whirlpools they were inexorably caught in, see that the people on the ships were asleep. The rescuers huddled in a corner, piled on one another like sacks of wheat.

Kital slept on his side with his hands under his cheek, and wherever Isika's body was, she gasped, but she was with Efir, flying, circling, looking for anyone awake, anything she could speak to.

And then she saw him. A tangle of black hair and cloth, he stood on the deck of the ship, glaring up at the Othra. There was a red glint in his eyes, and he moved jerkily, as though he wasn't quite awake. Isika drew in a breath. He raised a fist and shook it at the Othra, and when he spoke, his voice was cracked and hissing.

"You know me from the temple, girl, and you turned your back on me. You cannot steal from Fate. I own the world, and I will have this boy whose fate was set as soon as his family betrayed him. He is mine. You can't steal from me!" His voice boiled; it rippled and screeched. Isika was shivering uncontrollably. She wanted to flee from Efir's vision, but she forced herself to stay.

Tell him I will not stop seeking my brother.

Efir spoke to the demon thing. "The World Whisperer will not stop seeking her brother."

The man's face twisted in hate. "I own the seas, I own the sun's rising and setting, I own the death of leaves, the seasons trotting out their steps without sight, without understanding. How will a girl steal from me? Look at my power! Look at these ships! I am everything—I am the end. You cannot steal from me!"

Isika was shaking violently now, her teeth rattling. She couldn't stand the red glare of the horrible man much longer. She forced herself to tell Efir one last thing.

Tell the goddess I can, and I will. Tell her that just as I have a choice about how I will rise every morning, I will defy her, I will destroy this spell and take my brother back.

She heard Efir speaking, saying her own words, and the sound filled the skies above the ships. The tangle of hair and clothes, this man being used like a glove for the goddess, jerked and foam bubbled out of his mouth as Fate shrieked in anger at Isika's defiance.

Isika came to herself on the beach, every part of her aching. Benayeem's face was close as he stared at her with terror.

"Isika?" he whispered. Isika realized she was leaning against Gavi and that Jabari was pinning her arms to her sides.

"I'm okay," she said, and her voice was hoarse. "You can let me go."

"What has happened, young one?" Ivram asked. He loomed over her, his staff dead-looking in his hand.

"Who is the World Whisperer?" she asked, slowly rising.

He stared. "Where did you hear that word?" he asked.

"The Othra said it before, and they used it just now, speaking with the goddess Fate," she said. "They called me World Whisperer."

Ivram staggered then, and Jabari caught him by the elbow, his face wreathed with worry.

"I'm all right, young one," he said to Jabari, straightening again. "Child, you flew with the Othra?"

Isika nodded.

"I saw Kital. I saw the rescuers asleep on one of the ships.

I spoke to the goddess, who was," she paused, shuddering, "speaking through the body of one of the sea people. Efir spoke for me. The goddess is violent and angry, but I know we can defeat her, we must! Ivram!" her voice cracked. "Please tell me what this means! Why did they call me that?"

"They said it because you are the World Whisperer, child," he answered, and as he spoke, tears filled his eyes, and his staff glowed briefly before dying out again.

 sika stared at Ivram. "Yes, the Othra told me I am the World Whisperer. But what does it mean?"

"You can't be serious," Jabari said to Ivram, getting to his feet, looming over Isika. He frowned down at her.

"The Othra have spoken, young one," Ivram replied.

"They haven't told me," Jabari said. "Why haven't they told me?"

"But think of how they have attended her, protected her!"

"Please!" Isika said, her hands balled into fists. "Tell me what you are talking about."

"World Whisperer was the title of your grandmother," Ivram said. "More than being our queen, she was the one selected to tame the creation, to soothe it and put it to rights, to heal it and calm it after poison has touched it. Mugunta is always trying to destroy and taint the creation, and the world cries out to the Whisperer for healing. This is what Efir means when she says you are the World Whisperer. You are the one who has taken the Queen's place." He looked into her eyes, and she nearly took a step back, his eyes were so piercing.

"Does that mean I can rescue Kital?" she asked.

Jabari snorted. "Don't you hear what he's saying? This goes well beyond Kital or any one of us! If what he's saying is true, we must all defer to you!"

The rangers gave each other confused glances, and Gavi shifted his weight from one foot to the other. Ivram turned to regard Jabari with a cool glance. Isika felt sick to her stomach.

"I don't care about any of that," she said to Jabari, meeting his angry eyes. "All I want is to get my baby brother back."

A rush of peace filled her heart, and she looked up to see the Othra circling overhead. She felt tugging inside her, the strongest pull she had ever felt, and she realized that the ocean, the sick and betrayed ocean, was calling to her. She walked toward it, ignoring the mutterings of the others. When Jabari grabbed her arm, she tugged it out of his grasp and ran, evading his grasp. Isika waded into the ugly, sick water, and she did not fall.

THE SORROW and terror of the sea washed over Isika. She spoke to it in her mind. *All will be well*, she said, and a small part of the water cleared, just around her feet. She took a step forward and felt the poison soaking into her, meeting the flame of her heart and fizzling out. Ripples of clear water flowed from where she stood, and she waded farther in until the water came up to her thighs. The poison flowed into her and evaporated. A few fish woke up, and sea plants swayed under the clear water.

The healthy water spread outward, rushing along the beach and out toward the ships. Isika grinned. Fate needed to see that Isika would never let go. As the water resurrected, its life revived her as well, and she had the strength to keep moving. Voices called to her from the beach, but she ignored them, concentrating. She waded farther until the sea came up to her chest. Small fish darted around her feet. She could see the ships clearly now. The fog lifted, and the sun shone brightly on her head.

She pulled her feet from the bottom and swam. Could she swim all the way to the ships? She didn't know, but she swam on. Waves were starting to make the rushing sounds of crashing on the shore, and the water she swam through was cold and clear. More and more fish darted around her, swimming through her legs, brushing against her arms. They were happy to be free, and they passed their joy into her body. Once again, she was covered in tiny lights outlining her arms and legs as she pushed through the water. But she was exhausted already, her chest and arms burning from the effort of swimming. She gritted her teeth and kept going until she could barely move. And then she heard them.

They came shyly toward her, the two naia, the dolfina with their strong, quick bodies, nudging her with their minds.

Thank you, the bigger one said.

It is my pleasure, she said back to him.

Can we help? The smaller one asked.

I would be grateful for it. I am not as good at swimming as you.

A naia swam to each side, and she felt the joy and kindness of their souls as they nudged their heads under her arms, swimming swiftly through the water toward the ships. Isika watched as the luminous water spread from them until none of the green, slimy water remained. Slowly, the boats stopped spinning. They were bigger than she had thought, and she wondered how she would climb onto them, but then she saw that the four kidnapped rescuers had awoken and stood looking at her over the ship's railing. A boy threw her a rope, and immediately one of the sea people tried to draw it back in, but the other rescuers grappled with him, and Isika quickly clutched the rope.

Thank you, she breathed to the naia, and they quivered under her touch. Wave after wave of joy flowed into her, a stream of sunrises and sunsets, the thrill of a clean dive, the sea spray, the salt in the water, the healing of the ocean, and Isika took a deep breath and hauled herself up the rope.

Her arms burned, but she climbed onward, using her feet to grasp the rope while she moved higher and higher. As soon as she could, she used the side of the boat as a lever, pulling herself to the railing. The rescuers had disappeared now, and Isika heard scuffles on the deck. She took a deep breath to prepare herself, then hauled herself over the ship railing, landing on the deck on both feet.

Immediately, her eyes went to the place where she had seen her brother last. He was still there, sitting with his arms wrapped around his knees, and she drew in a breath at the beauty of him, sitting there, very nearly her child rather than her brother, his tiny arms and giant eyes in his face as he watched the fighting. But then her breath was knocked out of her as something heavy hit her in the side. As she fell to the ship's deck, she realized the weight was a person tackling her, and she heard the horrible voice call out, *hold her*.

Isika fought. She had taken beatings many times, so she had the strength to withstand the pain of the person pummeling her ribs with his fists, but in all her life, she had never fought back. To her surprise, it gave her more strength. Isika felt power surge through her, though her opponent had her pinned. Laughing, she managed to get her feet under his body, and she kicked out, launching him toward the main mast. He hit it with a thud and crumpled on the deck.

Isika leapt to her feet and stood with her hands ready, looking to see if anyone else was coming. But everyone else had gone still, frozen. The man with the tangle of black hair approached from the ship's stern. Isika breathed in deeply, calming herself. She had healed the poisoned sea, and the Othra called her the World Whisperer. She was not just some girl.

You are annoying me now, the goddess said, and she spoke the words into Isika's head rather than through the man's voice. Isika could hear the power and venom behind the words, and she shuddered.

"You have no power over me," she shouted, her voice strong despite her fear.

The man laughed crazily, his head tipped back and spit flying from his mouth.

"I have power over everything," he said, as conversationally as if he was talking about the weather. "Especially you."

Isika's eyes narrowed as she stared at the man the goddess was using as a puppet. She looked around at the other sea people. They were frozen and silent, watching the man in fear and disgust. She felt intense pity, then, for the people who stole children, whom the goddess used like this, with no regard for their lives at all. Born into a life of theft and no doubt thrown aside when she was tired of them.

"No one can steal from me," the man said, his eyes red and wild.

"I can," Isika said, and she lunged forward, across the slippery deck, her bare feet flying as she closed the distance and leapt on the man. He screamed as she grasped him, and Isika felt the wild power within him, the strength of his muscles, and the desperation of the goddess writhing like a worm. Isika clamped down on his arm and said, within her mind, *Go.*

Never, the goddess shrieked at her.

Efir, Isika called out. *Help me.* And with a blast of wind, the giant bird came and plucked the man out of Isika's grasp. Efir flew with him, dropping him into the sea, not far from the boat. Isika ran to the ship's railing, staring at the man being thrown around by more than the waves. Suddenly he went still, and there was a new lightness in the air. People visibly straightened and sighed as the air cleared. Isika grinned at Efir, who circled the boat, trailing light behind her.

Thank you, she said. *Will you bring him back now?*

Efir swooped down and plucked the man out of the sea as though he was no more than a doll, carrying him carefully back over to the ship and depositing him on the deck. A woman ran to the man and collapsed on his chest. Her long, straight, black hair was braided, wrapped with golden thread, and strung with mirrors. She sobbed against the man's still body, then began to check him over, rolling his ragged sleeves up to hold his wrists, pulling his eyelids back to check his eyes. The man was unconscious but breathing.

Just then, one of the other sea people walked forward. He, too, had the jet black hair of the sea people, and his hair was wild on his head. He scowled at Isika.

"You may have gotten rid of the goddess," he said, "But you won't leave easily. We just have one more child to sell. And with powers. This is going to be a large bag of gold, men!" He smiled, and Isika flinched from his broken teeth and his malice.

"No!" The shout came from beside Isika, and she turned to look wearily. She couldn't believe how tired she was. She had no strength to fight these strange sea people, the thieves of children. She wanted to run to Kital, but he was hiding behind a pile of sacks, and Isika willed him to stay there, safe and out of sight.

"No!" the voice said again, this time firm and quiet. It was the woman who crouched over the man the demon had inhabited.

"She has returned Torar to us, and we will honor that gift. He will live, and we will know him as husband and brother again, rather than the crazed lunatic the goddess turned him into."

The man made a quick motion with his hands as though he was praying. Isika recognized the man's fear of the goddesses—that they would hear the woman's words and strike.

"You must not speak so," he said to the woman.

"You know it is true, Bevar," she said. "He is your brother. You must see that he was unrecognizable. We will allow these children to go free as our thanks."

Bevar's face became even more furrowed and angry as he looked from Isika to the four rescuers he had kidnapped, measuring the woman's words. Isika was barely holding herself upright now, but she was afraid to show any weakness. Just then, there was a clattering on the boat, and Jabari leapt over the railing, following the rope Isika had climbed. Gavi jumped over soon after, Ivram and Ben in their wake.

Bevar's eyes widened at this new intrusion. Isika willed Jabari not to attack anyone. He seemed to understand the immense tension because he merely rushed to the rescuers, grabbing their hands and hugging them.

The last thing Isika heard was Bevar's words, "Very well, they can go," before everything went black, and she slid to the deck.

When Jabari saw Isika walk out into the water and not die, he closed his eyes. His head was clouded by opposing thoughts. One side screamed that it was demon magic, that she was in line with the Mugunta. The other side considered her words, *World Whisperer*, and wondered whether this might be the truth. He didn't know why he felt so clouded, why thinking was so difficult.

He opened his eyes and watched Isika wading farther into the water, healing it as she went. Around him, rangers gasped, and one woman cried out in surprise as the water came back to life. It wasn't as surprising to Jabari. He had seen her do it before. He looked up and met Ivram's eyes. Ivram looked back at him and what Jabari registered in the elder's face was deep disappointment. Jabari flinched away from it, knowing why Ivram was disappointed. Jabari had been trained to await the queen's return, to seek her with all his heart. Yet now the World Whisperer might be back, and Jabari was resisting. He had wanted to distinguish himself by finding the queen, but he hadn't realized he would feel overshadowed by someone who was just a girl.

Something was happening in the water—a flurry of motion—and Jabari recognized that the naia had come to Isika to help her swim out to the boat. He felt a burning sensation from his head to his feet. Was he *jealous*? Was that all this resistance was? He ground his teeth, frustrated with his mind and especially his emotions. Beside him, Gavi put a hand on his arm.

"Not much going on lately, is there?" Gavi said, smiling.

"No," Jabari said, laughing and sighing. "It's been

boring." He turned to Ivram. "Do we follow?"

Ivram gazed at the boats, watching Isika, who now climbing a rope into the nearest ship. Jabari caught his breath. She was courageous; he had to give her that.

"We wait. The sea is almost clear, but I still fear its effect."

Jabari clenched and unclenched his fists. Waiting was the last thing he wanted to do. He never waited for anything! He was the active one, the one who charged ahead. Was it merely that she was more powerful than him? He, Jabari, the most gifted of his generation? Was that why suspicion and anger boiled in him? He tilted his head and stared at the sky, watching the Othra float high above the ships. They had chosen her, they who had only ever been mysterious and evasive with him. He needed to come to terms with these feelings, or he could make wrong steps, wrong judgments, and hurt someone who had become a friend. As he watched the Othra, one of them—it was too far to tell who— plunged toward the ship and lifted a person from the deck, dropping him or her into the sea. Jabari gasped. The Othra never interfered with adversaries this way.

"It's time to move," Ivram said. "Rangers, stay here and wait for us. Jabari and Gavi, Ben, we swim out now."

Gavi gulped beside Jabari, and Jabari thumped his brother on the shoulder.

"I wish something interesting would happen," he said.

"Before we die of boredom," Gavi replied, though his voice was a bit shaky.

They waded into the water slowly, but it didn't poison

them. As soon as Jabari could tell that he would live, he dove straight in, swimming with long strokes. He turned his head and saw his brother just behind him, then Ivram, with Ben trailing them all.

It didn't take long to reach the ships. The air somehow felt cleared of confusion, and as Jabari hauled himself up the rope, he felt more prepared to support Isika than he had on the beach. He thought maybe he could win the fight within himself and believe in her. At least, he thought, until she did something outrageous again.

As soon as he pulled himself over the railing, he felt the looming tension. One man lay on the deck with a woman crouched over him. Turned away from them, Isika faced another man, her feet spread, her chin up and defiant. He smiled to see her with such a familiar look on her face. He caught sight of the rescuers, his missing friends, and rushed to hug them.

"Very well," the man said, "they can go," and Jabari spun as he heard a thud. Isika had fallen. She lay in a tangle of wet clothes and limbs on the ship's deck. He rushed to her, but Ivram got there first. He picked up the girl with the strength of a young man, holding her to his chest as he straightened to face the man who had made the pronouncement. The man wore the gold of the sea people on his wrists and around his neck. He was young, with a beard shadowing his face. His skin was light brown, and his hair was wild on his head.

Ivram spoke. "Thank you for your wise decision. We will not forget it. Do you have a boat for us to reach the shore?"

The man considered Ivram for a moment, then nodded

curtly. He gave a quick command, and men rushed to lower two small boats and a ladder. Jabari looked at the people aboard the ship. He couldn't believe they were just going to let these sea people, the same ones who sometimes stole children of the Maweel, sail their boats into the sunset. But he knew that he and the others were at a disadvantage on the ships. Too much blood would be spilled if they fought.

He sighed. Just then, out of the corner of his eye, he caught a furtive motion. He looked and saw a small boy peering around a pile of sacks near the ship's prow. *Kital.* He was little, still nearly a baby, with giant eyes and tiny hands gripping the sacks. Jabari nudged Ben, who caught sight of his brother and went to him, his arms out. Kital looked at the space between his hiding place and his approaching brother, and when Ben was close enough, the little boy ran into his arms.

Ben sighed and laughed and pulled his brother close.

They climbed down the ladders and into the boats, Ivram holding Isika until he reached the bottom of the ladder and handed her to Jabari. She was utterly still, the way she had been after she healed the river, and he thought of how much more poison she had taken into her from the sea, as well as facing the demon, as the rescuers had told him. When they reached the rocky shore, he climbed out of the boat, still holding Isika. It was impossible to be mad at her when she was so helpless, and he felt his heart soften toward the girl who could heal a sea.

"We will make camp here," Ivram said. "And wait for Isika to grow well again."

CHAPTER 30

*I*sika awoke to someone calling her name. She was warm and dry, and she could smell the salty tang of the sea. She was having a good dream, and she didn't want to wake up, so she frowned and snuggled deeper into her blankets.

She heard her name again, but this time she recognized the voice that called her and she sat bolt upright. Kital sat on the corner of her blanket, his little legs crossed under him, watching her with a frown on his face that quickly faded when he smiled, and his dimples flashed at her. She lunged at him and pulled him into her arms, hugging him until he squirmed, and she loosened her grip.

"My little boy," she said. "I missed you so much!"

"I waited for you for a long time," he said simply, his eyes huge.

She was surprised by how seriously and calmly he said it. "How did you know I would come?" she asked.

"They told me," he said, pointing at the three Othra, who were feasting on fish at the shore.

The Othra. Isika sent a warm feeling of thankfulness to them, then looked around to see where she was. Gavi sat by the fire, cooking as usual. Ivram perched on a rock beside him, talking with a tall girl Isika assumed was one of the rescuers. Jabari stood nearby, practicing archery with a piece of driftwood, sending arrow after arrow into a circle drawn on its surface. The sleeping pallets were rolled out near the fire, and the other rescuers sat on them or lay propped on their elbows, chatting with the rangers. A wave of happiness broke over Isika. Things were perfect, now that Kital was with her. She lay down beside him and stroked his round cheek.

"I found you in the end," she said.

"Have you ever had potatoes that were roasted in the ground?" he asked. "They're delicious!"

She smiled into his eyes and felt her happiness stretch even more.

GAVI BUILT A FIRE, and they sat around it casually, almost as though nothing had happened. Kital ate and ate, and so did the four who had rescued him. There was the tall girl, who Isika learned was Ivy, Ivram's daughter. She was a couple years older than Isika, born late to Ivram and Karah. She wore braids to her waist and, with her long legs, bore a resemblance to a tall, graceful stork. Then there was a rescuer with white skin and bright yellow hair. And a boy who wasn't from

Maween, but not from the Worker village, either. He had long black hair that he wore in a braid, and gold rings in his ears. Isika felt curious about the jewelry and wished she was brave enough to ask him about it. And there was a dark-skinned Maweel boy who was short and broad in the chest. He sat and chatted with Gavi by the fire. The four young people seemed exhausted, not yet recovered from their close proximity to the poison of the goddess.

"Why does Kital seem okay when the rescuers are wounded?" Isika asked Ivram.

"It always hits the older ones the hardest. If a child grows up poisoned, it will deeply affect him. But a few weeks of this kind of poison will be quickly repaired in a young child." He sat quietly for a while. "It's one of the deepest healings we have to do," he said. "When we get the rescued ones, and they have been living in poison for a long time." He looked at Aria, then at Isika. "Sometimes, wounding is very deep. But your brother is resilient, and he will be like new in no time."

Kital certainly seemed fine. He was poking at the fire with close supervision from Gavi. Isika's little brother was adorable, with his curly hair and light hazel eyes and the dimples in his cheeks. She watched as he stood on tiptoe and held his hand up as high as he could reach, demonstrating something big for Gavi, who nodded and grinned at him. Two rescued ones.

A shadow crossed her heart. No one had rescued her. She had to rescue herself. But she shook the thought away and took some of the potatoes that Gavi held out. Beside her, Jabari sighed.

"More potatoes," he said. "I can't wait until we get back home and eat a feast!"

Isika grinned at him. Since she woke, Jabari had been kind and comfortable with her, surprising her after their last, tense conversations.

"You are a true Maweel," she said. "Used to the best food." She would never ever complain about potatoes. To her, they were still delicious.

"We have fish too," Gavi said, joining Jabari and Isika. "But there's a wild herb near the river that goes well with fish. I'll gather some tomorrow. It'll make you cry and beg for more."

Isika smiled at him. Kital climbed into her lap. Isika was with her friends, she had her brother, and they were headed back to the city. All was right with the world.

THE COMPANY LEFT the cove and walked back along the rocky path with the cliffs towering overhead, traveling slowly because the rescuers were still weak. Isika took one last look at the cove that had given their brother back to them, and in her mind, she called goodbye to the naia. She got goosebumps when she heard an answering farewell echoing through the water. They fell into a pattern, Isika walking with Gavi, Ivy with Aria, talking together in low tones. Aria helped Ivy when she stumbled over rocks in the path. Kital skipped from sibling to sibling, holding Isika's hand for a while, then walking with Benayeem, then back again. He approached Aria for the first time when the company stopped for a break.

"I think you're my sister," he said.

"I think you're right," she replied, smiling at him. He was irresistible, with his dimples and dancing eyes, hopping from one foot to another while he talked to her.

"Can I walk with you next?" he asked.

"Of course you can. Sometimes we have to help Ivy, though."

"Ivy helped me so much when those sea people took us," he told her. "She held me when they made us stand on the deck all day. I'm sorry she's not feeling well now."

Isika tried to convey her gratitude to Ivy with her eyes. The tall girl returned her look with a tired smile.

They came to the river on the third day, traveling slowly as they were, and everyone cheered as Gavi pulled out his fishing net and waded into the quick-moving current. That night the fish tasted better than anything Isika had ever eaten, paired with the wild herbs Gavi had pulled from the river-bank with Kital's help. She didn't cry as Gavi had suggested she would, but she did beg for more.

The next day, the rescuers looked a bit stronger in the river air, but they still seemed to wilt like seedlings whenever the sun shone strong.

Ben came to speak with Ivram and Isika. "I sense something deeply wrong with them," he said. "I haven't known how to say it, but I hear their inner music going out. I think they'll die if we don't do anything."

Isika gasped, pain filling her chest at his words. "I thought they were doing better," she said.

"We have to get them to the healers," Ivram said. "I haven't seen this before. They should be feeling better by now.

"They have food, so they're a bit stronger, but take a good look at them," Ben said. "Can you see how dimly they shine? We have several more days of travel. I don't think they can make it that far." He looked at Isika. "I'm trying to learn to listen to what I hear. I think it's you, Isika, the way you worked with the people back at that house. You need to try to heal them. We don't have time to get them to the healers."

Isika stared at him in surprise, then looked at the rescuers, and grew afraid as she saw what he was talking about. Each of them had a hollowness to their appearance, as though they were caving in. Ivy was the worst. She sat leaning on her arms, and Isika could see that she looked scooped out, robbed of life. Isika took a deep breath, then walked to the older girl and sat down.

"How are you?" she asked.

Ivy looked at her. "I'm dying," she said. "They hurt us too much for healing. I'm not afraid of dying, but I wish I could see my mother again." Her words ended in a sob, then she inhaled deeply. Her skin was gray instead of its usual golden brown. Isika looked into her eyes and saw the tiny light that was going out. She was horrified. After they had been plucked from danger on the ship, could they just die sense-lessly like this? Anger at evil and love for the people who had rescued Kital rushed through her, making heat rise in her face.

"Let me try something," she said, leaning forward.

Ivy frowned. "Are you a healer?" she asked.

"No. But I have healed. And this worked before." Ivy nodded, shrugging as though it didn't matter.

Isika put her forehead against Ivy's the way she had with Ben after he fell in the poisoned river. Immediately she felt the deep poison roiling inside Ivy, formed of hopelessness. The goddess had planted a deep doubt in Ivy, doubt that there was a Shaper, that there was anything truly beautiful or good in the world. The doubt left a deep hole, and into that hole, all the sadness of the things that had happened to them —the beatings they had received, standing for days on the rolling deck of the ship, going hungry and without water— had eaten like acid into her soul. Isika shuddered. What the poison had done to Ivy was horrible, such a brutal wound on a young woman. Such things didn't belong on this sunny little river bank.

"Come with me," Isika said, and they walked toward one of the silverwood trees, Ivy hanging heavily on Isika's arm.

They sat at the base of the tree with their legs crossed beneath them. Isika rested her back on the bark of the tree, and Ivy faced her. Isika felt the humming of the tree right away, the bright sparks of life that ran up and down its branches. She longed to climb all the way into the canopy of the tree, but she knew Ivy wasn't strong enough for climbing. She rested her forehead against Ivy's again, and this time, all the sorrow and despair came flying out of the older girl, quickly, quickly. Isika sent it into the ground, then sent light and hope, the ingredients Ivy needed for sustenance and life. Isika drew it all from the tree, and from below the tree; the water, and below the water; the earth. All around, she saw light and fire and water. Sweet days of sunshine and lying on a hammock, reading a book. A woman Isika recognized as Karah sitting in a lamplit room, singing a lullaby. A dancing, laughing little girl.

She opened her eyes and drew back so she could look at Ivy. The color had returned to the older girl's face, and her eyes were full of light, a deep brown with fire at their centers. She grinned at Isika.

"What have you done, you beautiful thing?" she asked, reaching out and giving Isika a bone-crushing hug. Ivy leapt to her feet and did a couple of perfect cartwheels along the riverbank. The others watched her with open mouths, and the rescuer with the long black braid came to Isika, who sat, smiling, at the base of the tree.

"Do you think—" he asked, and she held out her hands.

"Come here," she said.

SHE HEALED ALL OF THEM, and afterward, she went to sleep, curled at the base of the tree, her mind whirling with the things she had seen. She dreamed, and in her dream, a large animal came to her, the largest eagle she had ever seen, or the largest cat she had ever seen. The animal changed shape continuously as it ran toward Isika until it settled into the form of a large cat with the wings of an eagle, wings as tall

as mountains as she thundered into the camp. Isika knew her
to be the Shaper. She picked Isika up in her mouth and
tossed her on her back, and they flew. First, she showed Isika
the beauty of the world, and Isika gasped as she saw tangled
forests and the expanse of the sea, islands like jewels, the
white, long desert. Then the Shaper took her over Azariyah,
the city of the Maweel.

Isika saw through the Shaper's eyes, and she was
dismayed by what she saw. Little bits of poison clung to the
corners of the houses.

They do their best, she said into Isika's mind. *But it is
insidious.*

She gave Isika pictures that flashed through her mind; of
the insides of homes that had people crying in the corners,
arguments in the palace, kids who were lonely. She saw the
claw marks of the goddesses, the tracings of demon magic,
people turning against one another in their hearts.

They have been without their queen for a long time, the
Shaper said.

But I am just one girl, Isika told her.

*True, there is only one of you. But you should never be
alone, for you are more than just one girl when you are
together. You have Benayeem and Aria, yes, you have
Aria,* when Isika shook her head, *you have Ibba, you have
Kital. You even have Jabari and Gavi and Ivy. And more, you
will find more. You are many, do not doubt, child. Do not
doubt. It will take time. Learn now of my ways, and do not try
to be more than you are. Grow slowly, for this is the way of the*

great trees that do not fall when the winds come and beat against them.

Isika pressed her face to the great animal's back and cried for who she had been and who she was now, and how she barely knew herself. Nenyi hummed, and the richness of her voice sang through Isika, calming her.

THE DREAM FADED, and she sat up. The sky was black, filled with bright stars, and Isika was surprised to find that her face was wet with tears. She felt such loss and longed to return to the dream. She stood and walked toward the river, sitting alone on the bank. The stars were like thousands of sparks from a fire, clustered into shapes in the sky. She sat and let the breeze dry her tears, and then she walked back to the camp and joined the sleeping people on the ground, folding herself into her bedroll and falling into a deep sleep.

CHAPTER 31

Traveling upstream on the river took four days instead of three. The boats sat lower in the water now that they had five extra people, but everyone took turns paddling, and they made a light chore of it. Isika loved the days on the water. The river's strength and beauty flowed around her, and the air grew slightly chilly as the season of cooling began, but not enough to be uncomfortable. Everyone was in great spirits, laughing and teasing each other. Now that Ivy was well, Isika learned that she was the most spirited of them all. She never stopped making jokes or teasing people. Isika watched her, marveling at her. What would it be like to be so full of joy and self-assurance? Maybe that was what it meant to grow up in Maween.

Ivy, Jabari, Gavi, and Aria were all good friends, and sometimes in the evenings, after they had eaten and banked the fire, Ivram took out a little flute and played. The music that spooled out of his flute gave Isika chills, making her want to run or dance. Then Ivy and Gavi did jump up and dance. Sometimes they danced together with intricate, energetic steps Isika didn't know, and sometimes they danced freely side by side. Isika's soul was very full as she watched them, especially when Kital left her lap to join them and moved his little arms and legs as though his soul might explode for joy.

Sometimes, though, Isika had cavernous doubts about whether she belonged. She felt lonely and different and wished she had come as someone normal, someone who could be easily folded into the Maweel, not as the descendant of a lost queen. She was isolated by who she was, even though it wasn't her fault.

On their last night on the river, Ivy stopped dancing in the middle of a song.

"That's it. It can't be just Gavi and me. Isika, Benayeem, Jabari, get over here. You too," she said to the other rescuers, but they shook their heads at her.

"No way, Ivy. I know you. You'll get me doing some ridiculous dance where I look like an overgrown bird," said the one called Deto, the boy with the long black braid.

"Not this time, I promise," Ivy said.

"Yeah, no. You had your chance, and you blew it."

"I apologized for that! Anyway, Isika, you're coming. Jabari, get her and bring her over here."

Jabari walked toward Isika and held out his hand. She shrank back, embarrassed, but when she looked into his eyes, he gave her a look of sympathy and said, "You might as well come; she won't leave us alone until you do. I should know. I grew up with her."

In the end, it was Isika and Jabari and Gavi and Ivy. Ben had slipped off somehow, the wretch.

"Dancing is forbidden in the Worker village," Isika said. "I have no idea what I'm doing."

"It won't take long," Ivy replied breezily. "The music lives in you, I can tell. Not like Gavi. I've had the hardest time teaching him how to dance. It took years." Gavi shook his head and his shoulders, bumping Ivy with one of them.

"I've always been glorious, don't listen to her," he said, grinning, and put his hands behind his head, shaking his hips from side to side.

Isika burst out laughing.

"There!" Ivy said. "That's the first rule of dancing. You need to have fun, so laughing is the first step. I'm going to ask my dad to play an old song, from before the queen was taken. It's a song of harvest, all about gratitude, so it's really happy. Dad?" she called. "You ready?" She turned to the rest of them. "This dance has steps, so watch Gavi and me. Or watch me, actually, Gavi will show you what not to do."

Gavi cocked an eyebrow at her, then closed his eyes and swayed his shoulders back and forth.

Ivram began a quick, light song on the flute, another that made Isika feel like bursting out of her skin, and Ivy and Gavi danced with intricate footwork that used their whole bodies. Isika tried to follow along, feeling completely unsure of herself, but ignoring the other people in the fire-lit circle. She especially ignored Jabari, who danced beside her. The music swelled until it was all around her, and moving her arms and legs and body with the sound was a new kind of joy. When she dared a glance at Ivy, the older girl nodded, approval in her eyes. Isika looked then at Jabari, who danced beside her as though he knew the steps perfectly. She narrowed her eyes at him, and he shrugged.

"I grew up in the palace," he said. "Of course, I know it."

But Isika found that she didn't care. She didn't care about anything, actually, because the stars were bright overhead, the smoke from the fire smelled delicious, and Ivy was laughing and holding her hand out to Isika. They twirled and turned together there, above the riverbank, after days of fear that were finally over.

WALKING BACK into the city was at once a relief and a new worry. Isika knew they would all go their own ways, and she was nervous about what the others would tell Andar and what would happen to her and her siblings. The dirt path became the city's wide paving stones, and she watched her feet walking on the road, clad in her new boots from Teru and Dawit. At least she would see Auntie and Ibba, no matter what else happened.

People came out of their homes to greet the company and call out words of welcome, especially to the missing rescuers. They also called out a ritual greeting to Kital. "Welcome home, little brother, heal well, rest well," they said over and over, walking out to touch his head or offer him some bread or a piece of fruit so that his pockets were full and he had to hand many of the things he received to Isika. His face was full of wonder at the beauty of the city, the pure white and brilliant colors of the buildings, the flowers growing against anything that would hold them up, trailing over rooftops or arbors, dripping off fences.

On the palace steps, Andar, Laylit, and Karah stood waiting. Karah ran down the steps as soon as they came close, sprinting toward Ivram and Ivy, her red hair flying behind her, sobbing and laughing, catching them in her arms. Ibba was there too, and she ran toward Isika, hugging her fiercely.

"I *missed* you," she said.

"I missed you too, little sister. And I'm back now," Isika said. Then Ibba caught sight of Kital, and the two of them grabbed onto each other and hugged the way little kids do until the hug turned into a kind of wrestling match, and Isika had to pull them apart, laughing. "Okay, okay, kids. Settle down."

It was then, with her face full of laughter, that she looked up into the cold eyes of Laylit and felt the first shudder of unrest. Andar watched Isika thoughtfully as Ivram stood beside the two of them, speaking in a low voice that Isika couldn't hear.

Andar raised his voice to address them. "How happy I am at this reunion," he said. "I know you are exhausted. Rest well, children. Tomorrow we will meet to discuss the happenings of your journey. Come to the palace, and we will talk and then have a welcome dinner. For now, be at peace in your family's home."

Isika sighed with relief, and, turning, found herself crushed against Auntie's well-padded shoulder.

"Come home now, young one," she said, and Isika exhaled

with relief. They climbed the steep hill to Auntie's house in a haze. Isika lay on her bed, and without even eating or bathing, fell into a deep sleep.

SHE HEARD voices in the kitchen when she awoke, and sat up and stared around her wildly, in a haze. It came back slowly. Isika was fully clothed, she was in the room she shared with Ibba in Auntie and Uncle's home, and she smelled delectable scents coming from the kitchen. She grinned.

Kital and Ibba were in the kitchen with Auntie, taking turns stirring something in a large bowl. Kital was covered in flour.

"We're making morning flatcakes!" he said.

"Or...bathing in morning flatcakes," Dawit said, standing to greet Isika with a hand on her shoulder. She smiled at him and ducked her head, feeling shy.

He held a book in one hand, and Isika stared at it. Of course, she knew how to read; they were taught at school in the Worker village, and Isika had occasionally led the complicated chants in the temple, but she didn't have much experience with books. Her eyes flew to the shelf behind him and grew wide. There were dozens of books, maybe sixty or so, assembled in an array of colors. They were beautiful.

Teru walked to where Isika stood and planted a kiss on her forehead. "Sit and eat, child, and then we'll get you ready for your day at the palace."

Isika's heart sank. She was tired. She didn't want to go

anywhere near Laylit's cold eyes. She sat obediently, holding her face over the hot cup of coffee Auntie handed her. Light streamed through the large windows on the other side of the kitchen, lighting up the bright curtains that rippled in the breeze. Isika looked at her cup thoughtfully, entranced again by the delicacy of the work. How could anyone make such a lovely thing?

"Auntie, you said this was made in the city?" she asked.

"Yes, the potter who made that is not far away."

"I think I'd like to learn how to do this," she said, and she felt a rush of happiness as the words left her mouth—the idea that she could choose something to learn and do that thing. What else could she learn? How many things were there to discover? How many books were there to read? Ideas raced through her mind. She wanted to make pottery, but she would also like to learn how the light cloth of the tunics was made and how the buildings were made out of earth.

"You'll be learning and going out as an apprentice," Auntie told her. "I can speak with the potter for you."

Uncle looked up from his book.

"They'll be wanting to decide what the child does," he said.

Isika felt as though he had thrown cold water on her. People had decided what she should learn her whole life. She'd had a moment of bliss as she imagined she could to pick for herself. She shrank into herself. But then Auntie spoke.

"She'll decide for herself if I have anything to say about it," she said, slamming a pot down on the stone countertop harder than was necessary.

Isika smiled, meeting Uncle's eyes wryly. Her heart lifted. It was good to know she had an ally in Teru, however undeserved. The older woman barely knew her. Isika admired what a wide, open heart she must have, to embrace others so quickly and easily. Maybe she could teach Isika how to do it.

Ben shuffled into the room, rubbing his face, and joined the other three in eating pancakes and jam. His eyes were sleepy.

"I'll never walk anywhere again," he said.

"You'll have to," Isika said, "because you'll be carrying me."

"How can you ever get anywhere if you don't walk?" Kital asked. "I'm going to walk around the whole world, and I'm going to be a cook like Gavi. He said I could. I made the fish with him, and he said I had a gift. Is cooking a real gift?"

"It's a sort of gift," Auntie said agreeably.

"An underrated gift," Uncle said from behind his book, and she blew him a kiss.

ISIKA BATHED, and Auntie did her hair again, this time braiding it into eight braids, then weaving them around her head. She gave Isika another tunic and wide, soft pants. Isika sighed with pleasure as she put them on. They felt much better than her travel clothes, which had disappeared the moment she took them off, whisked away by Auntie to be washed, Isika supposed.

This tunic was deep purple, woven with gold thread. It had a sash that Auntie tied high on Isika's rib cage. Isika looked in the mirror and saw a transformed person, a girl, really, not someone who looked like a ranger or seeker. She took a deep breath, looking at her face. She saw her mother's face in it, and also, she supposed, her grandmother's, the woman whose portrait hung on the wall in the palace. Isika saw the face of the queen in her own. And she bent her head then, because she realized how undeserving she was, how undeserving they must think her, to be the daughter of the daughter of the queen when she had spent her life as a Worker, feeding the poison of the goddesses. The Maweel had spent their lives in the way of the Shaper, fighting the Great Waste. For a heartbeat, Isika didn't know how she could walk before them, but she dared a glance at herself again and saw Auntie behind her, smiling at her with glistening eyes, and her spine straightened. She was Isika. She deserved to be herself, no more, no less.

They went out to the living space, joined later by Ben, who was bathed and fresh in a white shirt and blue pants.

His face was so different from Isika's, with his straight nose and light brown eyes. She wondered whether they would ever find out who their father was.

"Ready?" she asked her brother.

"Do we have to walk?" he asked. "Because it's breaking my former rule against walking. But yes, I guess I'm ready." He looked longingly at the other two children, who had been given a free pass for the day and were curled up on cushions in the sunlight, playing with the kittens that seemed to be everywhere.

They walked out to the road, and Isika gazed back at the

little house once more, then turned her face toward the palace. At the steps, she nodded at the guards, who stood aside and bowed a short bow as they passed. Isika was startled; they hadn't done that before. The palace hummed at her again when she entered. She put a hand on the wall briefly, looking up at the tall ceiling, but she didn't feel anything else, only the faint humming. When she and Ben reached the great room, she heard loud voices, which quieted the moment they were announced.

They entered the room. This time Andar and Laylit sat on thrones that were elevated above the rest of the room. They were tall and imposing, wearing heavily embroidered robes, the thin circlets of the regents on their heads. Ivram stood beside them, and nearby, Karah sat with Ivy. Jabari was slouched on one of the couches, and Gavi paced nearby. Ben and Isika bowed to the regents as they entered the room, the long bow of the Maweel, with their hands on their hearts.

"Brother, wouldn't it be better if we all sat?" Ivram said, and Andar looked at him for a long moment, then inclined his head.

"Let us be comfortable," he said, gesturing at the sitting area. The others waited until the regents were seated on the largest cushion, then seated themselves. Ben and Isika sat together, and Isika reached out and gripped her brother's hand. Jabari sat to the left of his father, and Ivram, Karah, and Ivy were together. Ivy winked at Isika. She looked breathtaking in her robes, but also as though she wanted to leap out of her chair and run around the room. Gavi paced for a moment longer, then settled on a cushion next to Ben.

Isika frowned. "Where is Aria?" she asked. "Shouldn't she be here as well?"

"Aria is resting," Andar said. "She has been excused."

Isika looked down at her lap, intimidated but annoyed. It didn't seem right that Aria wasn't there.

"Ivram has told us," Andar began, "of the events of your journey. Some surprising, some shocking. We know who Ivram believes your mother to be," Ivram shifted in his seat, his face cloudy, and the regent held his hand out. "Wait, Ivram, let me finish. I understand we are in your debt for returning everyone safely," he went on. "But apparently you led us into a trap made by a demon, which put our people in peril so that we lost one of our rangers," he added, and Isika felt the blood leave her face.

"She is our people!" Ivram interjected, and Isika saw that Jabari's face was troubled.

"Ivram would like to install you as our queen immediately," Laylit said, and the coldness in her voice sent chills down Isika's back.

"Laylit, I didn't say anything like that," Ivram said.

"Regent Mother, respectfully, without Isika, I would have been carried back into the city on a pyre," Ivy said, her eyes flashing.

"But what is this in her?" Jabari asked. "Is it a gift or demon magic?"

Isika flinched and stared at him again. Jabari wouldn't meet her eyes.

"I consider Isika a friend," he said more softly. "And Ben

too. But they were raised in demon temples, and I don't understand how that hasn't left a mark."

Andar held his hands out in supplication for quiet.

"We have many questions," he said. "We can see that you have a strong gift, perhaps the strongest we have seen in some time. But because of where you come from, we cannot be certain of it being a gift we can trust—"

Ivram interrupted, his voice like steel. "Andar, Mugunta doesn't gift in this way; he steals from others and feeds power only." He threw up his hands. "It's as though you haven't read the stories."

Andar frowned at the third elder, and Isika shrank into her seat. She didn't want to be at the center of an argument between the leaders of this beautiful country.

"I know as much as you do about Maween," Andar said. "And I know things can emerge from the Great Waste that are as beautiful as they are poisonous, things we have never before imagined. Therefore I declare what will be."

They all sat up a little straighter.

"For the next year, Isika and Benayeem will live with us in our city. They will learn our ways and apprentice with our masters. They will attend school and learn the gifts and magic of the Uncreated One. At the end of the year, we will reconvene to discuss their future."

There was silence. Isika felt as though she could finally breathe. What he had just described was exactly what she wanted to do. She lifted her head a little higher. She would be able to read the books she wanted to read.

"May I say something?" she asked, her voice quavering a

little. She sat up straighter again, determined that not to break down in front of them.

"Please speak," Andar answered.

"Thank you," she said. "I have no desire to be a queen. I doubt I ever will. I want to live here with Auntie and learn how to make cups so thin you can measure them against the moons on your fingernails. I want to eat at her table and take care of my brother and sister. But I want you all to know," and she made her back as tall as she could, "that my gift is not from Mugunta. I have dreamed of the Shaper, and I will never bow down to a demon again. That is all I take exception to, and Jabari," he looked up, startled, "how could you? You know me. That is all. May we be excused?"

Andar bowed his head to her. Ivram looked troubled as she turned and walked away from them, Benayeem just behind her. But she couldn't leave that place fast enough, and she didn't have any desire to go there again.

Outside, the air was clean and sweet, the flowers were bright, and they had nothing to do except be children in this beautiful place. Isika felt happier than she ever had, and she looked up at the sky and whispered to her mother, telling her that they had come to a good place, finally, and that Amani could rest, knowing it. Isika reached out for Ben's hand and squeezed it, and together they walked home.

***

GUARDIAN OF DAWN: World Whisperer Book 2, is out now. Read on for an excerpt.

ACKNOWLEDGMENTS

I can't even take a step into a page about acknowledgments without talking about my incredible, patient, supportive, long-suffering husband. His encouragement for this book has propelled it from the beginning. Thank you Chinua. I am in love with you forever.

Thanks as well to Kai and Kenya, my kids and best, most enthusiastic beta readers. Kenya gushed about the book, while Kai merely keeps pressuring me about the next one. (It's on its way, I promise!)

Thank you, Sara J. Henry, for your astute, sharp-eyed editing skills and for your support, and thanks Adam Heine for reading and giving me great input.

Thank you, Rowan Maximilian for reading and loving this book. Thank you, Leaf and Naomi, for the crazy support you show a girl who likes to write. Thanks, Mom and Dad for being so encouraging about my writing for so many years.

And thanks most of all to the readers of my blog, for being so kind and full of awesome. I really, really love you!

EXCERPT OF GUARDIAN OF DAWN: WORLD WHISPERER BOOK 2

Guardian of Dawn
    World Whisperer, Book Two

Chapter 1

Western Worker village, Shore of the Great Sea

The first time she saw the giant bird was the day she gave birth to her baby boy. Jerutha paced, gasping for air, while pain like hot knives spread from the lowest part of her belly to the very tips of her fingers. She walked the small birthing room wildly, shoulders held against the pain, and took a deep breath.

She tried humming as the spasm subsided. The birthing room she had prepared was peaceful at least. The herbs she had tied to the doorway released their gentle scent into the air. The walls were white and clean, and a few squares of sunshine fell across the simple mattress on the floor. She breathed. The ache in her heart hurt more than anything. She wanted her stepdaughter, Isika. She wanted her mother.

She couldn't have either of them, and the old midwife wouldn't be much comfort, coming only at the end of her labor to help the baby into the world. *Focus on the baby,* she told herself. When she had her child in her arms, she wouldn't be so lonely. Now, though, she had no one except her husband, Nirloth, the old village priest. Not so long ago, the house had been full of life. But Nirloth's stepchildren— Isika, Benayeem, Ibba, and Kital—were gone, and she missed them desperately. Since they left, a gray haze had covered the house as Nirloth grew sicker. His death seemed imminent. He skipped many days of temple work, and the villagers grew nervous that the goddesses would retaliate in anger.

Jerutha paced and swung her arms, preparing herself for the next wave of pain. What she would really like was to go into the forest to have her baby. Or to the sea. She could sit on its shores and let the pain drift out into the water. But she must stay in this room, alone until the midwife came. Another pain ripped through her and she gasped. She fumbled for the birthing ropes she had tied to the rafters, gripping them until her knuckles were white. The pain subsided, and she exhaled. The spasms were coming more quickly now. She whimpered, afraid. How could she do this alone? No one had ever told her just how much it would hurt.

Just when her terror felt unbearable, there was a breath of sweet-smelling air and a bird landed in the birthing room doorway. Jerutha froze. The bird was massive, as black as midnight, though when it lifted its wings, its feathers gleamed like jewels, purple and red in the light. She couldn't move from fear. A strange sound, a hum overlaid with words, came from the bird, though Jerutha could not say how.

"Don't be afraid," the bird said. "Rest."

It sang a low, quiet song, and Jerutha's terror and loneliness eased until she was filled with warmth and comfort. She lay on the mattress and dozed between pains. When she woke, the bird was gone. The midwife arrived and she rose to grasp the birthing ropes and deliver her son into the world.

The midwife checked the baby over silently. She bathed him, then Jerutha held her baby in her arms for the first time. A son. He moved his little mouth, searching for food, so she held him to her breast and he moved his face back and forth until he found her and latched on. She nursed him a long time, and when he seemed satisfied, she held him out in front of her. He opened his eyes and looked at her—a little mouse-bright creature, soft and new. She kissed him all over his face and marveled over his tiny body, his miniature hands and feet. A fleeting thought drifted through her mind. Who was the bird? How had he granted her this strange peace?

Jerutha and her newborn son lay curled together for hours, feeding and sleeping. The old midwife went home after she brought Jerutha the day's food; a weak porridge, filled today with chopped green vegetables for strength. She was staring at the baby's perfect, sleeping face again when a shadow fell over her. She looked up, expecting to see Nirloth, but was startled to see four strange men, dressed in the robes of priests, standing on the ground of their courtyard. It was unspeakably rude to tread on another family's grounds except for extreme circumstances. Jerutha's heart beat rapidly as she covered herself.

"Woman," one of the men said, and she shivered at the sound of his voice. "Dress yourself and attend us."

"Lord," she said, because though she didn't know who he was, he was clearly a man of great power. "I have given birth to a new son, not five hours ago."

"We have grave business with your husband and it cannot wait," the man said.

"Oh, but he is very sick," Jerutha replied, her heart still tapping a rapid, terrified rhythm.

"We know, and that is why it cannot wait. Please dress and attend us."

They turned and walked toward the house, and Jerutha knew they would go to Nirloth whether or not she was there. Wanting to spare him, she sat up and pulled her heavy outer dress over her head, wincing at the stiffness in her muscles, the pain in her abdomen. She may not have felt much love for the old man, but pity twisted in her gut as she thought of him lying alone in his bed. She picked up her baby and held him close, tucking his soft head under her chin. She felt the fierceness of her love for the tiny creature, the way it was already forming her, shaping her into something stronger than she had ever been, yet helpless to save them from whatever would happen next.

The men stood around Nirloth's sleeping pallet in the

dim room. Their faces looked repulsed as they stared down at the old man. He sat up and shifted so his back leaned against the wall.

"Jerutha," he said, as she entered. "Prepare some tea for these men." His voice was weak.

She stared at him, but he didn't look at her again. Surely he hadn't missed seeing the baby in her arms. She bowed her head and went to the kitchen, anger sparking deep within her. Who were these other priests? She wouldn't have lost her stepchildren if it wasn't for the ways of priest and goddess.

Isika, Ben, Ibba and Kital were considered outsiders because they had walked out of the desert from an unknown place with skin as richly black as the losh trees that surrounded the Worker village. The Workers had finally succeeded in driving the children away, even if by accident. Jerutha felt her anger flame higher, remembering. Isika and Ben had fled to rescue their brother when Nirloth, in the way of the Workers, had sacrificed him to the goddesses, sending him out to the deep ocean in a tiny boat. Had they succeeded in rescuing him? Where were they now? Were they safe? She laid her baby in a nest of blankets and bent to revive the fire, then filled the kettle and put it over the flames for tea.

Her mind raced. Who were these men? She had heard rumors, only whispers, really, of other villages, other Workers, but she had never seen one before. They seemed like priests, they were dressed like priests, but she had never before considered that Nirloth might have men to answer to. She stood frozen as she listened to what the men were saying.

"Nirloth, you have allowed too many cracks to enter the structure of this village," the man who had spoken to Jerutha said. "You haven't made the required sacrifices, the temple is filthy, and, worst of all, you brought black outsiders to work in the temple. You have ruined this village, its power is diminished and the favor of the goddesses is no longer upon it."

Jerutha heard her husband gasp, his breath becoming jagged and choked. Her heart caught in her chest and she scooped up her baby and ran into the room. He sat, clutching at his chest, and she rushed to him and helped him lie on his side. The man droned on, heedless of Nirloth's distress. Jerutha stared up at the strange priest. His face was a shadow in the darkness of the room.

"The goddesses are angry. You are no longer priest of this place, Nirloth. Hakar will take your place here and you will be his servant."

Nirloth continued to gasp for breath. He turned away from Jerutha without even glancing at the baby in her arms, and pressed his face to the wall. Jerutha looked up at the men.

"Please," she said. "You have said what you came to say. Please let him rest."

They looked at her and slowly one of the men, who hadn't yet spoken, nodded. He put his hand on the arm of the spokesman, and the four of them turned to leave. Jerutha nestled the sleeping baby beside her and turned to put an arm around Nirloth, who was shaking, his face still pressed to the wall.

He didn't live through the night. The only thing he said to Jerutha was something she barely heard.

"Tell Isika I'm sorry," he whispered. A few hours later, she stood and left the shell of her husband, walking out to the birthing room in shock. She lay on the mattress and nursed her new son. Nothing felt real and she was afraid.

She watched, numb, as over the next days, the strange priests performed the funeral rituals. She worried about what would become of her and her son. Even in her grief and fear, the tiny boy was clutching at her heart, a perfect being who comforted in the endless nights of worry.

The priests left the village without saying when the new priest would come back. During the weeks that followed, Jerutha settled into a kind of life that was hard and lonely, but peaceful; making porridge in the morning, tying the little baby to her so she could work in the garden. She began selling her vegetables in the market, leaving herself only the ones that were misshapen or overripe. The coins she gained helped her to buy grain for the porridge.

The baby was remarkably good. He blinked at her when she bathed him in the warmth of midday, and he grew more solid as the days went on, smiling at her when her heart felt unbearably lonely. The people of the village complained and muttered because there was no priest, and Jerutha felt as though she was always looking over her shoulder, waiting for more trouble to appear. She didn't know what would happen when the new priest arrived. She supposed she would move into her brother's house, though it was too small. She thought often of her mother in those days. Jerutha's mother had wandered into the desert, insane, when Jerutha was young. She had never recovered from her first daughter being given over, sacrificed to the sea long before Jerutha was born. Jerutha missed her and wished hopelessly for a familiar hand on her shoulder on the loneliest days. Sometimes when she felt the most despair, she smelled a fragrance like the one the bird had brought with it, and she looked up, but didn't see anything.

The moon grew and shrank four times and the baby could laugh, but Jerutha didn't see the bird again. She wondered about it often. Was it the result of a labor dream, or had it been real?

The priests finally came back on an afternoon when the sun had leached the color out of the sky. Three this time. One marched straight into the temple and began to ring the bells and burn the incense. The other two strode into the house, going from room to room, muttering to each other. Jerutha tried to make herself small, but she couldn't help overhearing what they said.

"We will take the widow to Batta," one said to the other. "The high priest wants her. She is young and already has a baby, perhaps he will marry her. If not, another priest will."

Jerutha felt the blood leave her face. She stumbled out to the garden. She fell to her knees on the ground, the baby banging against her ribcage, tied to her front with a long strip of cloth. He made a tiny sound of protest, and she sobbed. What were they bringing her to? How could she protect her son? She looked around wildly, thinking of running out into the wilderness, away from priests and men. But she sat back in the dust, knowing she wouldn't survive alone with a baby. She cried until she couldn't cry anymore and sat staring without seeing.

A shadow crossed the golden afternoon light in the vegetable garden she had planted with Isika, many months before. She felt a stirring of air and smelled the sweet breeze from her birthing day. Despite itself, her heart lifted. She looked up to see the bird standing before her. It was not as large as she remembered. It was taller than her as she sat there, but her memory had made it taller than a standing man. The colors rippled through its feathers as it opened and closed its wings once. Jerutha felt a strange rush of hope as the bird spoke.

"Isika gave you a promise before she left," the bird said, once again making its words flow into the air around Jerutha in a way she couldn't see. "She told you she would help you if you called for her. Tell me, young one. I will pass on your message."

Jerutha gasped as hope blazed up in her heart. And then she began to speak.

Read on...